this is the recalibration

by

michael ingram

Previously titled Deus Otiosus (Etc.)

Original cover art and sketches by Michael Ingram

beardsANDbicycles is a tiny publishing house in the Pacific Northwest.

Originally published in 2013. Printed in arguably the best hemisphere.

For more information about the author visit
www.deusotiosusetc.blogspot.com

ISBN-13: 978-0615756646
ISBN-10: 0615756646

in somnis veritas

CONTENTS

this is the recalibration[1]

etcetera

Luna,

I fucked up.

I'm sorry.

That's pretty much where we are right now – an admission of guilt and a weak stab at absolution. That's all you've seen. To you, I'm not a father. I'm an ash sitting in an aging urn or dusted onto a brown lawn or dumped onto a makeshift tombstone. I get it. My father was absent too – just a vapor, a mist, a blurry half-memory, a wispy cloud-dream. After he left, I told people that I was sired by a sperm donor, that I was once just frozen and half-living in a thin glass dish. -- *I remember looking up at the scientists – the white gloves and splash-goggles. I remember all the frost, the syringes, the rows of metallic bars. I remember melting.--*

I don't really know you all that well – at least not the current version of you. And you've only seen slivered versions of me, incomplete slices of my strangest selves. So I'd like to offer you the full context. You deserve the full context, nothing splintered anymore.

I'm obviously in no position to ask anything of you or to force anything on you because you have plenty of reason to be mad as hell at me, to ignore all the letters that I send, to return all the cards unopened, to skip most of our visits when I fly out, to hardly talk when you do come. I can't blame you. You don't have to justify yourself. The only purpose of this letter, if you read it, is to show you – not for my own benefit, not to get something off my chest, but just to be open and honest with you – where I'm coming from, where I've been, and how all this happened.

I don't want you to think that I'm trying to completely absolve myself because I know that I'm at fault for what happened, that I have made mistakes that led us here, that plenty of my actions were indefensible, that I'm guilty – at the very least – by complicity. But I just want you to know – and I think you deserve to know – that there is another trench and that you are being fought for over here as well. You've only been viewing things from one angle – an angle you didn't have the chance to choose, and I just want you to know that everything is a sphere and that there are no edges and that our shedding skin is just covering the same thing that's inside each of us. I want you to know that we are not so different, not as far apart as we might perceive.

You don't have to believe me, but after that week in June, after that summer of 2010, things changed for me. Back then – back when you were just a kid – I was pliable, spineless, impressionable. Nothing would stick to my ribs. I was creating my own edges, self-scaping my own cliffs. And the urgency of being right on the edge – even a false edge – forced me to remember that I was real. But the new edges, the deeper ones, the sharper ones became increasingly counter-productive.

Anyway, you know how things turned out, but I think you deserve to know why I can only see you in spurts now, in tiny measured segments. You deserve to fully know why you look at me like I'm a stranger, like I'm hollowed out and shelled in metal.

Even if reading this only confirms everything you already think about me, I'm okay with that. As long as you know the truth – heavy and unmovable – that's all I can do. This is what happened. This is who I am.

Dying To Know His Daughter,

your father

Part I

escape velocity

June 21st 2010

As soon as I woke up, before I even got out of bed or saw her note, I knew your mother was gone. Maybe it was some kind of intuitive thing, some kind of communication with a collective consciousness – her voice whispering into my psyche. I didn't really believe in presages or otherworlds then. At the time I just noticed there wasn't any steam coming out from under the bathroom door. On Mondays your mother would – and probably still does – start her week by waking up early to take a shower hot enough to irritate the sun, closing the door and filling the whole room with a foggy cloud that melted the paint off the walls and curled the baseboards, steam-soaking the mirror and floor. She would come out – with two towels, one on her head, one wrapped around her body under her armpits – all red-faced and sweaty, looking like she had just gone for a jog.

But on that Monday morning in June, I got out of bed, stood at the bathroom mirror – steamless and still – with my head throbbing, looking at my pitiful patchy beard I had been trying to grow since school let out for the summer. I grew up assuming that men grow burly beards on short notice. After my father left, I retained mostly just images of him, quick snapshots rough-edged and fading from the beginning. And in most of the images he had thick, full facial hair, always able-bearded. Even in the memories where he had unbearded himself for some reason, he seemed able to magically rebeard at will. I figured past a certain age, after some kind of passage into manhood I would grow into it – the heavy, easy beard – too, but it just never happened.

The air in the bathroom was hard, made of ice – cicles of it, sharp and frozen while dripping. Someone had spilled a bottle of Coumadin – a prescription anti-coagulant I started taking after experiencing heart palpitations --*"I've never seen this in someone so young, never prescribed this to someone your age."*-- towards the end of the semester. The round white pills – the number ten inscribed on the front – were scattered across the

15

porcelain sink, a few on the floor with wads of dust and cat-hair, lent and old skin stuck to the sides. I picked up and dry-swallowed three -- *"Take once daily."* -- and pulled my gray velvet pouch out of my pocket, funneled a handful inside and repocketed it with my lighter. I scooped the rest of the pills across the sink into the bottle.

A lot of your mother's essential things from the bathroom were missing: her hairdryer, whose chords had been twisty-tied and tucked between the plastic toothbrush tin and her face cream; all her bottles in the shower, most of which had French names and smelled of odd fruit mixtures. I always liked their smell, though I never admitted it to her. I was raised to believe that real men aren't supposed to appreciate the scent of fruits. But anytime she went out of town, I used them in small amounts of unadvised combinations, creating foamy chemical reactions on my scalp.

> *maybe Eris just spent the night somewhere else*
> *and it's mostly just cosmetic products, supplements gone*
> *and nothing long-term is missing*
> *and this is nothing*
> *and this isn't the real one*

There were even a few relics: a dirty towel left on the bathroom floor; some loose change next to the sink; one of your stuffed animals – a squirrel – that I got you for Christmas the year before. Eris said you might pop off and choke on the fuzzy squirrel's button eyes so she boxed and filed it in the closest, but I would still get it out for you when she wasn't around.

I'm sure you're too young to remember this, but your mother and I unspokeningly decided to internally divide the fridge for practical reasons. My side, the left one, was mostly empty – a few apples, a half empty container of hemp milk, a lumpy dull-orange grapefruit, and several bottles of local microbrews. The right side was much denser, partially because by default Eris had absorbed your section as well. There were several different flavors of yogurts, a half-gallon of skim milk, two gallon-sized jugs of water, a stoppered wide-hipped decanter of red wine, and a half-dozen unlabeled airtight mason

jars that I avoided for fear of struggling to open. When I closed
the fridge, holding an apple in my hand, I saw the note high up
above the magnets and outdated wedding invitations – at my
eye level.

"Don't try to contact us. We'll be back by in a few days for the
rest of our things. I <u>WILL</u> be taking <u>sole</u> custody."

The letter-stems were thick, intentional, pushed hard
onto the page, the lines all drawn with hard angles, protracted,
but the crosses and curves were inexact, the dots out of line. A
rushed hand had smeared everything, pulling the words up and
to the right in wisps.

it's not real
and she's exaggerating, just being dramatic
and this isn't the real one
and it must be a joke
ha-ha!
yes, it's a funny joke.
a dry one.
very black.

I peeled the pink Post-It note off the fridge and read it
several times, rubbed it between my fingers and thumb until the
adhesive on the back wore down leaving a gray, snot-like
residue on my fingertips. Looking around the apartment, I
realized that more of her things were gone than I originally
thought: her laptop, framed pictures of her parents when they
were young, her favorite snacks from the pantry, even her closet
had been picked down to the bone, empty plastic hangars
pushed all the way to the back corner. Really the only things
that remained were the bigger items unable to be taken in haste.

this didn't happen last time
and this is new
and this is what she said she would do

Though I knew your mother was gone and the memories from the previous night were beginning to solidify, I still assumed it would play itself out like the last time, that I would apologize and she would come back.

Back in the bedroom I heard my phone beep. I ran back, thinking maybe Eris had already reconsidered, that she was on her way home, that she was ready to accept my apology.

and why does my head feel so heavy
and my mouth so dry
and oh god fuck[2]

I picked up my phone – sitting on top of my pocket-sized notebook that I always carried with me – and saw a text from Mira.

"hey…can we talk?"

--Standing under a street light leaning, waiting, stalling--

I reached into my back left pocket, felt the flattened origami fortune-teller she gave me.[3]

---

[2] You're 18. I think you can handle the language. If I'm not honest then I'm doing both of us a disservice.

[3] I like to draw. I'm not great, everything flat and dimensionless, insipid, everything head on. But I'll include a few pictures – most on the cusp of kitsch.

[4]→I should text her back.

　　　→No, I should call, make it more personal.

　　　　　→But not too personal.

　　　　　→Keep it casual.

　　　　　→"Whoops. Did I call you? I meant to dial someone else. But let's chat while we're together on the line."

　　　←No.

←The timing is all wrong.

　　　→If anything, I should call Eris.

←The note said not to call.

　　　→But I think that means I'm supposed to call.

　　　　　→But none of this can be real, none of this can be right.

Your mother hated when I kept my phone on vibrate, said it made me unreachable. But I couldn't collect my thoughts – weightless, floating, untied, untamed – so I flipped the ringer off.

she can't really take her, can she?
and she's not being serious.

I wiped the note residue on my pant leg, and I guess because of the Coumadin, my hand felt like it had a glove on, everything vibrating through a paper-thin membrane.

she can't do that and i have rights and i can't just sit
and i can't just stew in my thoughts.
sequestered.

I needed to see everything at the right distance, in the proper proportion. I needed to burn off some building energy, aimless and uncontrolled. Plan-less, I went out the front door, down into the atrium of the complex. Through the small glass pane of four windows, frosted with condensation, next to the entrance, I saw Eris' red Jeep was not in her usual parking spot under the protective awning, an expensive spot she had insisted

---

[4] When I get too emotional (or need to make a decision) I visualize things as a tabulation so I can get my thoughts organized.

on shelling out the cash to own. Since we shared her car – I hadn't owned one in years – we split the expense.

Perched on top of the metal mail unit was a full grown lime green katydid – knees high, antennae like thin whiskers. He stood still, staring. In our unit, I found a curved magazine with Eris' name in the white box in the bottom corner, an energy bill, and a letter addressed to Cetus Tyde.

I don't know what your mother calls me around you – Hurley, Dad, that guy, asshole – but my legal name is Cetus, though few people know or use it. It's a family name – I think it has to do with aquatics, maybe whaling – from my father's side that I intentionally rejected, so I always went by my middle name, Hurley, claiming as I got older that I was never given a secondary name. Only two people still called me Cetus: my father and my friend Noah – though he usually used my high school nickname, Gumby. I had never given my father my address, so I knew the letter was from Noah. Inside the card he wrote a short note:

Mother Fucker,
I don't mean that to sound pejorative. I genuinely hope you're sexually involved with a mother. Writing to let you know I set up camp near Hamilton. Come see me sometime and we'll kick it. I'm sure you can guess my locale.

Still unsatisfied, I walked back upstairs, chained and unchained the front door before tossing the mail on the kitchen table and walking down the hall past your room. Somewhere in your first few years I developed an association between you and baby powder. Even after you were too old to need it, I instinctively conjured up its smell, sweet and musty, when I thought about you. I guess the smell[5] is stored in my mind or nose or wherever it is our bodies file away sensory information.

Drawn in by the smell-memory, I sat down on your floor. You probably don't remember this but the walls of your first room were painted pastel pink with white pigs stenciled around at random, some moving in groups, others flying alone.

---

[5] I remember hearing somewhere smell is the strongest of all mnemonics.

I did most of the painting and stencil work with Eris as the creative critique. In the bottom corner of the wall there was a tiny handprint stained in white where you had crawled unnoticed into the room while we were painting and explored your own artistic talents[6]. I convinced Eris to let us leave it up, beautiful in its spontaneity, sad in its reminder of our limitations, a symbol of the things we could approach and imagine but not achieve.

Stacked on the floor were several construction paper cutouts of squares and circles with a pair of blunt-tipped four-ringed training scissors on top. Eris had been helping you practice your shapes, trying to hasten the development of your motor skills. She would slip her fingers into the outside finger-holes – yours on the inside pair – and guide your hands across the proper curves, show you the hard angles. Next to the stack of paper shapes was an abacus I bought you, which you were too young to really use. You mostly just looked at it, sometimes tried to chew on the sliding corks, unintentionally loosening your teeth.

I put my ear to the floor, listened to the air conditioner click on, listened to it hiss and rumble. Even though you'd only been gone a few hours, I didn't know what to do with myself. Monday summer mornings were reserved for you. After I finished teaching for the semester and it was warm enough out I would take you to the pool early in the morning before the crowd. Again, you probably don't remember this but you would sit on the edge of the pool peering curiously into the water – calm and sterile-smelling – until the bottoms of your pink feet wrinkled, the skin turning white and folding in on itself. I bought little yellow arm floaties with green ducks, but you weren't really interested in getting in the water so we just sat on the edge and looked at each other – you with these really wide eyes like you were expecting to see a miracle happen at any moment. Even at a young age you were able – as I thought only children were – to experience all the sensations to the fullest capacity, to dull nothing – a skill I've struggled to acquire. Sometimes I'd cup my hands in the pool and squirt

---

[6] Are you an artist now? Do you draw or paint, write or sew?

21

water at you and you'd giggle while the thin stream fell harmlessly on your legs.

Right after you turned two – the summer before all this happened – I finally coaxed you into the pool at the stairs down in the shallow end. The water reached up and splashed around your knees and you squealed wildly, unashamed of your reservations. At first you sat down on the stairs unwilling to move any further, but after you adjusted, you braved it out and lunged off the steps towards me. Water went everywhere. It was in your eyes, your mouth, your nose, your ears, but you floated towards me wearing your green ducks, smiling, looking exhausted but accomplished. I'm sure you don't remember any of this, but these are some of my best memories of you. This is what we did together.

Even though I had slept in so late, I felt drained, felt empty, enfeebled by the thought of not having you around. I was still a little hung-over from the disaster the night before, the details still fuzzy towards the end of the night. My muscles and ligaments felt stretched too far, felt like they might play an off-key note if plucked, might send a strange new note vibrating through my body.

I tried to explain this to you before, tried to explain my vibrations. It was at one of our supervised visits when you were still in elementary school. I asked you if you felt our bodies talking. You looked over at the social worker who quickly escorted me out. It came out wrong. It always came out wrong. What I meant to say is that string theory says that matter at its most fundamental level is made up of tiny vibrating strings and that the vibrations of these strings define everything about the object. The vibration is the identity, the distinguishing element. It hasn't been proven yet. It's just an idea. But I believe it is true. I don't have any data, nothing empirical. I haven't been using the scientific method. I believe it because it feels true. I believe it because I feel something similar inside my body, something other than my organs, something that vibrates and speaks with the vibrations inside everyone else. I believe our bodies speak. I believe we are never apart, are always talking. And I believe our emotions are just a response to these vibrations – being spoken and absorbed into our bodies, everyone's strings buzzing and balancing, tuning and harmonizing between us all. Sometimes the vibrations are too much, too unfamiliar, too overwhelming.

Anyway, I'm telling you all this now because while I was sitting on your floor watching the air from the vent wave your white curtains, I felt things I'd never felt before, new vibrations all over my body. Through the window I saw soft junipers and white oak trees, still and quiet, their leaves sagging from the humidity. I wanted to be completely still[7], but I couldn't. My body was moving, crawling everywhere. I tried my best not to move anything, to settle the vibrations soaring through me.

I ended up sitting on your floor most of the day. Even though it seems so counter-intuitive now, I wanted to hang around in case your mother came back. Despite all the evidence to the contrary, I was still convinced she would show back up, still convinced I would call to apologize, still convinced that I wouldn't have to fight for you, that everything would work itself out, that everything would always be simple. I clicked my phone back onto the ringer and sifted through the contacts in my phone until I reached your mother's name.

Of everything that you're about to read, this is the part that I regret the most, this is the part that I see inside my eyelids at night when I'm trying to sleep alone. Maybe I'm over-exaggerating it, but this felt like the fulcrum, the axis of everything that was about to happen. People I've talked to have told me that this was all bound to happen anyway – some fatalistic bull shit – and that there were thousands of other tiny moments for everyone involved that could have also served as the center. They told me that every moment is always the center. Maybe that's true, but I felt a choice. I felt personal responsibility here, deep conviction. All I had to do was call. All I had to do was issue a heartfelt *mea culpa*. It would have only needed to be half-sincere. I could have faked it, strained my voice to force a quivering breakage, put drops in my eyes.

---

[7] It's been scientifically proven that time passes more slowly when you move. I wanted time to pour over me. I wanted to glide, frictionless through time. I wanted everything over, wanted the resolution.

23

Maybe I would have had to buy her flowers afterwards, maybe pick up her half of the rent the next month. It would have been easy. And I want you to know that I clicked her name and held my thumb over the dial button, thinking of what I would say to apologize, of which words would change her heart.

But while I hovered over her name, the text from Mira flashed, still unanswered at the top of the screen and the origami fortune teller crinkled in my pocket. I clicked my phone back to vibrate. I clicked my phone back to vibrate.

"Do you think I look gay when I wear skinny ties?"

"It's chic, not gay. Wear the red skinny one."

Your mother and I were standing on opposite sides of our bedroom, her by the walk-in closet, me nearest my sliding door closet covered in a collage of art work – posters and old water color prints.

"This one?" I asked holding up a tie. She nodded. "This is pink, not red. Are you sure? What about brown or green?" I held up several other options, things with deeper shades, with more contrast. "These are more earthy. More manly. Don't you think?"

"Sure, I mean wear whatever you want, but I don't like the other ones. I like the red one."

I wanted to be agreeable, accommodating. And I needed to engineer a flawless date night – something solid, something to settle her growing uneasiness about me – for your mother's birthday. I patted the gray velvet pouch in my pocket, felt the edges of the ring pressing against the fabric.

> *i can't ruin this and i've ruined too much*
> *and should i bring my gray sports coat in case i get twitchy*
> *and in case i start sweating?*

I would sweat like crazy when I was a few pills under and even more when I wasn't, when my body told me that I needed to be. The fact that I was already thinking about the possibility of getting twitchy and sweaty made it seem all the more likely it would happen. So I opted for the pragmatic approach and wore the red skinny tie with a solid white button-up and gray slacks to hide my sweat. I brought my coat to cover up everything if it got out of control.

> *it's just good preparation.*
> *and men are prepared!*

I'm sure you've heard fragmented half-stories about my father – more ghostly than even me. If he taught me anything in the few years he was around, it was the importance of being prepared and appearing capable. And though I trained myself to resent all my memories of him, somehow his advice still lingered and tacitly influenced me.

I got dressed and sat on the bed fanning myself with one of Eris' hair styling magazines. Aware I was watching her, she took her outfit into her walk-in closet to undress and change. I watched your mother's shadow moving under her closet door, checked to make sure she was still dressing – still moving – and went into my office.

I want to preface this next part by telling you that it was casual. It was loose. Optional. It was whatever. It was just weed and pills. It wasn't anything major. I was in control. Regardless, I had no business bringing those things into your atmosphere.

I grabbed my bubbler – already packed tight with weed, the top layer singed, the edges still green – from a drawer in my office and went out to the porch where I pulled my gray lighter out of my pocket and lit the bowl. And I didn't see what I was doing then, not really, and I burnt it down, breathed it all in, held all that dirty air that tasted like sweet sand deep in my chest, held it until my blood smoothed out. I opened my mouth and let the pale smoke fall out and lit the bowl again and breathed and released until it was all just a silky black ash that I dumped into the compost bucket by my potted plants. I went back in, rinsed my mouth out and rubbed a fabric softener sheet over my clothes. Eris was still rustling around so I tapped lightly on the closet door.

"I'll be right out. You're sure you're not going to freak out tonight, right?"

Around the time I started the Coumadin I had been having trouble with routine things: going out to eat, sleeping regular hours, remembering simple tasks. These – and the off-kilter vibrations in my chest – were the symptoms that led me to the doctor in the first place.

"Come on, yeah, it's no big deal. I'll be fine."

She stepped out of the closet wearing a black, thigh-length, pencil skirt that hugged her hips and a coral red, straight-cut top. She liked it when our color schemes matched, said it made us look more connected. A thin layer of face powder dulled the natural shine of her face.

We left the apartment without saying much, everything rushed, implied. On our way out, I put my notebook into my back right pocket and grabbed my ink pen, and I felt my front left pocket for my lighter and tiny gray velvet pouch. As far as I know, Eris never knew I carried around the gray velvet pouch, never knew about all the pills, never knew how long I'd kept the ring in there. But she did know I carried around the lighter. Even though I was smoking weed daily, I just carried it around for comfort. In high school I carried around cigarettes too – menthols. Occasionally I would smoke one but really they were just for show. But I held on to the habit of carrying around a lighter at all times, just in case anyone needed one. Anytime I left the apartment, I patted each pocket to make sure I had everything I needed.

FRONT LEFT:	FRONT RIGHT:
lighter	pen
pouch of pills	
BACK LEFT:	BACK RIGHT:
(empty)	notebook
	wallet

Eris locked the apartment door, her left hand hanging in a loose fist at her side.

"Hey I'll drive this time," I said.

When she under-hand-tossed her keys at me I started to feel the waves forming in my chest, the low rumbling vibrations. That's where it typically started – my chest – before spreading upwards to my throat and downwards into my gut. I think it's because she tossed the keys under hand.

why didn't she throw it overhand?

27

does she think i can't catch?
and she just throws more accurately underhand
and it's the more graceful, girly thing to do.

When we got to downtown Cincinnati, all the street spots outside the restaurant were taken and it had started to drizzle. I turned on the wipers, everything clear in one frame, blurred in the next.

→ The rain gives me an excuse to drop Eris off at the front door.
　　→Dropping her off at the door makes me look altruistic, like a leader!
　　　→ "I saved my woman from water!"
　　　　→I think that's what she wants to see from me right now.
　　　　　→The saving.
　　　　　→The altruism.
　　　　　→The dryness.
　　　　　　→By the time I park the car and get in she will have already confirmed the reservations for two under her name.
　　　　　　　→I can avoid eye contact, can avoid people noticing my eyes, with those dirty bags underneath, the red veins streaking through the glassy yellowed-whites.
　　　　　　　　→**Excitement**
　　　　　　　　　→**Approved**
　　　　　　　　→**Chest Vibration**
　　　　　　　　　→**Settled**

When I walked, chest low, arms like boards, around the corner towards the entrance after parking the car I saw your mother standing under the awning out front with her arms wrapped around her body, holding her elbows in her hands like she was cold. She always seemed cold.

is she actually cold-blooded
and is there maybe just a fraction of reptilian blood in her veins
maybe a distant amphibious uncle

and either way
↓

←   ←   ←   ←   ←   ←   ←   ←   ←   ←   ←
↓

→She has not gone in yet.

    →A firm, strong statement has not yet been made.

        →I'll have to make eye contact.

            →I'll be at risk of receiving the disdainful looks from the hostess, see her recognize the high in my eyes, possibly even get my pockets searched.

                →Chest Vibration
                   ↓
             Returned[returned]

"Apparently you're not allowed to go in unless you have your whole party."

A stiff-haired middle aged man dressed in a black tuxedo nodded at us and opened the door, which led us into a small, overheated room. When the door behind us shut, a nearly identical man opened a second set of large doors – these windowless and made of deep brown wood, no rings visible – which opened into the actual restaurant. It was darker than I had expected; rows of dim, half-lit string lights ran across the ceiling in elliptical patterns. A stern-faced, firm-jawed woman stood behind a black podium.

"Is your entire party here?"

I nodded with my eyes on the ground and touched Eris' elbow, applying just a slight amount of pressure. She took the hint and stepped forward.

"Yes, we have a reservation for two."

"Last name?"

"Cede."

The hostess grabbed two menus and led us towards our table. I followed a few steps behind, eyes still down. My vision started to spiral, my heart shaking from the weed, and I tried not to trip in the darkness, my eyes still unadjusted. A small cone-shaped overhead light illuminated our table. Eris and I sat in silence both straining through the dim lighting to look at our menus. Even though they were difficult to read, we stared too closely, too intently. Through the blackness, I saw other tables lit up around the room but the space between tables was dark and empty, floorless and made of black water. I kept peaking over my menu, trying to catch a sign – a flick of an eyebrow, a twitch of a mouth corner, something – that Eris wasn't already checked out, that it wasn't too late. But she read her menu thoroughly, stoically. My ears buzzed as the conversation from the dark crowd compiled, everything thick, hazy in my head, the vibrations taking ahold.

"How do you think Luna is doing?"

Though your mother and I had our differences, there was no doubting her commitment and capability as a mother. I'm sure this won't make sense, but in my mind I passed off as an adequate father – better than my own at least – but parenthood came much more naturally to her. Maternal instincts, I guess. Eris looked up from her menu. The skin above her eyebrows was wrinkled, her lips tight.

"I'll call Julie after we order," she said scanning the restaurant looking for a waiter to flag down so we could place our order quickly, so she could get out quickly. My mouth was getting drier, my tongue growing, the weed settling in, the Coumadin slowing my body down, the blood in my chest loose and slippery. The floor was so dark, so black I couldn't see my feet.

> *the floor is made of water – black water*
> *and the air is made of bubbles, so tiny and dry and sharp*
> *and my mouth is so dry*
> *and there's sand in my mouth*
> *and it's on my tongue*
> *and it's in my throat*
> *and my teeth are crumbling*
> *and my lips are stones*
> *and i need water*
> *and i can't breathe in the black water and*

I grabbed my sports coat draped on the back of my chair. In what I viewed at the time as a brief moment of empathy – but

I see now more as a tactical maneuver to avoid losing face – she put her menu down and looked right at me.

"Hurley, it's not a big deal. Just relax. You're fine." But in another vein, she finished the forced nicety with a breathless, "Jesus."

I honestly think she meant well but these kinds of statements always escalated the situation. I logically knew everything was fine, that I was not in fact underwater and that I could in fact breathe, and to have someone acknowledge my unnatural behavior only made me more aware of my social fallacy, my inability to live in the moment and act in context, my inability to stay soberly in full-consciousness.

Our waiter, a tall man with slicked-back dark hair and green eyes, stood next to our table with his hands behind his waist. He looked, both in appearance and posture, like a magician hiding something in his hand. While he talked, it became harder to distinguish the singularity of his voice from the collective buzz of the crowd. I think he was listing the specials or explaining the wine menu. But I was starting to spin, everything moving in loops around me. I watched Eris listening to him, her facial expressions following right along with his voice inflections. They were both looking at me.

"I'm sorry. What was said?"

Eris lowered her head then repeated the question.

"Hurley, our waiter asked if we wanted to start off with a bottle of wine."

Her tone sounded like one she would take up with you when you had gotten into something you shouldn't have.

"Oh, it's up to you. Get whatever you want," I said coughing into my left shoulder.

this is over
and this is pointless
and it's too late
and it's always been too late
and this ring is so fucking heavy

"We'll take a bottle of the house Cab." She folded the wine menu and passed it over.

31

He swiftly walked away. I knew she would soon say things, negative things, unproductive things, so I stood up – my knees wobbly, my feet in flippers – and went to the restroom before she had the chance. Through the darkness, I followed the candles on each table, followed the wavering light towards the restroom.

It was bright. Much brighter. Clinical, my eyes quickly narrowing. One long wall served as a urinal. A slow, steady stream of water ran over a fake rock wall that led down to a trench at the bottom – a fancy piss trough. I'm guessing you've never been into a men's restroom but this type of set-up is unusual, nothing blocked off like that.

A man entered, shouldered past me, went straight to the middle of the trough, unzipped, and let out a guttural sigh. I walked up to the far right side of the wall and unzipped but without partitions I was bladder-shy, so I stared down at the floor, watched a sweat bead plink into the water, until the man finished, washed his hands and exited.

I shuffled over to a stall – each made of marble. Inside, I took out of my gray velvet pouch – brushing up against my lighter – and pulled out a Coumadin and a small perfectly round white pill with the letters OC inscribed on one side. I'm not sure what it was --"*some kind of equalizer*"-- but I dry-swallowed both hoping they would cancel out whatever was happening inside my body.

I dug out the ring – clear sharp stone perched on top – and put it loosely in my left front pocket, giving it quicker access in case I needed it as an emergency gesture to salvage the night. I wiped my brow and sat down on the closed lid, unpocketed my ink pen and notebook – mainly I carried it around for research. For years, I had been polling people, asking a question – which had several sub-questions buried inside – and tallying the responses.

→Do you have kids?
    →If Yes
        →How many?
        →Age?
        →Sex?
        →How often do you see them?
    →If No
        →Thank you, goodbye.

I'll explain why as we get a little further into the story because it won't make a whole lot of sense just yet. I also used the notebook for list-making. I would turn it upside down – using the backs of the pages from my research tallies – to take notes from back to front of things that I saw, placing them into categories. These lists helped me to make distinctions and decisions. Anyway, I was standing in the stall when I pulled out my notebook, flipped it upside down, and wrote some categorical notes.

Unmasculine
-Peeing in stalls

At the sink, I splashed some water on my sandy tongue, splashed some on my face, washed away the sweat collecting in the creases on my forehead and dabbed my face dry with a few coarse white paper napkins folded inside the dispenser on the wall.

Back at the table, the pills mixing well with the weed, I felt softer at my sensational edges. Eris and I sat in silence again, shifting in our seats. I picked up and put down the salt shaker, unwrapped and flapped out my cloth napkin, circled my index finger across the brim of my empty wine glass. My brow began to sweat again, along with the rest of my body. I didn't realize until after I hit puberty in full force – when my voice started jumping octaves without my command – just how many pores, orifices, and sweaty crevices the human body contains. The pressure on my chest increased and spread deeper – my heart squeezed by a firm, internal hand. Eris looked up at me as my breathing became more noticeable. I loosened my tie and tugged at my shirt collar as she scanned the room hurriedly and leaned over the table towards me.

"Pull yourself together."

Her eyes widened as she emphasized the last word. I put my hand in my pocket, flipped the ring in my fingers, wore it on the tip of my pinkie like I had done dozens of times before.

"I don't know what's wrong. Water."

With my free hand, I reached for my glass of water, missed and knocked it over. Thankfully the glass didn't shatter but water spilled across the table ending in Eris' lap. She hopped up, dabbing her pencil skirt with her cloth napkin, tinted red.

The dimly lit patrons from the surrounding tables secretly looked at us out of the corner of their eyes while the water stretched its arms across and deep into the black tablecloth, dripping from the corners. Our waiter walked briskly, elbows high, toward our table with several white towels draped over his shoulder.

"I'm so sorry."

"Oh it's quite alright, Miss. Accidents happen." He looked down at me. I avoided eye contact. I took the ring off my finger and left it loose in my pocket. "We'll move you to another table while we get this cleaned up."

In the center of our new table, a flat, white candle floated in a wine glass half filled with water. A basket of freshly baked, pre-sliced Ciabatta bread with two small plates for oil and spices was brought out in a wire rack, and our bottle of Cabernet Sauvignon followed shortly thereafter, which our waiter promptly poured into our oversized wine glasses, the deep red liquid barely covering the bottom. I never understood why wine drinkers fill their glasses so sparingly. When we placed our orders, I kept my eyes towards the floor, towards the black water. As he turned to leave, I raised my glass.

"Happy birthday," I said as we clinked and drank. She sipped. I gulped.

"I'm going to run to the restroom to dry off a little. You're not going to knock anything else over while I'm gone, right?" she said sarcastically.

I poured myself a supple glass of wine from the bottle our waiter had set on our new dry table and watched your mother walk away, her legs veiled in the void.

> she's not going to come back
> and she's going to ditch me.
> or the waiter will come over
> and he will start flirting with her
> and he will invite her back to his place for unabashed sex
> and they'll do it in front of my face
> and would she say 'yes' if he did?
> and would their bodies be seamless?

My stomach gurgled as I took another healthy sip of wine and ran my fingers over the lighter in my pocket. I grabbed the bottle and filled my glass again.

> the floor is made of water and it's so dark
> and everything is so wet everywhere
> and we will drown
> and no one will ever know
> and no one will see me at the bottom
> and how long has she been gone?
> she didn't leave me here did she?
> she wouldn't do that

I downed a third glass, poured a fourth almost to the brim. My empty stomach groaned again as the wine sloshed around inside me so I chewed on a piece of the crispy, dry Ciabatta bread to get the wine taste out of my mouth. Our waiter and one of his sharply dressed sidekicks brought out our plates.

"Do you need anything else for now, sir?"

He looked suspiciously at our almost-empty wine bottle. Over our waiter's shoulder, through the darkness, a short man[8] smoothed a dry tablecloth across our former table. I looked

---

[8] Identical to the two doormen, well dressed and too serious.

back towards our waiter, not at his eyes though. I aimed at his Adam's apple.

→I should ask him if he has any kids.
→I should log it in my notebook.
    →The words will fumble out, the weed-pill-combo softening, expanding everything in my mouth.
        →**Not worth the risk.**

I shook my head, and he turned on his heels and left again. I reached for the wine bottle and the last of it dripped out, deep-red and warm, into my glass.

fuck!
shit.
fuck.
shitfuck.
black water everywhere inside me
and if i drink the rest i can just hide the empty bottle
and say i sent it back for a better option
and that could turn this whole night around
and showing some initiative is what she needs to see right now
and this ring is too heavy for her hand

I chugged the rest of the wine and tucked the bottle under the darkness of the tablecloth, pictured it floating and bobbing under our table. I swished my mouth out with water to rid myself of red teeth stains and wine breath. She folded her skirt as she sat down, deliberately not making eye contact with me.

"The food looks good," she said reaching for the spot where the wine had been. "Where's our wine?"

"I sent it back for a classier option." I said it with practiced confidence, with unmatched bravado.

"Oh, great. What did you order?"

shitfuck.

36

I had not actually ordered anything so she would know I lied because when our waiter came back he would not have a new wine bottle.

"You'll just have to wait and see."

The saliva evaporated from my mouth, my expanding tongue stuck to the rippled-roof. And the sweat started up again, this time in full force across my whole body. I put my hand back in my pocket, fingering the ring. I couldn't keep my eyes open and my stomach was burning.

> *i'm suffocating in the dryness, in the black water*
> *and no one will ever know and Luna will never know*
> *and i have to see her before and*

Eris wiggled her lower jaw. It sort of felt like someone had sucked the oxygen out of the room, like jumping into a freezing river as the vibrations spread out across my body. I was nauseous, sloshy, everything inside me made of a melting liquid.

> *this is it and is the ring still round and will it fit*
> *and it will clean off the rust and*

"It's okay. I have something for you," I said

I stood up from the table, and everything in my field of vision spun, the room on a swivel. I felt a sharp pain in my lower left abdomen, had to lean down and put my arm on the table to keep from keeling over. People from the surrounding tables turned their heads, their faces bright under their table lights. They were no longer trying to hide their glances, watching us through their peripheral vision.

With my sleeve, I wiped the sweat from my brow trying to catch my breath, trying to regain control of my body, of my sensations. The buzzing in my ears returned, all the vibrations soaking through me.

"Do not ruin this. Sit down and pull yourself together," Eris said in a harsh whisper.

I tried to sit back down but my knees locked up and I started dry heaving.

37

"That's it. I've had enough."

Eris pulled seven ten-dollar bills from her purse, set them on the table. She grabbed my hand and led me out, dry coughing and burping every few steps while I patted my pockets. I pointed to the car, and she buckled me into the passenger seat where I sat rocking back and forth flicking my lighter on and off as she drove us home.

June 22nd 2010

Tuesday
morning

On the first night after she left with you I tried to sleep
but it never came, not even in increments. The clean scent of
shower-fruits and Eris' apple mints had soaked into the sheets,
and the empty indent on the right side of the bed made the
whole thing feel uncomfortable and lopsided. I kept having a
sinking sensation in my stomach, like I was falling through a
dreamsphere, the queen mattress, pillow-topped and malleable,
leaning down to the left. But I kept my eyes closed, kept
running live-dreams across the inside of my eyelids, dreamt
consciously of tree buds opening and closing, breathing. When
the backdrop was red instead of black, I opened my eyes and
stood up, light-headed, eyes heavy.

Even though I didn't make the apology phone call, at
least part of me[9] still expected her to show up sometime in the
night. I left the hall light on and every few minutes I would
check the clock and the angle of the bedroom door to see if she
had come back. But the strange shadows burnt hard lines into
the walls, and she did not return.

Still in my underwear, I opened the shades fully and let
the morning sun in full throttle. My pupils struggled to adjust,
shrinking quickly to limit the light intake. I dressed in pre-worn
skinny jeans and short sleeves and gathered Eris' remnants
around the apartment, all the relics still scattered across the
bathroom. I scooped the change into my hand and brought it
out to my desk, put the dirty towel in the laundry room, and
picked up your stuffed squirrel. The right eye popped off, hung
from a single loose string, just as Eris had said it would, so I
picked up the brown button, unthreaded the twine, and put it
inside my wallet on my nightstand. I went into my office,
pulled my flask out of the drawer and took a few pulls.

the edges are too sharp
and my insides are too soft

---

[9] Probably my idealistically inclined right brain.

39

I looked out the window, looked at the floating porch which squared off at a right angle straight out from the door. I converted half the porch into a vegetable garden, where I honed my amateur horticultural and husbandry skills. Eris objected at first but eventually allowed me to grow what I wanted as long as she didn't have to be involved. My red bell peppers and tomatoes were almost ready to harvest, though the yellow summer squash still needed a week or two before it was ready to be planted.

The compost bucket, all loam and eggshells, was in the far corner. Eris was just getting used to the idea of having a garden on her porch, so when I brought up and explained the idea of composting too, she freaked. Always a germ-phob, ever since you came along she made us all obsessively wash our hands and use hand sanitizer. Apparently she was convinced that by keeping you away from germs you would never get sick so the thought of having trash and worms anywhere near our apartment made her lose it. I tried explaining how the human immune system builds strength by exposure to the very thing that it is defending against, but she wouldn't listen to anything logical.

I walked out and still at the top of the compost bucket was the tail end of a shriveled joint. I tried to light it, rotated and sucked out the last few harsh hits. The thick Midwestern heat made me more aware of my body, of my skin, of the holes forming in my chest, of the corrosion, the black water still dissolving inside, slipping through the singed slits.

I sweat liberally, my body self-cooling as the skin on my forearms and the back of my neck warmed. I knew the next day my skin would be burnt, would feel stretched too tightly over my bones. I grabbed three Coumadin out of my velvet pouch – knocking my gray lighter out in the process – and popped them into my dry mouth.

it helps and it's good
and it's just temporary

40

and they can't just sit in there with the ring
and it's not heart disease
or is it?
and is there something inside me, some kind of infection,
something unwelcome growing and multiplying, laying eggs
and rotting my heart out from the inside,
shooting its filthy seeds down my blood stream, out to fill up my limbs
and oh god what is Eris doing with my daughter
and what is she telling her?

While I watered my plants, I imagined Eris telling you stories about me, stories that weren't true, stories about the quality of my character to try to alienate me from my only daughter, trying to brainwash you, mold your mind, pit you against me, trying to build walls of cement in the air.

--"It's your father's fault that he's not around."--
OR
--"If he wanted to be with you, he would have changed."--
OR
--"He doesn't deserve to be with us. He's just a bum."--

The thought of Eris emotionally pulling you away from me, the thought of her planting ideas into your young trusting brain gave me an overwhelming urge to get out of the house, to confront her for not coming back, for putting all the onuses on me again, for orienting you against me. In my mind I would speak frankly, concisely, laconically revealing Eris' true character to you.

--"Your mother is an incorrigible strumpet, a serial dater."--
OR
--"Your mother has a pathological need to control us."--
OR
--"Your mother is a thief, a white-collar bandit."--

Filled with a youthfully enthusiastic ambition – a chest busting with well-intentioned venom – I went back inside for my bicycle.

41

i need to see her
and i have to see her
and this will change everything because i will not,
cannot be denied anything.

Biking often helped me clear my head, made me feel connected and dislodged all at once, helped me burn off emotions that I didn't know what to do with, helped get rid of the awkward excesses. I grabbed my bicycle out of my office in the apartment, tucked a t-shirt and my wallet into my pouch that I hooked underneath the seat, and snapped my phone into the case mounted to the handle bars. I took a few more pulls off my flask, flicked my gray lighter on and off, adjusted the flame height, and pocketed it along with my notebook, velvet pouch, and origami fortune teller.

FRONT LEFT: FRONT RIGHT:
lighter   pen
pouch of pills

BACK LEFT: BACK RIGHT:
origami fortune teller   notebook

Feeling reckless, feeling like metal and steel, I left my helmet behind and pedaled off in the direction of Julie's house, where I figured you and Eris would be staying.

I'm not sure how much your mother has told you about our relationship, about how she and I met and how you were conceived. And if she has talked to you about it, I'm not sure how much of what she's said is factual. So even though I know it's uncomfortable to think – or in this case – read about your parents having sex, I feel obligated to tell you my side of the story, to emphasize a few things from my perspective. I met your mother at my brother Brody's wedding. Since you haven't seen him in over a decade, I'll catch you up.

1 – At the time he was a professor of Greek Mythology and literature at the University of Cincinnati.

2 - He lived a few miles south of Hamilton, in downtown Cincinnati, with your Aunt Bailey and cousin Colton.

3 - Even though he and I lived just a few miles apart, we didn't see much of each other, didn't ever really cross paths.

4 - He and I weren't – had never really been – close, had always forced things.

5 - I had been dreading his wedding. It wasn't because I thought it was a bad idea. I just knew my father would be there, and I was determined to avoid him.

I'm not sure how much information you've gotten about my father either, so here are his highlights.

1 - He left when I was 11, moved to California with a younger girl.

2 - I saw him once a year until I was 14. I'll explain later why we stopped seeing each other.

3 - He and my mom never officially got divorced, never legally separated. After I went to college he came back from California, got back together with my mom. They resumed their marriage like nothing had ever happened.

43

4 - My mother always held on to his last name, Tyde.

5 - He patched things up with Brody too, but I kept the door tightly locked on him. Before the wedding, I hadn't seen or spoken to him in three years, our last meeting ending poorly.

Since Brody appointed me as one of the groomsman[10] I didn't have to worry about sitting next to my father during the ceremony. I skipped the rehearsal and the dinner afterwards, so the day of the wedding, I arrived just before it started and followed the lead of everyone else. From the steps by the alter, I saw my father sitting in the front row, naturally filling out his tailored suit and sitting smugly next to my mother. I avoided eye contact with him altogether, though I could feel him watching me, hoping to catch my eye if I turned even for a second in his direction. He had been trying to contact me since our last encounter a few years prior, but I had been diligently avoiding him.

I first saw your mother sitting at a table of strangers while I gave my obligatory toast at the reception. The first thing I noticed, the thing that initially caught my eye was her shiny face. The lights in the reception hall bounced off it, creating a blinding shimmer like a coin in sunlight at just the right angle. We sort of alternated looking at each other, deliberately not making eye contact – each conducting an independent physical inventory of the other. We eventually crossed gazes but both turned away bashfully.

Later in the evening, out of the corner of my eye, I caught a glimpse of her maroon dress under the flashing lights on the disco-style dance floor. As the lights flickered on and off in retro ecstasy, her shiny face glowed and faded alternately, her blonde hair white under the intense lights. Our dance patterns eventually intersected, but we moved past each other again without pause though with definite mutual interest. It wasn't

---

[10] I was up there more to even the sides than anything else. It was purely cosmetic.

until we ended up next to each other in line at the open bar that we first spoke.

Just to make sure we're on the same page[11], Julie was one
of Eris' best friends from the hair salon. Her and her husband
Mark had two daughters, straddling you in age, so naturally
play dates became a regular occurrence, and we were each
other's de facto babysitters. They lived in a new subdivision just
northeast of our apartment, about a twelve mile, mostly flat
bicycle ride I figured.

I was right about the distance to their house but wrong
about the topography – or maybe I was just out of shape since it
was summer and I wasn't biking to work every day. I had made
the drive in Eris' car plenty of times, but I'm always amazed at
how different the lay of the land is when you experience it first-
hand rather than through a windshield. A nasty head wind
followed me at every turn, taunted me in circles, my head
spinning, the sun hot on my neck.

When I turned left into Julie's neighborhood I saw Eris'
red Jeep parked in the driveway of their home, a two-story
standard suburban set-up with a dull-peach trim, the siding a
faint mauve. All the houses were brightly colored: cream-
yellows, sea-greens, scarlets, powder blues. And they were
close together, everything snug and leaning into each other. It
was a painting. Fauvism. Strident and wild, vague at the edges.
But they had a clearly demarcated yard made distinct by
varying shades of green, Julie's yard being much more fertile
than either neighbor.

A black truck was parked on the curbside by their
mailbox – fashioned in the shape of a fire truck to match Mark's
profession. I had a hunch the black truck belonged to Mark's
brother, John, who I had only met in passing several times. He
always had scabbed knuckles, had always just been in a scuffle.

Pulling into the neighborhood, I felt a sharp pain shoot
down my right quadriceps, felt something pop and tighten. I

---

[11] I'm not sure if you know them or not. Maybe they're still an everyday part
of your life.

hid my bike behind a pair of large, rounded burning bushes by the entrance sign, and not wanting to draw attention to myself, I shuffled, trying not to limp, towards their house just along the main road, third on the left. The neighborhood was quiet, their yard uncluttered.

> *this truck must be john's.*
> *but i should check.*

I cupped my hands up against the tinted windows. Inside I saw a police badge sitting in the front seat, along with a huge plastic container of what appeared to be some sort of body building supplement.

> *definitely john's*

I hobbled– my limp getting harder to conceal, the muscles getting stiffer, more taut – over to Eris' car to see if I could figure out what she had been up to, to see if she carried around an explanation for not returning the night before. It was mostly full of things I recognized from our apartment, things she had gathered quickly when she left – some blankets, a red plastic basket of toiletry items in the floorboard, a box of your toys sitting in the passenger's seat, your car seat – which I kept telling Eris you were too big to still be using – a pile of linens she had not sorted out yet, and a laundry basket full of shoes.

> *why hasn't she unloaded all this into Julie's house?*
> *and is she planning to come back soon after all?*
> *and had last night just been extra punishment?*

I patted the origami fortune teller in my pocket and looked back at John's truck. Last December, Julie and Mark had introduced John to Eris at their annual holiday party. Since that party John had been coming to Eris' salon regularly.

In my head I pictured myself bursting through the front door, screaming obscenities and accusatory statements about her character and the character of those who offered her solace.

→"How could you leave and not come back?!"
→"How could you threaten to take Luna away from me?!"
→I will yell between heaves of angry tears.
    →Belligerently.
        →I should have come drunker, should have packed
        my flask.
        →I should go in smelling of whiskey and tree bark,
        smoke and fiery lubricants.
   ←No.
        →It's better to appear level-headed.
        →Restrained.
        →Tempered.
        →Intentionally angry.
        →Everything measured, but still loose, unpredictable.

But just as I got ready to break and enter, I heard voices back by the porch. When I would pick up or drop you off, really anytime I saw Mark, he would invite me out to see his new porch. He talked about it constantly, had apparently installed a new patio area, complete with a hot tub, a grilling station, and gazebo-themed sitting area. And Julie had planted a garden filled with perennials: hot pink anemones, tiny sharp-petaled bluestars, leafy bunchberry, gazanias bursting with fire. Truthfully I was more interested in the garden than the stonework.

I heard splashing in the hot tub, so I made my way carefully around to the side of the house. The muscles around my thigh coiled and clamped down over the bone.

i will run in arms high, will belly-flop into the hot tub,
come up yelling, tongue-snapping.

"Do you guys want something to drink?"

The voice calling from inside the house belonged to Julie. I recognized the squeaky sopronic vibrations, the soft wet timbre.

"Actually, yeah, that'd be great. Maybe a glass of red wine."

It was unmistakably Eris – breathy and nasal, a faint whistle chirping in tiny bursts with the egression of air through her white teeth

"A beer would be great."

The guttural, friction-heavy voice surely belonged to John. They sounded like they were sitting in the hot tub together. I heard the door creak open and click shut, and it was quiet except for a few watery sloshes. There were voices, hushed and hurried. I couldn't hear them clearly so I crept, keeping my right leg straight, along the side of the house to get within earshot.

"…and you're too good for a guy like that."

bastard

"…be honest with you? I just really wish none of this ever happened and…"

I took shorter breaths, quicker and audible. I heard more sloshing around in the hot tub and muffled feminine giggles, high pitched throat whistles. I was hot, sweating. My blood was flowing, unstuck and sweeping through my limbs. I was on fire. Everything was shaking, tiny earthquakes under my skin, between my muscles. The angled shade created by the side of the house receded, spilling the strong sun across me as I craned my neck closer to the edge to hear more of the conversation. Sweat dripped off my brow onto the twisted rhododendrons planted in a semi-circle. I unpocketed my notebook.

Unmasculine
-Peeing in stalls
-Sneaking around outside an acquaintance's house
-Identifying rhododendrons

I took the ring out of the pouch and placed it on my pinkie. Over my shoulder, I heard their garage door open. Mark had fired up the weed eater which drowned out all the tiny disloyal voices coming from the backyard.

50

--I just wish none of this ever happened.--
--I just wish none of this ever happened.--

My skin buzzed everywhere inside and out, numbing all my senses, numbing my fingers. Starting to panic and quickly losing bodily fluids, my cramp worsened and my vision blurred. I shuffled my way back towards the front of the house and peered around the front corner to gauge where Mark was trimming. Thankfully he had gone around to the other side of the house to start. But I could feel a pair of eyes on me, something looking down.

this is it
and the sky will open
and this is it

Head spinning, I looked up and saw their neighbor, staring and pointing down at me from her upstairs window with a phone in her hand. I was caught. Eris would soon be notified, would come around the corner with a towel wrapped around her. John would be proudly shirtless and thick-chested with a hand on the small of her back. They would say things, spew negative sundries about my lack of character, about my wilted moral fiber, about my inadequacies.

run

I moved quickly, stayed low to the ground. I ran with my arms because my leg was useless, dragging behind me in the grass, my knee bending awkwardly. I felt like I was running on sand, couldn't get any traction, my legs buried. But I made it to the entrance of the neighborhood, grabbed my bicycle out of the bushes, pushed off with my good leg. My feet were on fire, churning through the wild lava inside the earth, my feet pushing through the ground. The pain in my cramped thigh – a stone pressing against the skin – reverberated down to my toes and up into my spine as I forced it to keep pushing. I checked over my shoulder, half-expecting to either pass out or see John's truck cresting the hill with a noose and thick tree branch in the back. But I didn't see anything, and I pushed the ring off my pinkie, watched it bounce into a drainage ditch.

Over my shoulder I saw your mother standing in line behind me. Already socially lubricated by a half-dozen low-cal beers, I was loose enough to lead the way into a conversation.

"So how do you know the bride and groom?"

"Actually I don't know them at all. I wasn't really invited. I came as a guest of a friend," she said swinging her arm around the room. Apparently she had befriended everyone. "What about you?"

"Don't tell anybody, but I don't know anyone here either. I'm actually trying to crash the wedding."

She laughed. Casually, with restraint, ready to play along. "Nuh-uh. I saw you giving a toast."

"Yeah I just walked up and grabbed the mic and started talking."

She leaned into me, her elbows inches away from my chest.

"So where's your friend? Or did you say date?"

"Oh, no, it's not a date. I came here with one of my good girlfriends," she said speeding up. "She is one of Bailey's friends from high school. I guess her real date bailed on her so she asked me to tag along so she didn't have to make the trip to southern Indiana from Ohio alone."

"Oh so you're from out of town?"

"Yeah I live in Cincinnati – that's where Bailey's from too. We both went to St. Ursula but I didn't really know her that well."

"St. Ursula, huh? I didn't have you pegged as one of those conservative, highbrow types."

"You've heard of it?"

"Yeah. Do you know where Hamilton is?"

"Yeah! That's actually where I live, but I always just tell people Cincinnati since people have heard of it."

"That's where I used to live before I moved here for school. I just graduated a few months ago."

"No way! Small world." She turned her head down and combed her fingers through her hair, blonde and wavy at her shoulders. "So what about you, where's your date?"

"None for me. I didn't even get 'and guest' on the invitation."

We ordered our drinks – a red wine spritzer and a domestic light beer – and went our separate ways again. She was energetically drunk, interested but not ready to settle, and I had to stay on the move to avoid being cornered by my father, who I was able to keep a watch on above the crowd-level, both of our heads sticking out of the top. So I moved through the night with one eye on my father and one on Eris whose shiny face I could see, even through the crowd, moving from group to group around the room. Partially because I had to constantly recalculate my coordinates to avoid my father and partially because of her erratic movement, Eris and I just kept circling each other, our clear eyes synching up while we moved around the room.

Our orbits collided again at the end of the reception. I had been tasked with handing out sparklers for people to light so we could emblazon the path for the newlyweds to their get-away car. While I went around handing out sparklers, I scanned the atrium for a bright flash of light, something sharp and concentrated. Call it kismet or whatever you want, but when I had two sparklers left I turned around and saw your mother standing right next to me, scanning the top of the crowd.

"Hey it's you again!" she said when we both turned and saw each other.

"Yep. You need a sparkler?"

"Yeah sure."

"Here I'll go ahead and light it for you."

We carried our dwindling sparklers outside to join the collective bodies fortifying a path between the door and the limousine hired to carry away the bride and groom. Both sufficiently drunk by this point in the night, Eris and I hunched over laughing at nothing, our hands on each other's shoulders.

"They better come out soon or we're gonna need some new sparklers," she said while both of our sparklers sizzled at the bottom of the stick.

this is nice
and this is good
and this is right
and no one can ever stop us
and where is my father?

I had lost him, briefly forgotten he was there. So I scanned the crowd looking for a thick head of hair standing tall above the rest. He stood idly beside my mother, laughing and pointing at something. But then he was moving, walking in big strides, bumping shoulders and looking serious, stern. He was still pointing. He was moving and pointing and waving.

"Hey I think that guy is trying to get your attention," Eris said.

He was coming right towards me, looking right at me, his eyes black, unblinking, eyes like stones, tiny jewels stuck inside. But my mom grabbed his elbow and whispered something into his ear that sent him off course.

"I'll be right back."

I did a loop around Eris, throwing my father off my scent and ran back into the atrium where I saw Brody and Bailey getting ready to make their grand exit. I picked up the box of sparklers, pulled my lighter out of my pocket and ran back out to Eris.

"Hurry! Here they come!" she said pointing towards the doors.

Brody and Bailey ran down the stairs, hand-in-hand. Eris and I lit and waved our sparklers frantically, screaming and cheering. When I look back, it feels like a cheesy movie montage, but I think for your mom and me it was essential for the course of our relationship to feel transcendent in that moment and to be rootless and lost together in that collective effervescence. Something about weddings makes people feel things more intensely because as we all yelled and watched them duck into the limo, I was on the edge of tears, but I really can't explain why. I looked over at Eris and her eyes – heavy and hazel – were watering too. We were both caught in a weirdly binding, collision-type moment. Our bodies weren't touching but there was friction between us, something happening. I've always sort of believed – more so now after all that's happened – that our bodies have some kind of invisible magnetic field that surrounds our skin, not like a shield, but like a magnet that pushes and pulls us in certain directions. It's not like a fate thing or even something measurable by an oscilloscope. It's just a manifestation of our tendencies. I think our magnetic fields collided that night, the sparks fooling us into seeing attraction.

After the newlyweds got into their limousine graffitied with chalk lettering and rainbow colored paper streamers, the crowd dispersed, but Eris and I stayed right where we stood, blinking, still recovering from what we knew we had both felt – an unbalanced electrocution of our hearts and veins.

"Do you want to go get a drink or something maybe?" she asked looking around.

> *i need to get out of here*
> *and she's cute and has so much energy*
> *and so much life*
> *and is so bright*
> *and i'm a little drunk*
> *and my skin feels alive*
> *and this could work*
> *and this could be good*

"Yeah sure."

"Great. There's a bar at the hotel I'm staying at. That work for you?"

"Sounds good."

"Great. Let me just tell my friend not to wait up for me."

I said my goodbyes – handshakes, cheek kisses, back slaps – to everyone, careful to avoid my father, at the reception. Walking the few blocks to her hotel, it started raining – not hard but enough for the water to gather in holes and gaps in the pavement. Without regard for her summer dress, Eris jumped off the sidewalk and splashed, rippling the full moon, into a tiny puddle beginning to form in the pavement. Your mother was the kind of person who would jump in puddles when it rained just so people would think she was the kind of person who would spontaneously jump in puddles. I think it was just a subconscious means of testing me while providing multiple contexts – a social chameleon – within which she could operate.

Inside the hotel bar, we sat next to each other on tall armless circular chairs. The bartender, an intangibly masculine woman probably in her late thirties wore a white button up blouse with fluff near the top. The room smelled of dry whiskey, smelled like a campfire. Eris and I were the only two people in the room, except for an older man in a suit sitting in a leather chair next to the window watching the rain fall and swirling the ice cubes around in his drink, sipping occasionally. Horn-heavy jazz music played quietly over the stereo system.

"I'll have a beer. Something local. Maybe an IPA."

"Perfect. And for the lady…" The bartender spoke deeply, the words folding out of her gut. I turned towards Eris.

"Red wine."

Your mother's unusually shiny face – not oily, just bright – gave her a luminous quality that made her more human, less intimidating.

> she's too pretty to be here with me
> and she's had many sexual partners, developed early,
> was kissing with tongue by the fifth grade
> and i don't belong here
> and how does she not see it yet?

"So why did you ask me to come here with you? Are you just the kind of person who likes meeting new people or something?"[12]

She gave me a drunken smile – smug, her lips thinning – because of my straight-forwardness. The bartender backed

---

[12] I've since discovered that she really does like to meet new people. But she likes it because she has this incessant need to see how people react to her. She needs to meet new people so she'll know who she is.

away, skillful in the art of pretending to clean something in order to give us some space.

"Well, truth be told, I just got out of a really long, serious relationship…"

"Oh boy, here we go."

"Shut up," she laughed. "I'm serious. But he was, you know, like the stereotypical guy, all muscular and hot-headed."

she dated my father
and do i look like my father
and she sees my father in me

"I'm familiar with the type."

"Anyway, he ended up cheating on me so I dumped him."

"And so you asked me to come here because…?"

"Because you seem like the complete opposite of him. And you're nice."

"And cute," I added.

"And very cute."

i should ask her.
no, it's inappropriate timing
and it's a date!
and it's not a date.
it's casual.
it's conversation.
innocent coquetry at best.
and i should ask her.
and i need the numbers.

"Can I ask you something?"

"Sure."

"This is going to sound really weird so let me preface it by saying that it's for some research I'm doing." I pulled out my notebook, licked my finger and rubbed it over the point of my pen.

"Okay…What?"

"Do you have any kids?"

58

"Not yet but I've always wanted kids, lots of them. I can't wait to be a mom."

"Oh okay. Well thanks." I marked the tally in the corresponding category of my ever-growing sample set.

"What kind of research are you doing?"

"It's nothing, really. It's…hey did you feel that…I don't know, *electricity* when we were waving those sparklers?"

"Yeah it was one of those spine-tingling moments. Totally weird," she said taking a sip of her wine.

We sat there and talked until the neutrinos or radiation or whatever kind of mass or magnetic energy from our encounter cleared out of our veins. My alcoholic confidence and talkativeness were wearing down. She put her hand on my wrist and looked at my watch.

"I'd better go. It's getting late," she said reaching into her clutch for a mint.

"So I'll call you up sometime?"

"Well I'm only in town until tomorrow night, then I'm going back to Ohio. So 'sometime' probably better be sooner rather than later."

She brushed my arm again and laughed an unwarranted and sloppy laugh. Her offer felt more like a drunken bargain, a cheap, last minute, obligatory suggestion.

But I still woke up the next morning thinking about her, about her energy, thinking that her spark might pull me out of my rut. So I called her up, and we met for lunch at a café near her hotel. Rain still drizzled down from the night before, so when I walked her back to her hotel room we tried to fit under the same umbrella. Our elbows touched, sending charges up and down our forearms and she slipped her arm, soft and rattling, around mine. We got as close as we could but we were both still getting wet, so I walked a step behind her holding it over her tiny frame. It felt cliché, but it made me feel useful and I think it made her feel desired, so we went with it. She asked me up to her room, and of course, I came up.

I wish none of this ever happened.
I wish none of this ever happened.
I wish none of this ever happened.
I wish none of this ever happened.

I flipped and inverted the phrase, followed the curves of the letters, looked at the spaces between the words, boiled it down and steamed out its assumptions. The themes of the phrase – regret, insatiability, wanting to start over – made me think of Noah and his letter, made me envy his chosen lifestyle that allowed him to live multiple lives in succession. When he finished with one, he shed it off in favor of another, something fresher, softer. He was a snake. A palimpsest. While I pedaled away – knees circling and jumping like pistons – from Julie's house with no particular destination in mind, I had a deep desire – somewhere down in my marrow – to swap skins with Noah, to adjust my reality, turn it into putty and put it in the kiln to see what came out hardened.

I didn't want to go back to my empty apartment yet, not alone, not before it had been sterilized it, cleaned of anything covered in Eris-dust. So I stopped at a familiar gas station to rest and rehydrate, to avoid confronting anything. Still cramped and weak with anger, I pulled out and swallowed a Coumadin and another of the white round pills with OC inscribed on it.

Outside the gas station kiosk I noticed a man – old only in the eyes – sitting on an upside down white bucket leering at me. He had on a ragged long sleeve t-shirt with the word 'ALBEDO' printed in large block letters across his chest and rocked back and forth rubbing his hands up and down his sleeves, thin and frayed, like he was cold. Instinctively, I tried to avoid eye contact with him as I limped inside.

I'm sure she's still like this, but in case not, your mother refused to drink tap water, even if filtered, so we always bought the gallon jugs at the grocery store. And she wouldn't let me buy the smaller ones because she said they were inefficient. So unable to bend my right leg, I habitually shuffled towards the back wall of shelved gallon jugs.

i hate gallon jugs
and they're too cumbersome, too pretentious
and i should get something else,
something smaller, something totable
and i should stick it to her
and mail her a cartoon of tiny water bottles.
UNFILTERED!
do they sell unfiltered water?

I backed up and went for the suction-lined, swinging cooler doors. My hands wobbled, grabbing as many tiny water bottles as I could handle. Cradling them against my chest, I shuffled up to the cash register. The clerk wore all black, all sleeves, showed no skin but her face and fingers. Ringing up my bottles, she leered – behind black-lined eyes – at me like the man on the bucket outside.

"$6.66."

I shuffled back and grabbed one more bottle.

"$7.99."

I gave her a ten and tore along the perforation on the plastic sleeve covering the top of the first bottle, the kind that required suction. The clerk sat back down on her stool and flipped through a magazine with pale, sharp-toothed men on the front. My frontal lobe and the back of my throat numbed but my leg loosened while I chugged.

Outside, the man on the bucket was still rocking. He had a large facial pustule just above his lip. I walked – elbows tucked in, eyes straight ahead – by him and dropped my change from the water purchase into his mug which splashed as it fell in. He reached in and pulled out the two soggy bills and the penny. I smiled apologetically, my cheek's skin stretching out across my face. He stopped rocking and pulled out a pocketknife.

he's going to kill me, stab me in the gut and bleed me out
and the gothic woman will help, will laugh the whole time,

will drag me into the woods
and do strange things to my cadaver.

He reached into his knapsack and pulled out a giant red apple, used the knife to slice it into bite-sized segments. He held a slice up to me, dangling it from the tip of his knife.

"No thanks," I said limping past him.

"Leg cramp?"

"Yeah. It's just…"

"Here eat this." He pulled a yellow banana out of his knapsack, dirty and tattered. "It has a ton of potassium. It'll help."

He spoke with startling annunciation, all the hard consonants exact, the vowels sung softly. He spoke like he knew many languages, knew foreign ways to twist his tongue. I hesitated, not wanting to get tied down in a conversation with a stranger carrying a knife. He flipped over another bucket next to him and slapped his hand on the top.

"No I should really be going."

"You look like you need a rest to me," he said still holding up the banana like a gun.

is he going to shoot me?
i should oblige and he has a gun in his knapsack
and he shoots target practice often, at live mammals,
tiny and swift-footed and he has a knife
and he is a professional knife thrower
and he worked at the circus,
could cut an acorn in half from great distances.
i should oblige.

"I guess I could sit for a minute."

The bucket was cold and wet against my back pocket, so I pulled out my notebook, leaned to the right to keep the origami fortune teller in my back left pocket dry.

"You okay?" He looked at my hands wobbling as I peeled the skin off the banana.

"Yeah I'm fine. It's just been a weird day and a half. You live around here?" I asked hoping to change the subject.

"Yep."

He pointed towards a man-made ditch behind the gas station where I saw a tied off garbage bag and a white milk crate tied to a purple moped.

"That's where you live?"

"Well, it's just temporary. But it works. How's the leg?"

"Much better," I said between mushy banana bites. "I can already feel it loosening up."

"Bananas kill cramps. And I'll let you in on the secret too." He tilted his bucket, leaned in closer to me, lowered his voice. "It's all about the color. You've got to get them when they're still a little green and then eat them as soon as they're fully yellow. You can't let 'em get too mushy."

"Thanks," I said leaning away. His breath was awful: old fruit and sweet tea.

"So who is she?" He leaned away and bit another slice of red apple off the tip of his knife.

"What?"

"Who's the girl?"

"What do you mean?"

"You think I can't tell a torn heart when I see one?"

"Is it that obvious?"

I stared at his ready-to-burst facial pustule instead of his eyes, yellow and dry.

"Yeah. Let me tell you kid...what's your name?

"Hurley."

"Let me tell you Hurley, we've all had our hearts broken. Did she leave you or did you leave her?"

"She left me."

"For another guy?"

"I think so."

"Well then you're free," he said holding his arms up into the air.

I twisted my lips sideways.

"You'll be alright kid. You just need to get some distance. Go somewhere that you've never been with her. Go somewhere completely new. Experience something completely unfamiliar. You can't go to places that you used to go with her.

It might feel good. It might hurt so much that it's actually nice. But it doesn't do any good. It's not productive."

He threw the apple core over his back shoulder.

"You think that'll work?"

"I don't know. But that's why I'm out here. Because my old lady, well ex-old lady, she's never been this free. Best to my knowledge anyway."

I finished my banana, stretched and popped my knee, rolled my ankle around to test the leg muscles underneath.

"Well do you think it's working?"

"What's that? "

"Being here."

"Oh it's too soon to tell."

His hands dirty, his skin thick and tough, I wanted to know how long it had been. We leaned our bodies in opposite directions on our buckets and he whistled an unfamiliar tune.

"Can I ask you something?"

"I think you already did."

"Right. Do you have any kids? I'm just asking because of some research I'm doing."

"Yep, two of 'em in fact."

"How often do you see them?"

"Not so much anymore, I guess. I send 'em cards and stuff in the mail. But I tend to avoid going out there because of my old-lady, well ex-old lady anyway."

"How old are they?"

"Thirteen and Fifteen."

"Boys or girls?"

"You sure are asking a lot of questions." His pustule trembled and shook, wiggled with weight.

"It's for research," I said raising my head, looking at his forehead, looking at the spot between his eyebrows.

"Right. Boy and a girl."

I scribbled down the information, guessing at his age, not wanting to annoy him with more questions.

"Anything else?"

"No. Well, actually, yeah. What's your name?"

"Albedo."

"Oh, okay, I get it," I said pointing to his shirt.

"Yep. It's a family name. Just call me Al, though."

"Well I should get going," I said standing back up, feeling dizzy from the pills. "Thanks for the banana."

I half-waved from my hip, my arms suddenly hot and itchy. Al watched me signal my way back onto the road, turning westward. I didn't really have anything else to do and like I said, I didn't want to go back to the apartment. It was empty, heavy, the roof made of stone.

> *does Al know the truth*
> *and is she a cataract, a scar on my iris*
> *and can i really exorcise her spirit by announcing my own*
> *and i can't go home*

I tried to think of something Eris and I hadn't seen together, things that she'd never touched or tasted or imagined, places she'd never even thought about, places she didn't even know existed. I needed a place she would hate, something to spite her. I took out my gray lighter, flicked it on and off and texted Ryan:

"hey man, i need to pick up a package. be there in 10"

Ryan's apartment complex – built in the early seventies – was molded, untamed. The entrance sign was electric green, the roof of each unit was a moss green, the doors were deep forest green, and the dense and sturdy shrubberies covering the bottom half of the windows were a brown-green. I knocked on his door and in the adjacent window, a finger slipped through and lifted up one of the vinyl slates on the blinds. He was a sweaty man, sweatier than me, his brow always moist, the edges of his shaggy hair always wet. And he couldn't be still, not even for a second. His foot was always tapping, his knees banging together, his eyebrows rolling like caterpillars. When he answered the door his curly brown hair was matted with sweat and pointed in all directions, and he wore a pair of thick-rimmed reflective black shades even though the apartment was almost completely dark.

"How much do you need?"

"Just give me a quarter."

"OG?"

"Yeah, sure, whatever you have."

"You need anything else? Blue guys? More oxies? Something to rail?"

"What? No, just the weed."

"You got it, bro."

He offered no other greeting and walked – knees like jelly, elbows flapping – back into his bedroom to retrieve the package. On his kitchen table I saw an egg carton, gray and soft.

> *i should put his eggs back in the fridge for him,*
> *they'll go bad,*
> *stink up his whole apartment*

I cracked open the carton to see how many were inside. But there weren't any eggs. Instead the carton was hollowed out – all the half-rounded egg holders flattened – and several foldable plastic baggies were inside, each filled with colorful pills. A pale rainbow of relief.

→These pills look unfamiliar.
    →If I take them I might experience unfamiliar things.
        →Unfamiliar things, like Al said, might help me shake off Eris.

I slipped a baggy into my front left pocket next to my gray lighter and pouch. I looked down the hall to make sure Ryan hadn't seen me. It was dark though, hard to tell, all the shapes curving and growing limbs. The only light – real or artificial – coming into his apartment was the sunlight coming through the closed blinds, rows of white lines on the walls and floor. I looked for a light switch, a side lamp, something, but there weren't any built-in overhead lights anywhere other than the kitchen.

> *maybe i'll buy him a lamp for christmas this year*
> *and maybe some colored light bulbs.*
> *something sustainable,*
> *low output.*

Ryan came out of the darkness, emerged slimy with sweat holding a twisted plastic baggy of cannabis, some brief description of the strain scribbled across the front. Like he always did, he opened it up, stuck his nose in and took a big whiff.

"Mmm. That's some good shit, man." To me weed has always smelled like body odor. Or maybe the smells just mixed together in Ryan's steam-sweaty apartment causing me to create an irrelevant, subconscious association between the two smells. "Ten bucks."

"Still giving me the teacher's discount, huh?"

My knuckles grazed your brown button while I pulled the cash out of my wallet.

> *she's mine and i can't do this*
> *and none of this is right*
> *and this can't be real*
> *and it's so fucking dark in here*
> *and there's black water everywhere and*

"Yeah, o'course. I wouldn't have passed English without you, man."

"Right."

He would always smile and nod his head incessantly after saying something semi-serious. It was annoying, the kind of smile that said: Damn, can you believe I just said that? I wanted to punch him, to throw something at him. More so because what he said was true, though. He had been in my first English class as a teacher at Hamilton High School. He showed up completely baked after school one day to re-take a test. A baggy of marijuana and some crumpled rolling papers fell out of his cargo pants while he writhed around his seat during the test. I'm not really proud of this, but instead of busting him, he agreed to let me start quietly buying from him for cheap.

Your mother and I reached an unspoken agreement that our fling was just the result of post-wedding emotion, that it was just a fun ephemeral night. We lived in different states. It wasn't practical. We had only talked a few times since that night, always through the buffer of social media, never direct conversation. There was flirting, but it was casual, digital – smiley and winky faces made of punctuation, exclamation points and initialisms. Nothing was real. Nothing was serious. And even though I had convinced myself she had no interest in anything romantic or even a repetitious evening, I kept thinking about her, specifically the electricity I felt, the way our bodies snapped into place, felt cosmically synched. So I was glad when she called me up three weeks after the wedding, but her tone when I picked up wasn't what I was hoping.

"Listen, we need to talk."

"Yeah, I think so too. I'm really glad you called. I've been thinking a lot about you. And I know we decided it was just a one-time thing since you live all the way in Ohio and I'm here. But…"

"I'm pregnant."

Straight in. No posturing. No lead in. No pressing through a silk screen. My hands numbed, the tips of my fingers felt heavy, asleep. Things moved inside me – my organs digesting themselves – and I couldn't sit still, couldn't keep my feet from shaking. Your mother and I held our cell phones up to our ears and mouths, the only evidence of our continued connection was the sound of breathing into the mouthpiece. Her short, choppy breaths like small wind gusts in my ear – ghost friction.

"Are you serious?"

"I wouldn't joke about this."

"And you're absolutely sure?"

"One hundred percent. I'm never late. And I took the test like three times to make sure. I'm *definitely* pregnant."

"But I thought you were on birth control."

"I was. But I also started taking a new kind of medication, just borrowed it from my roommate to see if it would help me. I didn't even think about it, but I guess it somehow canceled everything out."

"And it's definitely mine?"

"Oh, god absolutely. Yeah you're the only person I've slept with since I broke up with Jim and that was only two months ago."

→Who is Jim?

   →I don't even know this woman.

      →And she's growing someone inside her, and it's partially mine.

      →And a piece of me is inside her and will always hold us together.

   ←I don't even know her.

      →Who is Jim?

         →Her muscular ex-boyfriend.

            →He can probably make his pecks dance.

            →And has staggering sexual stamina.

            →And he grows hair all over his body.

               →And then shaves it off and then grows it back again just because he can.

There was another pause in the conversation, silences broken only by breathing and unnecessary clearing of throats – tiny announcements.

(ahem) → *"I'm still here!"*

"And you're keeping it right?"

"Oh my god, that's not even an option. Of course I'm keeping it."

"Sorry I didn't mean to offend you."[13]

---

[13] I was only asking to try to be accommodating, to be supportive.

"No it's okay. It's just that I have strong convictions about that. Not for religious reason really, it's just…well it's not an option."

Over the next few weeks we talked on the phone more often, and in August, after I had driven out once to see her, I floated out an idea via video chat.

"Here's an idea. What if I move out there?"

She bit her lip and stared at the wall past the camera.

> she wants me to state my case and i should have made a poster
> and pasted pictures on a tri-fold science fair board
> and should have used lots of 3-D diagrams, block letters.
> no!
> bubble letters!
> lots of curves.
> everything light, soft.
> cotton swabs everywhere, taped all over the board
> and bright colored tissue paper and streamers!
> and it should have been a celebration!
> but i'd sneak in facts about single motherhood,
> and about the delinquency of bastard children.

She was looking back into the camera, waiting.

"I just hate to miss everything, all the appointments and milestones. I feel like I should be there for all that. I want to be there for all that. And there's no way I can be involved from two and a half hours away."

"I don't know." She said it slowly, unrolled the words, lengthened the vowels and turned them into water. "What would you do?"

"I can transfer, finish my teacher education program there."

Technically I was working through a teacher education program, though more than anything, I was sitting around with my rotating roommates in our slowly dilapidating house in the off-campus bowery. None of us were close, though I'd been there for three years and though the group changed, whoever lived there it was always the same, all of us wearing tank tops and too-tight shorts talking – with the windows open, the AC always broken – about obscure equations and philosophical madness, extending our college years further than they had any right to be stretched. The only thing that brought us together – the only reason we spoke in we's – was that we were all in the same battle against loneliness. Instead of sitting alone on weekends we vowed – though it was never spoken – to always sit together, to unite. A strength in numbers type of thing.

"I'm not tied down here and I just hate the idea of missing out on my child's life. And plus I'd love being closer to you."

I said that last part with trepidation, quickly self-conscious, unsure of how she would react. I pretended to scratch my face to cover my quivering bottom lip. We still hadn't really had that pivotal define-the-relationship conversation.

"Yeah, I guess I'd like that too."

Looking back on it now, I'm not sure if her reasons for agreeing were the same as mine, but I guess it doesn't matter. All I'm saying here is that I took the initiative, that I made the adjustment, that I picked up and moved, that more than anything I was determined to be there for you. By the end of September, three months after Eris and I first met and mated we were living together in our own apartment with your body folded inside hers.

June 22nd 2010

Tuesday
late afternoon

Bicycling through downtown Hamilton towards the apartment, I passed teal-topped buildings with endless windows and pointy-tipped limestone houses. I swerved past statues, some old – dirty-bronze, patina-green – bearing stern faces of old men, others new and brightly colored, abstract and spiral-shaped.

i shouldn't have bought that weed
and i shouldn't have taken that bag of pills,
shouldn't have eaten the blue chalky one
and it's dirty and it's tainted
and i'm dirty and i'm tainted

In German Village – at High Street and Third, about seven miles north of the apartment – I saw an untried diner. I must have passed it hundreds of times on my way to work, but I had never noticed it before, nestled between a dirty brick building and an old paper mill. An easily miss-able faded white sign with cracked block letters peaked under the pale green awning of a building overhead. Still unwilling to go home, still aching for something non-Erisian, I chained my bike and went inside. There were several booths along the side wall and a long bar by the front door. Sizzles, cracks, and clanks came out of the kitchen, partially visible behind a white half-wall. A handmade sign said:

73

The diner was empty except for three large men in beards chatting up a massive female cook at the front counter, so I sat down in a four-person booth by the back window. A tired looking waitress, her eyes dark and sunken in, soon came over.

"What can I get for you?"

Her voice was quick, strained, drenched in smoke. It was the voice of an old woman coming out of a young body, an overused body.

she has small children at home.
undoubtedly.
and i should ask her how many, what ages,
the history of their names,
how often their father comes around.

"Just a glass of water and some crackers."

She walked away with her eyes down, arms stuck at her sides, too heavy to swing. I looked at the menu posted on yellowed paper under a smeared glass covering across the table. Your mother would have ordered an iced tea and the soup of the day. Then she would lean over in the seat and help you with your food, or if you were with Julie, she would say she was going to call and check on you. I'd tell her that you were fine, but she'd get up and call anyway. After the meal she'd reach into her square purse for a mint and her pocket mirror. I pulled out my notebook.

Things Eris Has Not Seen
-Diner

--"I wish none of this ever happened." –

But I wasn't sure what she had and hadn't seen anymore, what she would and wouldn't do and say.

Things Eris Has Not Seen
→Diner
→The inside of Ryan's apartment.

I watched the waitress glide behind the white kitchen half-wall, her dyed-black hair hanging in a bun behind her head, loose bangs swinging freely across her face. I watched her set the water and crackers – three in the package – in front of me without making eye contact.

> *maybe her shift is almost over*
> *and maybe she likes to listen*
> *and she's an outsider*
> *and so maybe she can provide some clarity*
> *and maybe she is looking for the same thing*
> *and we can be the ant and the aphid*
> *and we can be a cinematic, box office smash*

Imagined Scenes with a Tired Waitress
By C. Hurley Tyde

Act 1:
(The scene opens with WAITRESS walking towards YOUR FATHER's table. The corners of her lips are barely – but noticeably – upturned.)

WAITRESS
Did you need anything else, sir?

YOUR FATHER
No, I don't think so.
(Or maybe YOUR FATHER would be feeling more ambitious.)
No I don't think so, but would you like to sit and chat for a while? You could tell me where you grew up and how you came to live in Hamilton. Myself? I've been here for several years now. I teach at the high school just up the road. My brother is a teacher too, well a professor. He's always outdoing me. I know you didn't ask, but it's rude for me to come on so strong and not let you know even the slightest thing about myself, about what brought me here. Not that you're really interested in me at all. Well you might have the potential to be, but it's probably too soon to tell. I think I used to believe people

75

are predisposed towards one another but I'm not really sure how I feel about that anymore. Actually, I think that's why I'm here. Truthfully I'm not sure of much of anything anymore. Or maybe I never was. I guess I'm still not sure what's real and what's not. The only thing that I know is real is that I only enjoy things after the fact, never during. God, I've said too much, haven't I? You must think I'm just the sort of person who turns all of his problems into epic ordeals.

WAITRESS
(She slides into the booth seat across from YOUR FATHER. *She tucks her tiny yellow pencil behind her ear and closes up her palm-sized black notebook that she uses to write down orders.)*
No, of course not. Please go on good looking man with interesting ideas.

YOUR FATHER
Oh I'm so sorry. I haven't even told you my name. *(pauses, contemplates)* But maybe it would be better to remain anonymous. Anonymity has always been appealing to me because it allows me to be anybody that I want to be, to wear whatever skin I want to wear. Maybe for now, we won't use names, not just yet. Let's identify each other by our thoughts instead of these meaningless linguistic identities stamped on us at birth. Let's be known for what we think and believe, for what we feel and know to be true!

(WAITRESS smiles ferociously and gestures for me to continue with a slight nod of her head. Her eyes, cold-blue and wet, might widen in interest.)

YOUR FATHER
I'll be known as Revolutionary. What should I call you?

WAITRESS
Call me Cliché.
(YOUR FATHER would stroke his chin and nod, pleased with his ability to enthrall her with his imaginary-enhanced confidence and charm.)

76

YOUR FATHER

What kind of music do you like? I can't really fit my musical interests into one genre, per se, though when I was in high school, I played in an electronic-based rock band called Rhythmic Epilepsy in the Key of C. It was mainly instrumental material, but we were really innovative for teenagers, though nothing ever really came of the band. We played for a few birthday parties, and my mom said we were great. *(shakes his head, throws up his hands.)* God, that sounds so fucking lame. Oh, pardon my language.

(WAITRESS giggles and tells YOUR FATHER not to apologize. Her smile reveals dimples that accent her smooth lips.)

YOUR FATHER

Well it still seems inappropriate using strong words like that after I've just briefly met you, especially a nice, innocent girl like you. Not that I'm sexist and think women can't handle strong language. And not that I think you're inexperienced or naïve to the ways of the world. I just wouldn't want you to think I'm always vulgar or crude. Well, maybe I am these things, but even so, I wouldn't want you to think that just yet.

(WAITRESS moves her hand across the table, reaches for YOUR FATHER. Her hands would be warm and soft and their fingers might lock, their knuckles clicking in place. WAITRESS and YOUR FATHER talk about how they want to know all about the world and its mysteries. They talk until the sun drops down low, until the daylight dims, until they are alone. Then WAITRESS says that sometimes if she listens in the quiet of night, she can hear the world whispering intricate secrets to her, things only she is supposed to know. She keeps these secrets until she sees something inspirational, then breathes them out into nature, which absorbs them, hides them in tiny curls like secret dimensions, until it whispers them to someone else. WAITRESS would say that she had to coin a name for it because there are not words for things that the scientists and dictionary makers have not at least imagined. Imbedded Truth, she calls it.)

End Scene

But I never did work up the bravery to call unnecessary attention to myself. I couldn't even pull out my notebook, couldn't ask her my questions in my quiet booth at the diner, though she tempted me with a tired half-smile.

"Anything else?"

Shifting around in my seat, I tried to avoid her eyes. The edges and knobs of my bones pang-ached from leaning on the table. I shook my head. She tucked her tiny pencil behind her ear, closed up the black notebook she used to write down orders and walked away, no tip on the line.

i should say something to her
and i should open my heart
and spill my chest on the table for her
and i should leave a tip

I pulled seven dollars out of my wallet, left it all on the table. Your tiny brown button popped out, bounced and rolled across the ash-blonde floor, so I crawled over, wiped it clean and put it in my front right pocket. Dusting off my knees, I waved casually to the waitress, her eyes twitching in their deep-set sockets, on my way out. She didn't see me, so I wiped my wet nose with my knuckles.

I had been looking for a reason to move away from Bloomington, to break free. But it had to be big, something heavy to break my inertia because my environment, the house I had been living in had some kind of gravitational hold on everyone inside, keeping us in an aimless haze well into our twenties. If I had stayed, that house would have likely ushered me stumbling and blabbering into my thirties. It was a place of delayed adulthood that allowed me to shrink the world, compress the universe into my backyard. Planets were just interesting ideas. Stars were just clear-edged dots on my ceiling.

But even though I wanted out, living a life unprovoked had made the decision to leave unnecessary. And really just in general I've always had trouble making decisions. If I can't visualize the logic, can't feel the cogency, then I can't make the decision. Outside of resenting my father, I had deliberately chosen not to choose anything. So I think, though I couldn't have articulated it at the time, I saw your conception as my chance to expand and view the world in its proper proportions, with unreachable infinitesimals and infinities. It was my opportunity to shake the film that had settled over my eyes and to do something real. I had spent so much of my post-adolescent life postulating and theorizing, never called into battle to test my actual competencies. You were my chance to transpose my conjectures about life onto a reality with actual moments and emotions at stake. So I left. I picked up everything and moved to Ohio.

Your mom had insisted on providing the bed and all the furniture, so I just rented a car, packed all my clothes and a few personal items, and strapped my bike on top. Even though the autumnal equinox had just passed, it was unseasonably warm that day. The summer temperatures refused to relinquish their hold. In typical Midwest fashion, Autumn would win the battle one day, bringing cooler temperature. Summer would then fire back with temperatures in the eighties the next day. It was a constant battle between the two that typically went unresolved until Sister Winter entered and froze them both into submission sometime in November.

I hadn't seen the apartment before moving in because Eris set everything up. She sifted through the local listings, went on all the tours, signed the lease – the whole deal because she had the good credit. I didn't have much to my name other than several thousand dollars in student loans and an IRA that I couldn't touch until I was sixty-five.

When I pulled in, Eris was parked along the curb looking at her watch. She turned off the engine and the AC. In my experience these types of interactions can go one of three ways.

1 - Make everything big. This is how things normally are with me and my brother Brody. He'll spread his arms out wide – too wide – and say "Get in here buddy!" loudly – too loudly.

OR

2 - Everything stays small because it has to. It's all tiny half-hugs, short cliché sentences – "It's good to see you." "You look nice today." – and comments about recent weather patterns.

OR

3 - When it's genuine it's quiet but not forcedly so. It's between the words, infused inside the touches, everything known, implied, codified, always there.

When your mother and I hugged, it was small, all awkward and forced. Brody had agreed to meet us there at noon to help with the larger furniture so we brought up as many of the small items as we could while we waited for him. Eris carried seat cushions and lamp shades. I carried boxes and ottomans. Noon passed with no sign of Brody. Only nearing the end of her first trimester, Eris was, looking back, probably capable of helping me with the furniture, but she used your tiny curled up body as a legitimate scapegoat. So she went up to the empty apartment to start unpacking and organizing the boxes

80

while I waited on the curb for Brody. Occasionally I would see her looking down at me – her eyes narrow – through the open windows. Brody eventually showed up and made several large gestures. I'm not saying it bothered me, it just felt dishonest, disingenuous in its size and scope. Which I guess for Brody – and that whole side of your extended family – was to be expected. After his display, the two of us quietly moved the last few pieces of furniture up the stairs and into the unit.

Even though we had decided to move in together, your mother and I had never officially had a conversation about our status as a couple, about what we would call each other publicly.

"Eris, my roommate, my friend."
"Eris, the mother of my baby."
"Eris, my casual girlfriend, the carrier of my seed."
"Eris, my serious live-in girlfriend."
"Eris, my family."

For me at least, it was all still unclear, too foggy, liminal. But the first night we moved in she initiated sex – unprotected, swift and graceless. Again, I know this might be weird for you to read, but stick with me. I wouldn't include it if I didn't think it was necessary. Afraid – or unwilling – to broach the subject of "us", to put some kind of definite label on it, sex, in her mind solidified things.

Afterwards I had this urge, this impulse to put my head in her lap, to lean my head against her stomach, warm and slippery. I wanted her to rub my head, to stroke my back, maybe lean down and put her head against mine, maybe whisper something inaudible in my ear. But when I pulled my head close to her stomach she scooted out from under me, flipped onto her side and asked me to spoon her.

For the first few weeks, things went on like that: the frequent sex, the excitement of our legs accidently touching under the sheets, the teamwork atmosphere, all the give-and-take. We were just kids playing house. None of it was real. It was a temporary arrangement, a cotton dream. Then she started showing, started rounding out and bursting through jean buttons, which meant that all forms of sex stopped. The air got tighter, all our words made of concrete. And by Halloween her morning sickness – which she assured me would be temporary[14] – lingered and became a regular occurrence. It started as something to joke about, a shared experience, something we finally had in common.

ME
Remember that time you threw up for three hours?

HER
Yes.

ME
I was there, you know.

HER
Yes.

ME
…
(ME lifts hand for high five.)

HER
…
(HER ignores ME.)

As it increased in frequency and severity it became less and less funny for both of us. By the fifth month of her pregnancy, our second month living together, she was waking up every night and, not so quietly, rolling out of bed. I'd hear the lid of the toilet bang against the tank, hear the all the half-burps and splashes, the rattling around in the bathroom. At first I tried coming in to offer some words of comfort, to hold her hair. The exchange usually went something like this:

---

[14] "No more after the first trimester!"

ME
You okay?

HER
(heave, splash)
What do you think?

ME
Well I think you look sick.

HER
Jesus, Hurley.
(heave, splash)

(*HER feet, swollen and pink, are curled up behind the base of the toilet.*)

ME
You need some help?

(*ME places a hand between her convulsing shoulder blades.*)

HER
Out!
(heave, splash, heave, cough)

I remember thinking how perverse it was for me to see all her bodily changes, the swollen feet and near-constant puking. I knew all those intimate details about her without knowing really anything about her past, about her friends or family, about the things that she thought about when she first woke up. The whole thing reminded me of living in a co-ed dormitory my freshman year of college. There had been a boy's hall and a girl's hall adjoined in the middle via a swinging door. We all felt excited to be away from home, felt bonded by our proximity, but in our most intimate moments we still held closely to our privacy. Eris and I didn't have a swinging door.

One night she came home red-eyed, mumbling as she unwound her scarf and peeled off her wool knitted cap, hanging them on the back of the door. I caught enough words to figure out that she was turned away from the tanning bed because she was pregnant. I'm sure she knew they wouldn't let her tan, and I'm sure she wouldn't have done it because she knew it could have harmed you. It was just an adjustment for her. And adjustments are hard, sacrifices are difficult by nature.

So that night we went out and bought a spray tan kit. She undressed for me – not in a sexual striptease way, just a practical this-is-my-body-now-and-yes-there-are-two-sets-of-organs-inside me-and-yes-I-have-blood-enough-for-two-and-I-need-your-help way – and I sprayed all the places she couldn't reach on her own. It was these moments of strange intimacy and forced physical openness that were our foundation.

"Make sure it's even. I don't want it to look patchy," she had said, legs spread.

"Why? No one else is going to see this, right?"

"Just make sure it's even, okay?"

Your mother went on maternity leave from her job at the hair salon sometime during the eighth month of pregnancy, which – since I was still in the process of getting the credentials to make me a "highly qualified teacher" – left us both cooped up at the apartment. Things were good then. We were still getting to know each other, learning each other's idiosyncrasies. I don't want to say we were falling in love necessarily because that feels too contrived, too cliché. It was more just that there was a subtle shift in our focus, a few glances that became more familiar and comforting with time, the recognition of body language and tonal qualities. When she wiggled her nose and upper lip, I learned that meant she was tired and trying to hold back a yawn. I knew she liked to have the back of her neck caressed just under her hairline. And she knew that when I woke up in the mornings, I liked to use the same coffee cup everyday even when dirty, so she intentionally didn't wash it for me, left it in the fridge, crooked old coffee lines cracked around the rim.

But with the connection finally being felt, the annoyances also became more alive and vocalized. We were no longer floating politely around the same apartment. We were now full participants in a life that had collided quickly and unexpectedly. She started criticizing the pre-sneeze frenzy I went into, which she once said was cute. She started making comments about my tight pants and every now and then, I'd find new baggy slacks on the bed with the tags removed. She was never subtle. I knew her outbursts were just part of the pregnancy, part of the emotional ups-and-downs and that there were just certain adjustments a new couple in cohabitation had to make. But I wondered if there was more to it. It seemed like she was testing my mental elasticity, intentionally trying to stretch me too thin, trying to break me and remold me into something that I was not. It made me more aware, more self-conscious about how I looked and stood and talked, made me question everything about myself. I pushed these thoughts out of my mind, thinking things would improve once you were born, once her hormones rebalanced.

June 22nd 2010

Tuesday
late afternoon

I flipped the tiny brown button from your stuffed
squirrel between my fingers.

what is Luna doing?
and does she miss me?
and does she know what's happening?
and if she did, she would not consent
and surely she feels something,
feels it in her body, something unnatural, something breaking, drifting
but she can't figure out what it is
and where it's coming from

I slipped the button down into my front right pocket
again.

is Eris really going to take sole custody?
and is she really going to keep me from Luna?
and is that legal?
and what are the laws?
and why don't i know my rights?
and she'll try anything
and she won't let me see her alone
and she'll treat me like a criminal
and if i resist, she'll move to the pacific northwest.
europe.
russia.
always moving, changing her name
and i will be forced to live out of a backpack,
to track them across the globe
and i'll need to learn more languages, something latin based
and i'll need a high-speed scooter because the gas overseas and

I pushed my thoughts away from the idea of constant
global travel and supervised visitations, court-ordered non-
custodial parenting, and I rode my bike south towards my

apartment in the suburbs that skirted old Hamilton. The roads were empty, everyone home with their family, napping, talking with calm blood and soft smiles on the telephone.

Hungry and still several miles short of my apartment, I pulled off into a familiar industrial park, a place I knew for sure Eris had seen and been to, one of her favorites actually. After going to Ryan's and the diner, I felt unchanged, felt heavier if anything, so my AI-induced quest to find something new in a town where I'd seen everything seemed silly now, fruitless.

Inside a cylindrical food kiosk, a tan-skinned, white-haired, elderly woman with chopsticks in her hair stood with a dwarfing hunch and a shawl around her shoulders despite the summer humidity. A portable fan spun behind her, her olive eyes heavy, stuck on the ground. The sign on the top of the kiosk window only had three items listed: Hot Dogs, Popsicle, Soda/Water. Normally I would avoid processed meats, opting for the locally and humanely raised, but I was starving and out of options. I could have gone home to eat, but I still just didn't want to be there alone in an apartment that had quickly become insular. I didn't want to hear all those buzzing noises that ring in my ears when it's too quiet, didn't want to count all the things missing. So I ordered three hot dogs, doused them in yellow mustard and red ketchup and swallowed them down, the taste of plastic hanging in the back of my throat. I walked with my bike towards a crooked creek winding under a steel-lined bridge.

> i don't get why Eris likes coming to this park.
> everything's concrete, all hard and made by men
> and there's nothing soft or green
> and nothing folding out from inside itself
> and nothing real

I peered over the parapet of the bridge and saw a school of fish swimming in a group of twelve. Their bodies, though blurred by the ripples of the water, were smooth, quick, their tales flicking, snapping like fingers. They were underwater bullets. Bullets with tiny brains. Or at least a clear sense of purpose, with a sense of confident rationality. They swam like they knew exactly where they were going and exactly how long it would take them to get there, each fish content to fill his position within the twelve. Everything was in unison, collective turns, synchronized stops and starts. That school disappeared down the creek and another group, identical both in size and demeanor, swam in the opposite direction against the creek's gentle current.

Eris has not seen this
and Eris is incapable of this
and my father is incapable of this

In the background I heard the playful yells of children, the screeches and kicking up of dirt, their voices reverberating in my chest like parade drums.

She can't be taken and
She can't be taken and
She can't be taken and
She can't be taken and
She can't be taken and
She can't be taken and
She can't be taken and

To the right of the creek, dozens of kids were running around through the mulch, weaving in and out of swings and under forts and jungle gyms. My feet were heavy, aching with childhood nostalgia. Kids run everywhere with an enthusiasm unmatched in any other age group. I pulled out my notebook, scribbled on an unused page.

-Encourage Luna to remain childlike (in terms of foot speed) for as long as possible.[15]

A young couple – late twenties maybe – sat on a metal bench whispering, watching their son chase another little girl – ducking under red plastic slides and hopping over tilted see-saws. The man, in a flannel shirt spotted with mud, leaned in

---

[15] Do you still run? Cross-country? Track? Anything like that?

and kissed his wife on the cheek. He pulled away and then quickly turned back and kissed her cheek again several times. I think he was imitating the romantic advances of a woodpecker or maybe a peacock. Defying the heat of the sun, she leaned up next to him and nuzzled her head against his chest. Their son kept running and blooming and chasing and circling the girl who walked away holding her mother's hand.

I never would have seen this, never would have experienced anything like this with Eris. I couldn't remember one time we had taken you to a park together and snuggled on a bench or done anything similar. She didn't like the idea of you playing where other kids had done "god-knows-what." She would be worried about how you might be developing allergies or how the sun might give you skin cancer – even though she tanned both naturally and artificially. When I brought up the hypocrisy of her concerns about the sun she shrugged it off as irrelevant. I'm not trying to say it was wrong for you to have been her number one priority and for me to have been on the backburner, but it made having any sort of natural moment nearly impossible. I jotted in my notebook.

-Maybe Al was right.

I popped my phone off the handle bar case and texted Mira.
"hey let's meet up tonight"
She texted me back almost immediately.

> she's been waiting on me, thinking about me
> and we can live in the cracks in the water
> and in the creases in the pavement

"awesome! where? what time?"
"my place at 9"

"My water just broke." She said it firmly with confidence and a surprising amount of restraint.

"What? Like, you're getting ready to have the baby?"

"No, a water balloon just burst inside my vagina."

She rolled her eyes and pushed herself up off the couch with her arms and tried to prop herself – legs straight – up, but she couldn't carry enough momentum forward to keep her upright. I circled around behind her, grabbed under swollen arms to help her up. There was a small wet splotch left on the couch.

> *what is that?*
> *amniotic fluid?*
> *and i have no idea what that is, but i bet that's it*
> *and maybe a small amount of urine mixed in*
> *and we'll need a new couch*
> *or we'll keep it, turn it into a good story.*
> *--Ha-ha. You see that stain there next to you?--*

I grabbed our pre-packed bag of supplies – she packed it weeks in advance – and helped her out to the car. While we sped through traffic she swore upon her mother's grave that if I didn't go faster she would eat me after the birth. We saw something like that on the Discovery Channel, where coyotes or dogs or something sometimes cannibalize their mates. Despite the empty threat, I drove as fast as possible, and twenty minutes later we were at the hospital.

"The baby's not due for another ten days."

I was talking to no one, to myself, I guess. Everything was moving fast, too quickly. It was unnatural, my eyes barely open. I helped your mother out of the car and stumbled through puddles of black water in the parking lot, the full moon slicing and rippling everywhere. That moment in my memory is just a surreal blur. I didn't think it could happen so fast. I'd heard about these twenty hour labors. I was told there would be lots of waiting, talk of centimeters, buckets and buckets of ice chips. I packed three books on post-natal care in our supply bag. I thought I'd have time to read, take notes, highlight things and prepare myself to become a father. But a few hours after we left the house we had a tiny person, you, in our care. We decided not to find out if you were going to be a boy or girl beforehand because we wanted to be surprised. I expected a boy because from a statistical standpoint there are slightly more boys born than girls – nature's way of compensating for my gender's recklessness. But I suspect – and this is just conjecture – that these numbers will slowly, over the next few generations, drift back toward fifty-fifty as modern women begin behaving more like modern men. Either way, I was glad to be wrong, glad to overcome the odds, glad to have a girl, to have you.

People often say that having their first child changes their perspective of the world. They say it infuses purpose, fulfills procreative destiny, provides a new meaning to the mystery of our existence. Men often say that it makes them come-of-age as a male, makes them love the mother of their child more intensely, more fully. I was just scared shitless – or at least I had all these vibrations in my chest and arms, even in the back of my head, that were completely unfamiliar, that were staggering in their reach and power. The paralyzing vibrations, the mix of emotions when added and split reached a recognizable quotient of fear.

I remember when the nurse placed your tiny frame wrapped in blankets in my arms, I was so afraid I would break you. You looked so fragile and confused. Your miniature facial features twisted and curled on your face – pink and hot. I stood there unmoving, afraid to step or walk or sway or breathe with you in my arms – vibrating wildly all over, weak and made of helium. Too confused and stunned to know exactly how to react, I think the nurses – and probably Eris too – interpreted my paralyzing emotional overflow as disinterest. But it was the first time I saw something and knew without a doubt that I was in love. It was the first time I was able to distill and identify the crazy vibrations that love can produce and store wherever it is our bodies store emotions.

Eris and I came and went to the hospital alone, no family or friends, no fanfare. In the rush to get there, I forgot – though I'll admit it was sort of intentional – to call my mom who came to town – uninvited and weeks early – in preparation for the event. Even though I had made her promise not to bring my father with her, I didn't call her post-natal out of fear he had tagged along and forced her not to say anything. And the no-phone-call probably served as some kind of subconscious, tacit assertion of my independence which I had struggled to claim fully. But I called my mom when we got home the next morning while Eris slept. It turns out she had made the trip alone so I invited her over to see you. Always politely overbearing, her mannerisms – crossed legs, closed shoulders, tight lips – showed a clear distaste for her lack of awareness and involvement in the whole pregnancy process.

I don't know how much you've been told about your grandparents from your mother's side, but Eris' parents refused to be involved in the pregnancy even tangentially. I first met them about a month after Eris and I had moved in together. Once we got settled in our new apartment and had reached our unspoken agreement of commitment, we decided we should meet each other's families. Her parents, much older than mine, had moved to Florida. Her semi-retired dad, a president emeritus at an investment bank, was gray-haired and sturdy. Both his handshake and hair-do were firm. Her mother, also a hair-stylist, was an older version of Eris – athletic, impatient, holding nothing back. When we flew down for the weekend, we all had a conversation about you and how Eris and I had decided not to get married which ended with both of her parents – strict in their moral convictions – having barely audible verbal explosions about our transgression and how our souls were at risk. We decided not to spend the weekend. I found out later that we were actually *asked* to leave. I think her parents disliked the idea of Eris raising you on her own even more than they disliked me, but eventually they stopped calling and started sending generic Christmas cards with a wallet size family photo and a check reading "Xmas" on the 'For' line. Unless things have drastically changed, I'm guessing you're familiar with the formality. You deserved better – a proper family: two sets of parents, grandparents, full siblings, nothing partial.

June 22nd 2010

Tuesday
early evening

With my body returning to equilibrium, I sat at my
kitchen table fiddling with my lighter, eyeballing my new bag of
weed, mentally debating the idea of an island as a paradise and
as a prison, struggling with the increasing unbearability of
consistent full-consciousness and the almost impulsive
decisiveness of the text invitation to Mira.

i shouldn't have invited her over
and it's too soon
and did it come off as an invitation to some sort of early evening tryst?
and is that what it is?
and it's nothing
and she's a friend
and what if Eris shows up while Mira's here
and she'll yell, make a scene, call all the neighbors together
and they'll all throw trash at me
and they've all been saving their trash – the worst of it – for this

*--bare feet slapping on patio pavement, splashing of hot tub water,
clinking of glasses--*

My body rattled inside, things shifting in my intestines,
axons and dendrites conducting electricity, sending signals and
impulses everywhere. I opened up the bag of weed, picked out
a few buds and dropped them back inside, hand shaking. My
chest tightened, the blood flowing through it made of dry
concrete powder. My doctor said this was normal, just a
symptom. *--I've never seen it in someone this young--* I steadied
myself, shuffled to the bathroom, hands on the walls and took
two Coumadin, the tip of my left ring finger suddenly numb.

I straightened my spine, improved my posture and sat
back down at the kitchen table, thinking about each breath,
slowing everything down. The clock on the wall said 8:13 pm
EST so even though I told Mira to come over at nine, I figured I
had about an hour before she, always fashionably late, showed

up. The weed was still on the table, the bag of mystery pills in my pocket.

I'm sure you've heard plenty of rumors about my drug use. And even though things ended up the way they did, this week that I'm writing to you about was a particular abnormality because there were sharp edges everywhere and I kept bumping up against them. I had to dull it all out for my own safety. And back then I only took pills and smoked marijuana, never did any kind of harder drugs, no needles or crackpipes, no melted spoons or tin foil. I didn't even really start doing it much until I moved to Hamilton because I felt so self-conscious around Eris. It felt logical at the time.

Proof[16]

1 - Eris is difficult to deal with.

2 - Eris is difficult to deal with because she makes me self-conscious.

3 - I feel self-conscious around her because she is critical of me, makes me feel inferior – emasculated.

4 - I feel inferior because I have a vague self-definition.

5 - I have a vague self-definition because of an innate lack of confidence.

6 – My innate lack of confidence ignites consistent self-criticism.

7 – Consistent self-criticism is mentally taxing.

8 – Mental overstimulation isn't sustainable.

9 - Marijuana gives my mind a break, naturally forces my thoughts to better places, calms my thoughts.

10 – The calm thoughts reduce the mental overstimulation.

11 – The reduction of mental overstimulation reduces the self-criticism.

12 – The reduction of self-criticism increases my confidence.

13 – The boost in confidence reduces the concerns over having a vague self-definition.

14 – The indifference to having a vague self-definition cancels out the emasculation, the critical words.

15 – The reduction of emasculation makes me less self-conscious.

16 – Feeling less self-conscious makes Eris easier to be around.

17 – Marijuana makes Eris easier to handle.

Q.E.D.

---

[16] Or at least an approximation of one.

The logic felt tight – unassailable – but the results were varied. The weed would either make me sketch out – make me more self-conscious – or it would calm me down and block the part of my brain responsible for self-conscious thoughts. I should have realized it then – and I certainly have now after all that's happened – but logic isn't always enough. There are tons of other variables. But the upside of the unpredictable results made the risk worthwhile, at least in my mind. None of this justifies the fact that I brought these things around you. I'm just giving you my perspective.

Anyway, that's why I started smoking weed that night. Because I was nervous, self-conscious, in a situation that was difficult to deal with. Normally Mira made me *less* self-conscious but it was all the other factors, the guilt-aspect, the is-this-too-soon? side of it that was making me freak out.

I opened up the plastic baggy again and – hands steadier – took a bud out. I pulled the bud off the stem and put it in my grinder – a smiley face scrawled across the front, x's for eyes. I dumped the crushed cannabis onto a piece of rolling paper which I then funneled into the bowl of my three inch glass pipe – burnt brown and dull orange. With the fleshy part of my thumb, I packed the weed in to get rid of the air holes. I already felt lightheaded, euphoric, swift-blooded – a common preparatory high I got just from feeling defiant, uncharacteristically treasonous and wild.

I flicked my gray lighter on and off several times, adjusting the flame before I held it over the bowl, turning the dark green into tiny balls of bright orange underneath, the bulbs spreading as I breathed deeply. Hold, exhale into the fan, repeat, ad nauseam. Then I pulled out an elongated pale yellow pill with what looked like the square root sign engraved on one side. I didn't know what it was and since I already had two Coumadin and a bowl working through my system, I broke it in half and dry-swallowed it. With all sorts of chemicals rumbling through my veins and muscles, breathing in and out of my skin cells, I picked up the bowl, still simmering and walked around the apartment, legs restless.

I was starting to see you everywhere. The living room wasn't the living room anymore; it was the place where you switched from laying on your stomach to crawling, from crawling to waddling, from waddling to walking. Your bedroom closet wasn't just your bedroom closet; it was your favorite place to hide when we played chase. The kitchen was no longer a place to make food; it was where you said your first word – "hold". Your accommodations were everywhere too: the socket blockers, all the hard edges of furniture softened with decorative fringe and coverings. Everything was made with you in mind. Everything was created for you, scaled to your fit. Even the locations that didn't have specific memories tied to them had the sad-gravity of memories never made. The front door wasn't just an entryway; it was the place where I had planned to take your picture before you left for your first day of school, your pink plastic backpack slung over both shoulders, pulled up tight.

I even saw you in my cat Tails. You probably don't remember him. When I was young someone, I don't remember who, told me once – or at least enough times for it to stick – that petting cats relieves stress. So when I was in college I adopted him instead of using Adderall during finals week, which yielded overwhelmingly average results. His wide-eyed expressiveness reminded me of you in your infancy when you stared up from your crib unblinking, saw everything for the first time, took it all in unobstructed, unbiased. I reached down to pet Tails but he turned his nose up at me, flicking his tail and walking away.

I set my pipe on the nightstand in the bedroom and got in the shower, instinctively turning the water to the hottest setting. Your mother and I hadn't been intimate since the last December, so I had started trying to entice her into the shower by creating a steam room out of the bathroom, leaving the door cracked open so she could feel the clouds of moisture. It hadn't worked and I typically just came out sweatier than I went in, but I remained diligent. It had sort of become a way of punishment. I forced myself daily to endure the scalding water pouring over my tender skin in a twisted, subconscious form of aquatic flagellation.

I undressed and waited for the water to turn into air, waited for the steam to build up and condensate on the mirror. The mirror didn't look right when clear. My reflection didn't look right if not clouded and streaky.

--I wish none of this ever happened.--

Once my reflection blurred, once my breaths were labored, deep and fog-heavy, and my sinuses loosened, I stepped into the shower and put my chest directly into the spout. I had always been too tall to get completely under the water, so I let it pound against my chest, against my heart. Then I leaned and curled forward to let it hit the back of my neck and run down every side of my head and back, watched it spray out and circle around the drain until the spiral tightened, pulled the water in. I got out, feet starting to turn into clouds, and dried off. My phone buzzed on the counter in the kitchen. With the towel wrapped loosely around my waist, I checked the message.

"here. can i come up?"

I texted back an affirmation and hurried back into the bedroom, got dressed, and cranked up the fan to dissipate the squandered THC.

I met Mira – and I want to go ahead and pre-emptively emphasize it wasn't anything sexual – when I took a job teaching at Hamilton High. My first semester I taught two classes: senior English Literature and freshman composition. I was nervous, apprehensive for my senior English class – Literature of the American Dream – because I thought that I wouldn't know enough, that my students would bring up things I couldn't answer. But after a week or so of fielding their questions I realized that, outside a few exceptions, I drastically over-estimated the knowledge and scholastic motivation of middle-class America's seventeen and eighteen year olds.

When I got to my classroom it was already full with students standing in groups, a few unspoken for stragglers standing at the edges or sitting in their desks with sharp pencils at-the-ready. They all looked much older than eighteen. Several actually may have been older, may have been held back early on, may have struggled to memorize their multiplication tables. Or spent their formative years in juvy. The boys had light mustaches and goatees. Some were tall, full figured, had arms with curves and lines. The girls had heavy make-up with bright colors, everything powdery, their posture exceptional, curvy in dangerous places.

Except for the few desked students, no one noticed me walk in so I started writing my name in huge, sloppy block letters on the white board. In the top right corner I wrote:

""'Makes no sense' makes no sense" makes no sense."

I started taking attendance and as I finished up through the W's and Z's the door squeaked open. A girl with short, straightened brown hair came in with her books pulled close to her chest and her vogue, thick-rimmed glasses shifting down the crook of her nose, a studded piercing in the left nostril. She had on bright green skinny jeans, ballet flats – one yellow, one blue – and a white v-neck shirt with the words "Follow Your Bliss" handwritten in black marker.

When I read the shirt, I knew we would get along, again not in a sexual way. I just knew we had similar tastes.

"Where should I sit?"

I first noticed it then, that she always aspirates her 't's and 'd's. They sort of have a breathy, whispered quality. And she has these really animated lip movements. Most people talk with their tongues but she really talks more with her lips, all wiggling and quivering. It's like they sort of twist and the last word of each sentence comes out of her mouth sideways, especially when she's nervous or really into something.

"I guess up here by me."

<u>June 22nd 2010</u>

<u>Tuesday</u>
<u>evening</u>

Mira walked, arms swinging at her sides, into my apartment wearing a thin, halo-esque headband[17] that made her brown hair – cut and styled short – stick to her forehead. She wore a white v-neck t-shirt with a quote handwritten in black marker across her chest.

"My hands and lips are roses. My hands and lips are blooming."

Her jeans ended just above her knees, a line of frayed fabric barely grazing the top. Up and down both wrists she wore colorful rubber bracelets and almost all her fingers had rings.

"I'm surprised you wanted to meet here," she said leaning her duct tape purse against the wall by the front door. "I figured you would want to meet at the hospital cafeteria or the library or something like old times. Is Eris out of town?"

→Should I tell her?
    →I should tell her.
        →She'll be a good friend.
        →She'll understand.
        →Support.
        →Console.
        →Comfort.
        →Touch...
            →I shouldn't tell her.

"Yeah she'll be gone for a couple of days."

--*"let me see your badge again."*--

"Cool."

---

[17] I think it was actually made out of pantyhose. I'm sure you know what these are called.

She flared her nostrils and slipped off her blue and yellow ballet flats, her favorite pair of shoes.

"You want something to drink?"

"Sure. You have any wine or something?"

"Probably."

I instinctively reached for Eris' decanter half full of merlot.

> *is it ethical for me to offer Eris' wine to Mira?*
> *and aren't there rules about that?*
> *and if so, they are vague,*
> *unwritten.*

--*"I like your black truck."*--

I grabbed the decanter along with a local microbrew for myself. Truth be told, I really never liked the taste of beer. I just forced myself to acquire a functional level of tolerance since it is one of only a few manly drinks. I've always naturally preferred – as I suspect many men secretly do – malt drinks or mixed cocktails with some kind of juice base but because of my father, I grew up thinking real men don't drink those. So I learned to refrain. But once drunk enough, I always stopped caring, started stumbling around ordering endless chocolate cake shots.

"What's that smell?"

I poured her a glass of wine, my arms light, airless, turning to steam from the weed – or maybe the yellow pill.

"What are you talking about?"

"You don't smell that?"

"What?"

"It's like. I don't know." She put her nose up, sniffing the room. "It smells like weed actually?"

"Oh. Yeah…that's…" I nodded my head towards the bedroom where my bowl still simmered.

"Really? I thought I smelled it in the hallway on the way in." I shrugged, trying to seem casual. It *was* casual. It was nothing. "Just when I think I know you…Anyway, give me the tour of your place? I've never been in past the main room."

104

She lifted her wine glass off the table, threading the neck of the brittle glass between her index and middle finger, palming the cup. I pinched the neck of my bottled microbrew and walked down the hall, my eyelids starting to droop, flipping on lights as I went.

"This is Luna's room."

She stuck out her neck, leaned her head in, keeping her body in the hall and ran her fingers up the door frame, across the metal latch.

"Super cute."

--"...and you'll be a great, strong male presence in her life – better than Hurley."--

"And there's my office," I said pointing across the hallway.

"An office? Do you grade papers or something in here?"

"Actually – and I don't know if you remember this or not – but the summer before you left for college I was working on some sketches at the library one day when you came in for our after-school meeting and said something about how they were really good. And I'll never forget it, you said 'You're always telling me to follow my dreams and to follow my talents. And this is great. You should totally pursue your art.' And so right after you left for school I converted this into my office so I could work on my artwork."

"Because of what I said?"

"Yeah. And, I mean, nothing has ever come of it but that doesn't mean that my time spent in here isn't worthwhile. It's more for fun than anything. And plus, when Eris and I got this place we intentionally got an extra bedroom, just sort of under the assumption that we would eventually have another kid. But the room was just going to waste before I converted it into a studio."

"Well I guess we're even. Because you're the reason I decided to go to school for art rather than something more practical. The joke is on us, I guess."

She moved around the outer edges of the office, circled the perimeter, brushed her hand across the tote bag – propped in the corner – with the painting that she gave me two weeks before. She looked at my bookshelf, filled with my research materials on top, squatted down to look at my novels alphabetized by author down below.

"What's this?" she asked standing up, looking at a comic tacked to my corkboard on the wall overhead.

"Oh, yeah. That's just something I submitted to the school paper when I was in college."

It was a comic strip re-enactment of President Bush signing the No Child Left Behind Act into legislation. A caricatured version of George Bush was sitting at a make-shift table grinning, hair disheveled. He was holding a bottled beer in a koozie that said 'Go America!' across the side, and the paper that he was signing in front of him read:

No Bush Left on the Ballot in 2004
No Country Left Uninvaded[18]
No Brain Cells Left Behind.

Ted Kennedy, also caricatured, stood with a nose bleed and a thumbs-up sign next to Bush. Karl Rove was reading a book with the letters "AYP" on the cover by lamplight in the corner of the picture.

"This is amazing!"

"Yeah, I thought it was pretty good too, but it was the last thing that the school newspaper ever let me publish."

"I thought Bloomington was pretty liberal."

"Yeah, I mean it is. More so than Hamilton anyway. But I guess there's always a line."

"Who's this?" she said picking up a picture frame on my desk.

"Oh, yeah, I don't know."

"You don't know?"

---

[18] I stole that one from Noah.

"Yeah, I bought it thinking I would put something in there, but then I just kept thinking that the people in the stock picture looked so happy. And so I just left them in there."

She sat it back down on the desk, glanced at the loose-leaf papers, the doodles and scribblings scattered on my desk.

"Is this what you're working on now?" She picked up one of the sketches.

"I don't know, not really."

"Oh come on, now you're shy all of a sudden? What is it?"

"Well my thing lately is that I'm trying to turn some of my favorite books into graphic novels. So that's a scene from Naked Lunch. Did you ever read that?"[19]

"Yeah, of course. And I bet this is from the scene near the end where Lee is using a street phone to call the Narcotics Squad when he finds out the people he is calling for are not on record. Right?"

it's intelligible!
i'll be famous!
lauded!
canonized!

"Yep. Anyway, let's continue the tour."

"Right."

We moved deeper into the apartment, but my feet were not on the carpet. My head was not on my body. And there was a sharp pain in my upper chest, a new self-induced edge growing and gnawing at me from the inside.

"Here's the bedroom," I said coughing.

Mira sat on the mattress – the sheets still twisted and hanging over the edge – and bounced, testing its comfort, testing its firmness.

---

[19] I know I'm not in any position to tell you what to do, but I'd strongly recommend reading that book if you haven't. Read it slowly, then quickly. Read it while listening to music. Then read in silence. Read it in as many languages as you can.

she's not expecting to sleep here is she
and she can't sleep here
and Eris would kill me
and Luna wouldn't understand
and it's too late anyway
and nothing will ever change
and why is it so cold in here?

Traces of your mother were all over the room: the white curtains hanging underneath the cornice, the red silk bedspread, the pictures of flowers and lakes, covered bridges and strange babies in hats sized for adults. My only decorative allotment was the collage of posters on my sliding closet door. Balanced radially around a picture of Vega-Szebb,[20] I had several dozen art pieces and indie rock posters. Eris said the whole display gave her a headache, made her head spin when she looked at them "all jumbled and messy like that" so we typically kept the collage covered by the second bare sliding door, kept it covered by the chipped tan wood spotted with light age rings.

--hot tub, whispered giggles--

"Victor Vasarely, right?" Mira asked looking at the center-piece of the collage.
"Yep."
She sipped on her wine glass and I took a pull on my beer as I stood – she still sitting on the mattress – swaying on my feet like a thin-trunked tree in the wind. My pipe sat on my nightstand, a thin wisp of smoke folding out of the bowl.

i should bring it up
and we need to talk about what happened
and she's waiting for me to bring it up
but not yet
and not just yet

"You want me to put on some music or something?"

---

[20] Google this if you're not familiar.

"Sure."

"Hey didn't you say you used to play in a band when you were in high school? Put some of that on."

"Jesus, I haven't listened to that in a long time. You sure you want to subject yourself to that?"

I always loved it when people showed an interest in my art, even outdated. It validated me, made me feel like it wasn't a waste of time. If people showed interest, then it had to be worth something, right? Though I guess I should have been more self-satisfied in my work, shouldn't have let people's reactions be the sole informant. Either way it was nice that she remembered and asked, so I sifted through the time capsule of accumulated junk – each tier peeled back reminded me of things I had wanted to but never found the time or confidence to accomplish – in the bedroom closet until I found my band's old recordings. The hinges snapped and the front plastic flap dropped off when I opened the two-disc set.

"You know, I've never even showed this stuff to Eris."

"Really? Why not?" She hopped off the mattress --*thank God*-- and sat down next to me by my art-covered closet door.

"I don't know. It never came up, I guess."

"So what instrument did you play?" Her hand went up in the air immediately after she spoke. "Actually, let me guess." She closed her eyes, wrinkled her forehead. "Bass guitar?"

"Seriously? Come on, bass guitar? That's what you think of me? No way, I played keyboards and auxiliary percussion."

"Oh, okay. Sor-ry. Do you still play?"

"Not really. I didn't even have my own keyboard or anything. All the stuff I played was my friend Noah's. He was the guitar player, the guy that connected the dots between everyone."

"You guys don't jam anymore?"

"Not really. Noah's sort of an expatriate at heart so he's never in town long enough to put anything together. After high school he hiked the Appalachian Trail and then traveled across the country by foot, hitchhiking and the whole deal."

"So he's one of those *Into the Wild* kind of guys, huh?"

"I guess. But he's not the kind of person that skipped college just so he could say 'Oh, yeah, I didn't go to school because I don't believe in the system.' He just did it because that's what he wanted to do. You'd like him. But hey talking about Noah reminds me of this story that I've *got* to tell you."

One of the things that Mira and I have always had in common is that we're both naturally introverts but once we get started talking about something we care about, something that makes our skin buzz, then the social floodgates crash open, the word-levees collapse. And plus all the chemicals mixing inside my body were making the normal social barriers seem more scalable, turning all the sharp edges into soft slopes.

"You can have some if you want," I said watching Mira eyeball the still-simmering pipe of weed on my nightstand.

"Yeah?"

She took the bowl, pipe-path gray and fogged, and cradled it in her palm. I lit it for her, and after breathing in, she shook her head, squinted her eyes – smoke going in and out of her nose and mouth – and passed the bowl off to me.

"Fuck. That was too big." She was still shaking her head, coughing out smoke.

"Hold on a sec." I left the room to get my baggie and grinder. When I came back in, she was cradling the bowl again, this time taking an intentionally tinier hit, breathing gently, smoothly.

"So what's this story you were going to tell me," she said still pushing out ropes of smoke.

"Right. So the first time I ever smoked weed was with Noah. You'd have to meet the guy to understand, but he can convince *just* about anyone to do *just* about anything. Anyway, it was our senior year and we were gearing up for George Bush to come to our school to officially sign this new bill into action. It was this huge deal that he was in town. Our plan was to set up our instruments at the entrance of the school the night before he was set to arrive, and then we were all going to camp out and start playing as soon as the sun came up. It wasn't like a subversive thing; I mean we weren't angry citizens. I don't know why, but we figured once we started playing, no one

110

would be able to stop us so we'd be on T.V. or something. We called it Operation Nicklebee.[21]

So the night before, we went out to Noah's cabin – he inherited this cabin out in the boonies from his grandfather – so we went out there where we kept all our music gear and Noah brought some weed. We didn't have any pipes or rolling papers or anything so we used some tin foil and a milk jug and the first hit I took was so massive I coughed so hard that I threw up in the sink."

It wasn't really that funny, but Mira and I were laughing and teetering on our tailbones, our highs growing and setting in. I refilled, took another hit, exhaling thick bills of sweet smoke and passed the bowl back to Mira.

"So anyway," I said trying to compose myself. "Once we were all pleasantly blitzed, we loaded all our equipment into his truck and drove to the school grounds. We set everything up and by this time it was like three in the morning. So we set up our tents, converted an apple into a pipe to smoke the rest of our weed and went to sleep."

"Wait, I've heard about this before. I thought it was just one of those weird school legends. People these days call it the Hot Box Rockers. You guys didn't actually pull it off did you?"

She took one more hit and passed the bowl – a bulb of orange blazing underneath the green, a thin ghost body waving its arms out the top – back to me.

"Well, see, that's the thing," I said as I inhaled another puff. "We were all so stoned that we slept in way too late. And so the next morning a cop pulled us out of our tents. They made us take everything down and sent us home before any of the media arrived."

"Typical stoners; think big, but act little."

"Yeah and thankfully we smoked all the weed so there wasn't any trace other than the apple which Noah ate while we were standing around waiting for our parents who had been called."

---

[21] No Child Left Behind. N-C-L-B: "Nicklebee"

I took one last hit, deep and heavy, pulled the smoke into the corners of my lungs, suffocating and singeing the edges of everything inside.

"So let's hear this music that almost escorted George Bush into Hamilton High."

After one semester in the classroom together Mira signed up for my spring class – an etymology course – even though she didn't need any more English credits. I first got into etymology in high school, and while I was existentially switching majors in college I dabbled in orthography, root origins and new root permutations. But it had been a long time since I studied the subject with any significant vigor. So I relearned the roots right along with my class, which gave the whole semester a sort of collective community vibe that brought everyone together.

Mira, an intellectual perfectionist, got a B on the first exam and asked if she could start coming in for extra help after school. My established policy was that I only operated during school hours, didn't stay late or arrive early, adhered only to the minimum time commitment required by contract. It's not that I hated being at school or wasn't committed to my students. Honestly I just hated spending time away from you. I know it probably seems contrived for me to say something like that with everything that's happened, but it's true. I didn't want to miss anything: a giggle, a burp, a spontaneous crawl session. I wanted it all, every moment of it. Heaping spoonfuls. Lethal overdoses. You were my foreground, my backdrop, my blood and oxygen.

But your mother had always encouraged me to get out more, to make my students a priority, a sentiment that, as I found out, she admired in theory but resented in practice. And Mira really pressed the issue, really wanted the extra help, so I agreed to meet with her after school on Tuesdays and Thursdays. Outside of her exemplary academic record and eccentric fashion, I didn't know much about her before we started meeting, but I quickly saw that she was like me. She walked into rooms with her eyes up, bright and searching, looking for confirmation somewhere. She liked geometry – both Euclidean and non – and shopped at indie book stores. She was always reading something, looking for new voices, looking for something to latch onto, something to be passionate about, a cause to bleed for. Though four years apart in age, we were both still finding ourselves, both going through something at the same time.

In those bi-weekly meetings, which ended up continuing throughout the whole semester, we discovered a kindred spirit for the arts and shared an intellectual intolerance towards (re) memorizing Greek and Latin roots. But more so than the academic side, those meetings were sort of an uncloseting of our souls, a dredging that cleared out our minds and solidified our thoughts. And again I don't want you to get the wrong idea; it wasn't a romantic thing at all. She had a pretty serious boyfriend, talked about moving in with him after graduation, and I was still emotionally invested in the idea of our family as a unit. But I actually think our romantic attachments freed both of us up to fully be ourselves. I know, at least for me, being with Mira blocked all my self-conscious thoughts, freed up my body to feel all the vibrations, all the buzzes and tingles in real time. So during those meetings, I felt at home in my head, in my body in ways that I hadn't in a long time.

After Mira graduated[22] that spring, we opted to continue our discussions over the summer. Twice a week we met somewhere in town – the Lane Public Library off Third, a pizzeria down on Main Street, or most often, the Fort Hamilton Hospital cafeteria just down from the school. Sometimes our talks – if the subject matter got touchy or if all of our other locations were closed – spilled over to the University of Miami-Hamilton campus across town where we could both blend in as college age, each on different ends of the spectrum. Again, it absolutely wasn't romantic in any way. We just got along great and had similar interests so it was just a natural thing. Nothing was forced. We weren't felling bastions.

We were always trading things – ideas, music, books, names of indie artists, indie zines and publications. She was an expert at finding weird new writing online, new age, genre-bending, mind-altering literature. The more obscure the better. But she hadn't read many of the classics – an indictment more on the public education system than anything else – so I gave

---

[22] With honors and an A in etymology.

her all sorts of outside reading spanning the gamut from *Ulysses* to *Mansfield Park*. She read quickly, eating the words, searching them for truths to take into her own life. But towards the middle of the summer I brought in a library copy of *The Bell Jar* to our meeting at the hospital cafeteria and that's when things changed.

"I can't read that," she said when she saw the pink and navy blue plastic-covered copy under my arm.

"Come on. This is a seminal piece of feminine literature. It set the stage and opened the doors for the modern female to free herself on the page. You'll love it."

"Look I'm not reading it. What else do you have?" She crossed her arms and looked down at the dirt in the cracks on the floor.

"Why won't you even give it a try?"

She raised her head slowly, incrementally, the gears visibly turning behind her fragile eyes.

"It's just my mom. She was obsessed with Sylvia Plath."

"Okay…"

"And she killed herself when I was a little girl."

fuck

"God, I'm so sorry."

"It's okay. I should've told you sooner. It's just…how do you or when do you bring something like that up? And I'll bet you can guess how she did it." She spoke casually, frankly, spoke with the confident frost of distance.

"Oh, fuck. Not an oven?"

"Yeah. And, I don't know, I guess I've just always thought that book," she said pointing towards my book on the table, "was part of the reason she did it. Like it justified her being crazy or something. And, to be honest, I'm sort of afraid that reading it will awaken something in me, some kind of genetic craziness that she passed on to me. And once it's awoken I won't be able to shut it off."

"Damn." We paused, both feeling the weight. "Well maybe it's one of those things where you have to face the devil, look him in the eyes, before you can conquer him, you know?"

"Yeah. Maybe. I just don't know if I'm ready. People in paper houses don't light fires."

"Tell you what. We'll read it together. One chapter at a time. You take this copy," I said handing her the library version, "and I'll go get my own. And if you want to stop then we'll stop. But we'll give it a try."

"Not yet."

I didn't bring it up after that, hoping not to offend her, fearing that I had crossed some sort of unspoken boundary and that she was going to shut down, shut me out. But a few weeks later we met in the upstairs section of the Lane library and she came holding the library's copy of the book.

"I think I'm ready. But," she quickly added an amendment "we've got to read it together. Are you sure you're up for reading it again?"

"Are you kidding? Good books always get better the more you read them. The first time you read it all you see is the plot, then the second time you read it you see the plot still but then you also see all the small details and all the periphery stuff that enhances the plot. And then the third time you read it you see it how you're supposed to – all together. If I haven't read it three times, I haven't understood it yet."

"Okay fine. But if we're doing this then I want to get my own copy." She slid the plastic-slippery book across the table. "You check this one out."

Her mother's copy had been destroyed,[23] so the next day Mira went to a used book store by herself to purchase a copy. I never asked her why she wanted a used copy of her own, but I think she wanted to glean some sort of vicarious experience through the previous owner. She needed to dwell on passages where the binding was strained, needed to see the reflections and notes left in the margins, needed to smell the remnants of another life that had endured the words. It took us a while, but over the next month we worked through the whole book, her

---

[23] I didn't ask by whom or by what means.

always speaking with unflinching candor about her mom and her emotions. She had a unique emotional vulnerability – not melodramatic but more of I've-lived-life-and-know-what-beauty-is sort of way. I don't think I really knew it at the time – or wanted to admit it – but her emotional enthusiasm, her raw inner energy during those last months of the summer drew me to her in a different way, made me feel vibrations that I hadn't expected.

But at the end of the summer Mira left for the University of Cincinnati to double major in art history and fine arts. When she left I figured it – our meetings, our consistent friendship – was over, that I wouldn't see her much, if at all. But that fall I was at her campus to see Brody's lecture on The Twelve Labors of Heracles, so I couldn't resist sending her a text message. We met up for lunch – and even though we could never get the timing right for anything more – we continued to meet irregularly over the next two years.

June 22<u>nd</u> 2010

<u>Tuesday</u>
<u>evening</u>

"What's that?"

"Vodka."

"Are you serious?"

"Yeah sure. Here…" I unscrewed the top of the spray bottle for her to sniff. "See?"

"Eris really has you on a leash, huh?"

"No, I just don't want Luna accidentally getting into the alcohol, so it just makes sense to keep it in the plastic crate with all the chemical solvents. She knows not to get into those. Plus I use it to clean sometimes."

I sat the clear spray bottle filled with vodka on the counter and stuffed the black crate with all the household cleaners back under the kitchen sink. Mira's eyes, the white parts, started to yellow, thin splotches of watered-down-red snaking across, the skin underneath loosening, drooping, falling off the bone. I grabbed two shot glasses and poured one for each of us.

"You want one, right?"

She nodded with her whole body, shook her shoulders. My eyelids felt heavy, my mouth dry, my tongue massive and in the way. We clinked our glasses, gulped down our shots, blinked our clouded eyes and held them shut, allowed ourselves to fully feel our bodies moving loops in our heads. When I opened mine, Mira was moving around the kitchen opening and closing cabinets, swinging them on their hinges.

"Where are your cups?"

"Above the sink."

She pulled down two red tumblers and made us mixed drinks, pouring the spray-bottle vodka generously, creating drinks strong enough to make our necks twitch.

"So let's hear this life-changing music you made."

"Right." She handed me a cup. "Which song do you want to hear?"

"What are my options?"

119

"Well let's see." I sat down by the stereo system in the living room and pulled out Rhythmic Epilepsy in Key of C's debut album. When I opened the case, the sleeve – which I hand drew and made hundreds of copies of – fell out. It was a ligature I developed to represent the word "Etcetera", the title of our most popular[24] track.

"Okay so on this disk there's a song called *Tetraktys* which is the opening track, followed by *Exponential Infinity*. And then there's the more popular *Etcetera* which, if my memory serves me, has some tasty keyboard."

"Well then I think we have a winner."

I clicked to the third track. Since you probably won't ever have a chance to hear the original copy – I've since lost it[25] – I'll try to set the mood for you. It opened with just the kick drum, driving and steady, muffled and deep, vibrating my fingertips. Then the clean channel guitars, arpeggiated and soft, came in followed by the syncopated keyboard chimes with a harpsichord alteration. And the bass guitar was there, ever-present but unheard, melodically steering everything, roping it all in. I took out my notebook, flipped it upside down, turned to a blank page.

---

[24] I admittedly use this word loosely.
[25] Though I'm sure copies still exist in the wild, tucked under car mats or sunken into closet chests across the Midwest.

→Sound Quality
    →Poor
        →Though not bad for being recorded in a
        subterranean cabin by teenagers.
→Musicianship
    →Keyboard: Off Beat
    →Drums: Herky-Jerky, Fill-Heavy
    →Guitar Work: Average
→Craftsmanship
    →7/8 Time signature is aggressive but sounds like a
    constant mistake.

Listening to that track, it was hard to remember why we thought we were any good. I guess it's hard to evaluate what you've made, what you've really done without some kind of creative distance. And more than anything, it just felt good to be making *something*, to be *doing* something, so the quality was sort of irrelevant at the time. But Mira closed her eyes and listened, nodded her head to the barely-findable beat anyway. When the drums picked up and the guitars got heavy, she got up off the couch and struck a rock pose – legs spread, knees bent, neck loose – and started playing air keyboards. We both started laughing sloppy wet laughs, our shoulders deflating.

"This is awful, right?"

"I didn't want to be the first to say it, but yeah…" she said between gasps for breath, falling onto the couch dramatically. "What kind of music do you even call this?"

"I think we called it instrumental math-core. You had enough?"

"Yes, *please* put on something else," she said composing herself. I paused the track and joined her on the couch, folding my knee flat across my leg, attaching my lips to the edge of my cup.

"So you said we needed to talk, right?" I said, my words slurring.

It happened two weeks before Eris left with you. It wasn't premeditated. It was just spur of the moment. Organic. No chemical additives. It was homegrown. In season. Ripe. It had no choice but to be harvested.

When I went to Fort Hamilton Hospital to get my blood checked again, I wasn't even thinking about Mira at all. I folded and tucked the prescription refill in my pocket and walked down to the cafeteria area to get some Jell-O pudding and a soda. She was sitting by the far wall reading a copy of *Giovanni's Room*, eating macaroni and cheese out of a paper bowl. She had on a typical Mira outfit that just barely stayed on the safe side of outlandish – lemon yellow skinny pants with her blue and yellow flats and a long sleeve, white shirt with slits cut up and down the sleeves and a quote handwritten across the chest.

"White: it is a complexion of the mind"

"Great book. You're not gay with only one foot out of the closet like Giovanni though are you?"

"What would it matter if…" she looked up and saw it was me. "Fuck Hurley? What're you doing here?"

"My Coumadin prescription ran out so I was getting an angiogram and my blood checked." I held up the cotton swab taped to my inner arm. "And I guess they found some kind of tachycardia – whatever that is – so I've got to wear this heart monitor for awhile." I patted the device hidden under my shirt.

"Heart monitors and angiograms? Aren't you a little young for that?"

I shrugged.

"Reading and eating macaroni in the hospital cafeteria? Aren't you a little too…I don't know. I feel like there's a joke there somewhere, but I can't find it. What's your excuse for being here?"

"No excuse. I just like hanging out here. I guess because it's quiet, and *normally* no one bothers me. Do you ever still come here to hang out?"

"Every now and then. Yeah it's usually pretty quiet so sometimes I get out of the house and grade papers or something here."

"Yeah and plus the food rocks."

I sat down in the empty, cold-metal chair across from her.

"It's good to see you."

"Yeah. Are you in a rush to get anywhere?"

"Not at all. You?"

"Nope," she said putting her bookmark back into place.

"So how long are you back in town for?"

"Well actually I've been meaning to call you. I'm here semi-permanently. I just transferred up to the University of Miami-Hamilton to be closer to my dad. I think he was starting to get lonely, starting to go back downhill a little."

"So you moved back in with him?"

"Well no. Kylie and I have our own place off Millville. We just moved in yesterday. We rent it from my dad who, of course, gave us a bargain to entice me to come back." She sipped her bottled water. "So what have you been up to? How's Luna?"

"She's good – getting bigger which is really weird. She's walking and talking and the whole deal now. Pretty soon she'll be driving and dating. It just all goes by so quick."

"Yeah I bet. What about Eris? How's she?"

"You know. I mean she's fine."

We looked down at the gray-tiled floor, dirty with lent and crushed chips.

"Oh hey, I've got some big news," she said. "You know how you used to always tell me to stop waiting for something to happen with my art? That I needed to make something happen for myself?"

"Yeah, sure."

"Well I called the The Arts Center awhile ago and they've been helping me plan this art show, like this exhibition of all my stuff. They've been promoting it pretty heavily." She said the last statement with a hint of casual, mock bravado, her chin waving like a flag in the breeze.

"Hey, that's awesome! When is it?"

"It's this Friday at seven o'clock. I was going to send out invitations and stuff but it's been so hectic with me moving back here and everything. I know it's last minute. I didn't even know if you were in town, but I'd really love it if you could make it."

"Yeah, of course, I'll be there."

When I turned my bike into the parking lot at The Arts Center – nestled up against the Great Miami River – I was already two pills and three bowls deep, my breath never fully in reach. The atrium inside was empty, all clean and white, the edges sharp and shiny. A sign pointed towards some noises down the hall.

It was shoulder to shoulder, standing room only, full with adults, well dressed and lemon-smelling and teenagers, dirty with holes in the knees of their pants and black knitted hats barely hanging onto their heads. Instrumental rock played quietly over the speakers, and the dimmed tungsten lights overhead caused the corners of the room to darken, soften the edges. I did a quick visual scan for Mira – searching for something colorful, something eclectic to catch my eye – but didn't see her anywhere in the crowd.

I blended in, dragging my feet around the room, admiring Mira's work. Her drawings and paintings – each of which had its own halogen spotlight – were spread across the walls, alternately black and white. She had the kind of talent that compelled people to buy her work – to look and think, to re-look and re-think – rather than just nod and speak in cliché generalities. Like most of her art shows in college that I went to, there were a lot of animal-themed pieces, specifically featuring the albatross. Her love for animals had become sort of her trademark, her artistic platform.

One particular sequential piece caught my eye. It was all on one canvas split into four equal sections. The far left section had a picture of a sea turtle floating in with the tide towards the sandy shore. The scene took place under a full moon with a pearl white, smooth-plumed albatross flying above the turtle. The whole piece was in water colors, soaked in cold blues and shadows. Though I'd never had any luck using water colors, I loved how they ran together on the page. It was so natural and organic, like a living creature. In the next segment, the sea turtle had reached the beach and had dug a hole filled with at least a hundred eggs. The light from the moon reflected off her shell--

"That one is my favorite too."

I looked over my right shoulder and saw Mira in a typical outfit – skinny, sky blue pants and a creased white t-shirt, words written across the chest.

"Art is Life"

"Yeah, wow. These are incredible."

"Can you believe how many people came out? I would have never expected this. Thanks so for much for coming." She gave me a hug, wrapping her arms all the way around my chest, clasping her fingers behind me.

"So anyway," she said pulling away "look around some more and then I'll have some closing remarks in like ten minutes. Then they're kicking everyone out right at eight." She wiggled her head on her shoulders to mock the curators.

While I did a lap around the perimeter checking out her other work – pieces crafted with acrylic paints, with charcoal, even one made from tiny bits of sand – I bumped into her father. He was hard to miss, a large man, both in belly and height. He carried a bushy beard that claimed most of his face, peaking in density and length on his neck. It dropped, wildly and darkly, down towards his cushy collar bones and reached out towards his shoulders. Mira told me in one of our after school meetings that her father used to be thin and clean shaven, but after her mother passed away, he started eating heavily and quickly became unkempt. She told me about the time that he took all those pills and she had to sleep all night in those chairs at the hospital, "the ones with the fucking red cloth and the wooden arms" always jabbing her in the ribs. He lost his job and briefly lost custody of Mira. But after cleaning himself up – and under Mira's supervision – he kept his beard more tamed and trimmed. Mira said that he kept his beard and belly as a reminder of his wife. The beard a cloak for his pain, a furry half-wall to hide behind, the belly a reminder that he can be full alone. Mira tolerated both, though she insisted that he at least keep his weight under control, which had become difficult for him, especially after Mira moved away to college. From a glance or even a brief conversation it was difficult to see how deeply affected Troy was by the loss of his wife because he was so positive and talked with incredible enthusiasm. But sometimes, behind his beard I could see the wrinkles on his face, the natural down-curve of his lips, the years of gravity taking hold of the corners of his skin.

"Good to see you, Troy."

"Hurley! Excellent!"

His voice boomed and shook my organs, shot rattling vibrations through my legs and chest – growing steadily heavier yet more hollow as the drugs crawled through me. An intensely passionate and euphoric man, Troy was how I imagined Santa Claus would look and sound when I was a child. I prepared myself for his unbearably strong handshake.

"So glad you could make it! I know Mira really appreciates all your support. She talks so fondly of you."

"Her work is great," I said pointing all around me. "What she has can't be taught."

Troy rolled his gums under his lips causing his whole beard to shift up and down.

"Are you two talking about me?" Mira said walking back over, seeing the two of us together.

"Of course," Troy said.

He put his hand on hers affectionately. People only had to spend a few minutes with Troy and Mira to realize how close they were. The bond was palpable. It was brazen and handsy. Unabatedly physical, though solidly unsexual. But people still looked, still muttered things under their breath when they saw this large bellied man with his hands wrapped around this young woman, with his sausage fingers on her creaseless palms, with her soft hand on his navel. It was sometimes a little much, but it was the kind of love – the doting and the openness, though maybe toned down – that I always thought I would have with you when you got older.

"I'm so proud of you," he said rubbing the outside of her hand.

The music in the room faded and one of the attendants – tall and thin with round glasses and stringy dirty-blonde hair situated around a scarlet scarf – stepped up to a podium made of spiky glass blocks.

"Thanks to everyone for coming out and supporting local art. As you know, our featured artist this evening Mira Mercury has agreed to allow fifty percent of the proceeds from her earnings tonight to go towards our future events. Now she'll be saying a few words before we close."

Mira walked up to the podium in wide strides with a firm, soft jaw curled into a smile that only those who knew her would recognize. When she got to the front, the attendant quickly ducked under something invisible and leaned into the mic. "And if you would, on your way out, let's have everyone pick up at least one piece of trash so we can keep the building clean. Thank you. Again, here's Mira Mercury."

Mira locked her knees and feet together, wavy and sparkling behind the blue glass podium.

128

"I just want to say thanks to everyone, again, for coming out. This is my first art show outside of school so it's great to get so much support. But specifically I want to thank my dad for supporting me and all my friends that encouraged me to be who I am. And I want to dedicate this night to my mom. She told me once that art is expression, and expression is life. So don't ever stop making art and you'll live forever." A few throats cleared, a few people chuckled. "Anyway, check out my website for information about upcoming events."

"Shameless," someone from the audience yelled out. There was a collective group exhale and a few laughs.

"My cards are on the table on the way out. Thanks again."

The crowd applauded one more time and then dispersed – couples nodding in pairs, teenagers slapping fives and walking slowly towards the door, some sidling – as Mira stepped away from the podium. Another wave of people moved away from the exit and towards Mira – the nexus for everyone in the room. She was barely visible over the hedge of prickly-bearded boys in plaid and middle aged mothers in musty flower print dresses with liberal art degrees. They circled around her asking questions, touching her shoulders. She pointed and nodded, moving her torso on a swivel, trying to glance over them to see her father. She raised her hand high up over the crowd and flapped her fingers at him as he waved and walked out with the hurried half of the crowd.

Waiting for the vapid pseudo-intellectuals and swooners to vacate, I walked – my legs feeling lighter, softer – back over to the sea turtle painting. In the third section, the hole that the mother turtle had dug was covered with sand and she was returning to the sea, leaving behind her children, her creation. In the last picture, a crowd of baby sea turtles struggled against the tide, tried instinctively to return to the ocean. It was presumably the middle of the night, in the hours where it's so black you can't see your feet and the clouds hide the moon. The albatross was not pictured in the last painting though in the left and right corners respectively there were facial renditions of both the sun and the moon, and there was a sapling fig tree, lushly green and the signs and the colors and--

"So, what'd you think?"

Mira was standing behind me in the salty light, and the last few people were trickling out the door. The woman from the podium hustled around the room picking up trash and shaking her head.

"It was seriously great. I'm really proud of you. Do you need some help taking everything down?"

"Oh you don't have to do that."

"I don't mind. I'm sure you need some help."

"Well, yeah, I mean, if you don't mind it would be great."

We started taking down the unsold pictures – some pieces sturdy and unbendable, others frail and fragile – and putting them into her sandy yellow plush-lined tote bags. When we bagged them all, we each hoisted them onto our shoulders and headed out to Kylie's car.[26] My body slanted to the right like a speed skater, almost tipping over because I picked up more bags than I could really handle. It seemed like the manly thing to do: over carry.

"You need some help with those, big guy?"

"No. Me? No, I'm fine."

She opened the car's front door and started peeling the bags one by one – placing each one carefully in the car seat – off my shoulder. Each time a bag came off, she brushed my hand, the touches feeling more intentional – involved more skin and pressure – as the weight lifted off my shoulder.

it's nothing
and it's breezy and it's casual
and it's all about dialectics
and long discussions and old books
and small words and big ideas
and art and life and real things
and dreams and the fucking pathetic fallacy
and renaming things and recycled energy

---

[26] She didn't have her own so she would always borrow her roommate's car.

"So anyway, great show tonight."

"Thanks again for coming. I know you've probably got a lot of other stuff that you could be doing."

"You'd think so. But not really. Eris and I don't really go out much."

Mira broke eye contact with me as I mentioned her name.

"So things are good with you two?" she asked with her head buried down in the car seat resituating her artwork.

"Yeah. Fine."

"Good."

She pulled her head back up and took the last picture off my shoulder.

"Hey, listen. This is the one you kept coming back to. The one with the sea turtles. You should take it."

"Really? No, come on, let me at least pay you for it." I reached for my wallet, my fingers shaking, my palms sweaty. She touched my hand to stop me.

"No way. It reminds me of you, anyway."

"Why's that?" I asked feeling my skin start to buzz, feeling my arms start to rise.

"Ever since we read The Rime of the Ancient Mariner my senior year, I've had this thing for the albatross. It was just so sad how it just kept following the Mariner. And since I first read it in your class, I just always think of you when I think of the story, of the bird. Anyway, you should have it," she said holding out the tote bag.

→I can hang it in the bedroom!
    →Eris wouldn't allow it.
        →The office!
            →She would still object.
                →I'll lean it against the wall.
                →Keep it in its case, still knowing what's inside.
                →I'll tell her it's something I'm working on.
                →She'll never look inside.

"Thanks," I said taking it out of her hands and leaning it against the front tire.

"Well listen, I've gotta get going. Kylie needs her car back soon. But hey, now that I'm in town, hopefully I'll get to see you more often."

"Yeah."

"And thanks again for coming." With our backs to the water – black and crawling, rippled streaks of golden-white from the street lamps – we were both stalling, loitering in the parking lot, not wanting to leave, not wanting to return to our regular lives.

hey, let's stay.
let's hang out.
let's drop off Kylie's car, rent one and drive down to the ohio river!
and let's pack a lunch – sandwiches and crackers, keep it light
and maybe pick up a two-liter, something quick
and let's bring our hiking shoes, just in case
and maybe we'll rent kayaks and head for the mountains
and let's make a mixed CD and listen to it the whole way down,
singing every word, feeling every word, making up new words!
and we'll rent a cabin maybe, invite everyone!
bring them all!
everyone we know!
all their friends too!
and we'll all meet and drink and touch each other,
hands trembling, elbows loose
and we'll all dissolve together,
lose ourselves in our thoughtlessness,
each word and movement a vapor in the collective steam,
our bodies sweating, dripping on the shag carpet.
yes there will be shag carpet!
and we'll laugh and touch and sweat all night until our eyes get heavy
and our shoulders can't take it anymore
and everything gets slow
and all the edges are gone
and we'll fall on the couch, on the floor,
in the windowsill, anywhere and it will all be the same
and we'll wake up, our eyes still hidden behind clouds

and we won't know why
and we won't know who is in our arms
did we ever get a name?
a friend of a friend – and we'll stand in the yard, in the dew
and drink syrup and sit in the sun
and sweat it all out

"Okay, well I'll see you later," I said.

I leaned past her to pick up the tote bag by the tire and she kissed my cheek. Just a quick swipe. No residue left behind. A quick, clean peck.

did she mean to do that?
and it was an accident.
a classic misreading of signals.
and it wasn't even real
and didn't even happen
and it's only my imagination

"I know I probably shouldn't have done that, but…"

It might be hard for you to read this since I was still with your mother when it happened,[27] but I just sort of leaned in towards her – it was totally just an instinct, some kind of muscle memory thing – and pressed my lips against hers. It probably sounds so wrong but it was just a knee jerk reaction. I hadn't kissed or been kissed in a long time. It wasn't even really a kiss. I just sort of touched her lips with my closed mouth. It's more like we were just standing really close together, looked more like I was whispering something to her. When I pulled away, I felt her hand slide in and out of my empty back left pocket.

"It's just that…well…I should get back home and you should get Kylie's car back to her."

"Right."

"Look, I'll call you sometime, okay?"

She hurried around to the driver's side of her car and ducked inside, looking at me with her chin tilted down, looking

---

[27] Hopefully you're seeing that the whole thing is more complicated than who was with whom.

at me from the tops of her eyes. Pulling out of the parking lot, she waved with her fingers, keeping her palm on the steering wheel. I put my arm up, and I stood there for what felt like a long time before I reached into my back pocket and found that she had slipped me a flattened origami fortune-teller.

Mira propped up her legs – knees all bony and sharp, calves soft – onto the couch. I shifted in my seat. She twisted her lips and scrunched her nose, on the verge of a sneeze.

"I think you know what I wanted to talk to you about," she said.

"Well just to make sure, why don't you lead?"

"I just need to know, really for my own sanity more than anything else, if what happened the other night was a one-time thing or if it was something that you had been thinking about too."

"I don't know. I mean…What do you think?"

"Hurley, I'm asking *you*." She folded her legs in, leaning in closer. I gulped my beverage.

too strong!
too bitter!
but real men don't complain about strong drinks.

"Look, we get along so great and I obviously like you and it's all so easy, but I've got a daughter with Eris so it makes things so much more complicated."

--*"You're too good for a guy like that"*--

"So it wasn't something that you had thought of doing too?"

I blinked hard and threw up my hands loosely, too casually – the booze opening me up, cranking my energy, the weed pointing all that energy inward.

"I mean, I don't know. I think I've told you this before. That if I can't visually see the logic behind something I have trouble deciding anything. And in this case I can feel the logic, but I can't see it because of all the complications. It's like my body doesn't agree with my convictions, you know? So I guess it's just easier not to choose. It's easier to not change."

135

--they're sitting in the hot tub, drying off with the same towel, cuddling on the couch, drinking from the same cup, hands on the same cup--

"But isn't not choosing out of lack of mental justification or whatever you want to call it – isn't that a choice? Isn't a non-choice just as deliberate as an active-choice?"

"Yeah you're probably right. But...okay so you know about my dad, right?" She nodded and burrowed her cold feet in between the cushions. "I just don't want Luna to think of me that way. It's like if I leave Eris then, you know, the underlying assumption there is that having Luna was an accident or a mistake. And I don't want her to feel, when she grows up, like she isn't supposed to exist, you know? And I guess I just feel like leaving Eris would lead to that."

My body felt stiff, strangely frozen.

"I get that. But I look at it this way," she said, her eyes drooping, her hands moving like dawdling clouds. My tongue tasted like powder and ash. I patted the lighter in my pocket. "I think we're all the sum of who we've been. So we are who we are because of what we've done. And so the past can't ever be a mistake or else our current selves are a mistake too, you know? So it's impossible for her to have been a mistake, whether you stay or leave. It's like each moment is a stepping stone towards something else, but sometimes we lose track of what's a stepping stone and what's solid ground. Just tell her that." She shrugged her shoulders, loosely reached down for her drink.

--quick kisses, wandering kisses, heavy petting (!)--

"Maybe all that's true, I don't know, but none of that logic will matter when she's pissed off at me for being absent. I guess that's really what I'm afraid of. If I agree to end it, then Eris will definitely get custody, and it's not fair for me to miss out on her life just because Eris and I aren't in love. My only chance to be with Luna is to be with Eris."

"But isn't it also just as crippling to create a household where love doesn't exist? You always hear about couples that stay together for their kids and then the kids end up resenting their parents because they fought all the time. And, I mean, isn't that unfair for you too?"

I leaned back and exposed my throat to the ceiling, rippled and crawling.

--pants being hastily undone--

"When I had Luna I gave up caring about what's fair to me."

"So you're just going to stay with her until Luna turns eighteen and moves out? And then what? And then Eris'll fall in love with you? Really? At some point, what's best for you becomes what's best for your daughter right?"

"I guess I just had this idea – and I don't even know where it came from now – of what a family is supposed to be. I thought it was supposed to be a group of people *strategizing* together and living and working towards some kind of common goal. And I know that's probably unrealistic to expect with Eris but I just don't want to be the one, when I look back, to say that I didn't value togetherness strong enough."

--naked, she lays on his chiseled chest afterwards, asks to see his holster, his gun--

"But at least you know that you're viewing things in terms of their potentials. Or what you want their potentials to be." The weed barged into our psyches, spliced and rewired our logic, veering our conversation onto loops built on top of other loops. "It's like that surreal moment when you're a kid and you think that your parents are perfect – the absolute standard to live by. But then something happens – like for me it was when I saw my mom start to be so sad that she couldn't function – and you realize they aren't what you thought, that they're just struggling people too. And until that moment it's hard to put things in context and realize what is actually strange and what is actually normal. But when you're honest about what you have – when you can distinguish between what you actually have and what you want things to be – I think that's when you can finally let go. At least that's how it was for me after…"

--she puts her pants back on, smells like him--

      This might sound insane and maybe confirm everything that your mother's told you about me, but while I was listening to Mira talk, my soul floated upwards into the aether, the visual scale growing smaller and smaller until, looking downward, my body was just a faceless, colorless dot inside a transparent roof. Everything was happening slower than it was supposed to, the timing off, my body frictionless, too soft. Then the lens zoomed back inwards until my consciousness was somewhere above the couch, watching my body recoil away from Mira.

> *why am i still resisting?*
> *and why is my face so red?*
> *and why are my limbs all curled and closed?*

      My body, my skin looked older – thicker and lighter – than I felt from the outside. As I forced myself back down inside my skin – that was supposed to be encasing my thoughts, my soul – I felt myself squeezing down, compressing through a magnetic energy hovering just outside my body. There was friction. Resistance. And then a snapping into place.
      Once back in my body – skin on fire, then covered in ice – I looked at Mira who was still talking. In that super-lucid, hyper-aware moment, I felt connected to her in a new way, felt a tingling sensation at each tip of my spine.

→To kiss her would be nice.
>   →I've wanted this for awhile.
>   →She's wanted this for awhile.
>   →It's time to stop holding back.
>   →If I stop holding back, I'll find out what's out there.
>   →Which is, at least metaphysically, what I'm after.
>   →Eris is holding nothing back.
>   →Body's Answer:
>   →Yes
>   →Kiss her leading to lengthy coitus with drug-induced stamina
>   →Mind's Answer
>   →Logical
>   →But too soon
>   ↓
>   **Physical Override**

Her deep-watery-blue eyes looked like miniature full moons – tiny cosmological portals – as I titled and leaned my head, putting an ellipsis in her sentence with my shaky lips.

By our third year together, your mother and I never went out together unless we had to, unless it was a special occasion, something forced. Our already low whole number had flipped to a fraction. And even at home we were only talking about topics related to you.[28] Because of our unique situation, our focus almost immediately became not trying to know each other but trying to know our child in the context of each other. So the divide that we both felt wasn't caused by one thing in particular and there was no conversation to formally verify its existence. It was just sort of always there in the background of what we were doing.

You probably don't remember this but for your first three winters we – you, Eris, and I – went over to Brody's house on Christmas Eve for dinner. But that Christmas, the one before everything changed, something felt different – somber and more serious. I think everyone in the room could feel the knots in the air bouncing off our thin skin, the knots in our bodies twisted and tight. But we couldn't see where they were coming from, who they hit on the ricochet.

After dinner we all sat in the living room and watched you and Colton unwrap and play with your presents – your brand new stuffed squirrel and his new pastel-colored blocks. Bailey took enormous amounts of pictures, and Eris, typically with an opinion on every topic, sat – arms folded, lips straight – in the single-seat recliner. She didn't talk to anyone unless they were playing with you. And even then she would only say things like:

"Be careful with that."
OR
"She really doesn't like to be played with that way."

As I'm sure you know, these sorts of terse comments from Eris were not unusual, but her demeanor and posture that

---

[28] "Who is picking Luna up from Julie's?" OR "What time did she go to bed?"

night provided an unfamiliar context giving her words a sharper edge.

As we were getting ready to leave for the evening, Brody pulled me aside while Eris was gathering up your presents and asked if everything was okay. I hated the questions. Always all the questions. The looks of concern. The squinting of eyes and crunching of teeth. The acting like he was better, wiser, always in the know. I made some excuse about Eris missing her family around the holidays. I guess it was partially true – you know the situation with your grandparents on her side – but I think somewhere in the back of our minds, Eris and I both knew something was coming, that something boiling in gray and red-rusted vats was about to ferment and foam everywhere. We all said our goodbyes and exchanged cursory hugs.

The ride home was quiet, not the comfortable silence of a veteran couple who had exhausted all their stories and developed a calm silence but an intentional, aggravated silence of a couple who had worn out their welcome. You were asleep in the backseat.

> all couples go through rough patches
> and all sparks fizzle out eventually
> and lightening only reverberates for so long
> but it can strike twice
> and we can recharge

I broke the invisible barrier between Eris and I by placing my hand on the outside of her thigh in the driver's seat. I half expected her to flinch on contact, to recoil repulsed by my forced affection. So I was surprised when she put her hand on mine instead. It was too dark for me to tell for certain and I was afraid to ask but she looked like she was crying. At least her eyes glistened, full and wet each time we passed a streetlight. When we got home we put you to bed – one of the few activities we both still had our hand in at the same time.

Eris and I hadn't had sex in months, but that night, like many others, I tried half-heartedly to make some advances. By that point, I had already conceded to the idea of living my life unfulfilled so you would not have to, that I would persevere

142

through a sexless life with an altruistically masculine devotion. But the fact that she touched my hand on the ride home bolstered me with hope.

Lying in bed, she had her back turned to me so I snuggled up next to her and started rubbing the back of her legs, rubbing tiny concentric circles right behind her knees. The lights were off and we'd been lying there quietly for a while, so she had sufficient leverage to fake sleep. She wasn't responding and her breathing was evening out mimicking that of a sleeper, so I assumed that, as had become the norm, I was being rejected, that the hand placement in the car ride had just been a fluke or maybe a sick tease. Looking back, it seems so counter intuitive now – that she was still so sexy to me, that I still wanted her. Maybe all the rejection was a latent turn on. Always a closet masochist, maybe there was a certain part of me that wanted to believe things would work out because it felt good to hurt, because I felt that's what I deserved.

But when I was about to stop and give in to sleep, Eris rolled over and kissed me once on the neck, kissed me softly, with closed lips. I wanted to kiss her back but my neck went numb. She kissed her way up towards my lips dissolving all that she touched, everything freezing and buzzing, my blood starting and stopping, everything falling asleep on contact. Her limbs moved slowly, deliberately. Swimming under the apple sheets she climbed on top of me, taking my hands. Even though the lights were off and my eyes were not fully adjusted, she looked different, moved her hips differently. Everything happened on fast forward, was blurry and unengaging. Afterward, she rolled off and went to the bathroom.

Even when your mother and I were having sex regularly, she wasn't a fan of post-coital cuddling or any of its variations, but when she disappeared into the bathroom like that I still felt a little violated. I wanted to put my head in her warm lap again. I wanted her to come back and tell me how good it was just to have me. I wanted her to belly flop on the mattress, roll around saying *God, that's exactly what I needed and…* I wanted her sentences to drift off, her mind to fire off unfocused, her eyes to soften, her lips to curl and dissolve into droplets of warm water.

But none of that happened, and while I waited for her to come out of the bathroom I felt overly self-conscious.

what is she doing in there?
and is she stalling?
and does she not want to see me naked?
and she is in there sitting on the sink with her knees tucked up,
waiting for me to fall asleep.

I sucked in my gut and laid my temple across my arm, flexing my bicep just to feel the hidden muscle grow and harden against my ear. The shower water started and steam leaked under the door, so I fell asleep thinking that it had just been some sort of test to see if anything was left, that it had just been a way to say goodbye. The next day your mother took you and left me for the first time.

I woke up with a massive headache, which in itself wasn't unusual. Since my teenage years, I had been prone to frequent headaches. They weren't migraines. I wasn't passing out and throwing up and the whole deal. It was just an annoying, difficult to pinpoint, pain on every surface of my head. After seeing an old Woody Allen vignette, I always imagined there were tiny people inside my head playing drums on my skull from the inside, trying to mine their way out. But as they played on my head that morning their beat was slurred.

I tried to put my surroundings into context but everything was fuzzy, all air and light and woolen felt, no sharp edges anywhere. I closed one eye and used the other, then switched. Blurry. I had lost one of my contacts. Leaning up in bed, the percussionists in my head started a drunken, sloppy cadence before switching to a bass heavy beat that thumped against my temples. A curvy shape stood next to the foot of the bed.

→Eris.
    →Eris left me.
        →Who is that?
            →Luna?
                →That's too big of a blob to be Luna.
                    →Mira!
                    →That's right!
                    →Mira came over.
                        →What happened?

"Hey. You're up."
"Hey."

I rubbed my temple trying to coax the percussionists into putting their drumsticks down, into postponing their recital.

"You okay?"
"Yeah, I think so. Can you hand me my glasses? They're behind the mirror in the bathroom."

I got out of bed slowly, testing my balance and stability, trying to find my equilibrium. Swaying in place, the percussionists switched to rolls instead of the thumping bass – a slight improvement, the pain less concentrated. Things are always more tolerable when they're spread out. As soon as I regained my balance, I realized I was naked, so I shuffled over to the dresser and put on underwear and jeans.

why am I naked?
shitfuck.
shitfuck.
shitfuck.
shitfuck.

With my one good eye, I started to piece things together, to grasp the implications of the mise-en-scene in front of my half-blurry eyes.

this is wrong
and no one will ever understand
and it looks so bad
and oh god, what if Eris walks in
and what if she has Luna with her
and what if she brings John with her to help her pick up her stuff
and she'll have him crush me into salt
and turn me into brine
and there's fucking black water everywhere and

"Do you have any Ibuprofen?"

"Check under the sink," I said, my voice rattling in my throat.

I heard wood against wood and the rattle of pills against plastic. She came back in with my old glasses – the prescription outdated. I took out my remaining contact and slipped them on, turning Mira's curvy hologram into a crisper, real-time image of her in a blue bra and yellow cotton panties.

"You're sure you're feeling okay? You look a little out of it."

"I'm fine. I'm gonna get dressed."

"Yeah me too. Can I wash up?"

"Sure."

Legs and hands shaking, I went to the dresser and saw my gray lighter, the velvet pouch of pills lying on top. Several more pills were missing, though I'm not sure which ones or who had taken what. All the substances successful in blocking out my self-conscious thoughts were fading away so I picked out and dry swallowed – swallowed hard, the pill, once smooth, now serrated on the way down – a round pill that looked like this:

"You want some water or something?" I said poking my head into the bathroom where Mira was leaned over washing her face, a wash cloth slung over her shoulder. I caught a glimpse of myself, eyes black, the area around my lips a faded blue.

"Yeah, that'd be good," she said looking up, combing her fingers through her ruffled hair in an attempt to smooth out the kinks that always inevitably develop overnight. I instinctively did the same.

The apartment was hazy, covered in a misty gray fog. I poured us each a glass of water from a plastic gallon-sized jug, turned on the overhead fan and opened the porch door, sliding the screen across the frame. Looking out at my garden, I pictured the roots of the tomatoes battling and cleaving under the soil, the winning sprout ready to shoot up.

"Are you worried that she's going to come back and see me?"

I turned around and Mira stood fully dressed in the living room sipping from her glass of water.

"What?"

"I don't know if you remember this last night or not, but you told me that Eris left you for good. Is that true?"

"I think you should go," I said turning back towards the window, eyes on Eris' empty parking spot.

"Look, I know you're freaked out right now but just relax. Nothing even happened last night. We just slept *next* to each other not *with* each other."

"Really?"

"You don't remember? Well, I mean you really wanted it to happen, but you feel asleep," she said suppressing a laugh.

"Oh god."

"No it was cute. I mean, we were fooling around and stumbled into the bedroom. You were pretty out of it by that point so I asked you if you really wanted to do this. You said absolutely and started undressing me. Sloppily, I might add," she said twitching her eyebrows.

"Then we fell onto the bed and kept kissing. You were trying to take all your clothes off but you were having a *hell* of a time getting out of everything."

"Oh god. Please stop."

She sat down at the kitchen table and started laughing, spinning her vial of lip gloss on the lacquered wood.

"Anyway, you passed out right after that. And I wasn't as gone as you, but I was too drunk to drive home so I just fell asleep next to you. Plus I wanted to make sure that you were okay."

"Thanks. Sorry."

"It probably wouldn't have been a great idea for it to happen like that anyway, right?"

"Yeah."

"And look, this doesn't have to mean anything. Okay? I know you're all over the place with Eris leaving and taking Luna. And the last thing I want is to come in here like some kind of home wrecker. I guess I'm just saying that I think it's best for us to wait to un-tether whatever this thing is," she raised her thumb and pinkie finger, pointing one at each of us, "until you work through whatever you need to work through."

"You're right. So we'll just keep it tied up for now until I get some things sorted out?"

"Sure."

I broke eye contact and looked around the still-hazy apartment, surveying the damage, everything gray. There were CDs out across the living room floor, reflecting lasers through the semi-smoke and the stereo buzzed – bouncing a faint high-pitched tension across the walls – from being left on all night. In the kitchen: a half-dozen beer bottles, a dirty blender, a crooked row of glass cups, and the linoleum floor looked wet, all shiny and slick. When I looked back over, Mira was standing by the door holding her purse.

"Call me later, okay?"

"Sure thing."

We hugged, both flat-footed – the top of her head landed right under my beard – and she said goodbye with her chin tilted down, looked at me from the tops of her eyes, kissed me on the cheek.

I went out on the porch to breathe in some smokeless air and look at my garden. Mira pulled out of the parking lot, and I grabbed my hand spade and a pouch of summer squash seeds. I warmed them with my palms and dropped them several inches deep in a soil-filled bucket next to the tomatoes and red bell peppers. Exhausted, I unloaded my body – full of bricks and filmy soot – on the couch inside and immediately fell back asleep.

I woke up from a dreamless, orange-pill induced semi-nap on the couch in the copper light of the open-window afternoon to the buzz of my phone on the coffee table next to me. It was a text from Eris.

"just fyi im coming alone to pick up the rest of my stuff latr 2day"

My phone had apparently been buzzing unanswered for a while because the time stamp on the text was a few hours past real time.

I blinked cinder blocks out of my eyes and re-read the message, searched it again to make sure it was real.

→The spelling makes no sense and there's no punctuation.
  →It must be real.
      →Did she already come?
      →Did I miss her?
  ←No.
      →So she'll be here soon.
          →I can't see her yet.
              →I'm not prepared!
              →**Get out!**

I frantically cleaned up the apartment, covering my tracks from the previous night. Looking back, it's not that I was ashamed. Hiding things had just become a habit. Plus she said she was coming alone, so you wouldn't be there as a buffer, a filter for the emotions that would surely leaven. I moved quickly, ignored my light-headedness, washed out cups, threw towels on the kitchen floor to wipe up the unexplained moisture, re-hid all the alcohol, tossed the empty beer bottles into the recycle bin,[29] and crammed the dirty blender into the dishwasher.

> *will Eris stay the night when she comes over?*
> *and will she wait around for me?*
> *and she'll have something to say*
> *and she'll sit by the door,*
> *waiting, seething, spitting gunpowder and lasers,*
> *stones and daggers*
> *and i can't see her*
> *and it's too early*
> *and everything is wrong*
> *and she'll have legal documents*
> *and make me sign things*
> *and i'm not ready*
> *and none of this is real*

I took a huge glass bowl out of a cabinet, filled it with the rest of Tails' food and gave him some extra water. I grabbed food, granola bars and a bag of trail mix, then ran to the

---

[29] Which your mother never looked in or used.

bedroom and sifted through my drawers for as many t-shirts and pairs of clean underwear as I could find. I stuffed my wallet and all my clothes in my backpack and rolled my bicycle out of my office. I dumped the last of the weed out of the bottom chamber of my grinder, poured it into a rolling paper, licked the edges and tucked the joint behind my ear. I attached my never-used one-man tent on top of my backpack and headed for the door, padding my pockets to make sure that I had everything.

FRONT LEFT:
lighter
pouch of pills

FRONT RIGHT:
pen
brown button

BACK LEFT:
origami fortune teller

BACK RIGHT:
notebook

On my way out I grabbed the letter from Noah sitting on the table.

Part II

dripping entropy

Biking along the shoulder of the road – gears and spokes ticking and clicking – I thought briefly about going back to Julie's again to demand to see you, to fight and make a scene. But sometimes the best way to fight is to withdraw the troops and develop a new strategy. Brute force – which I severely lacked anyway – would have only made things worse, given the courts even more ammunition. So I glided into the small parking lot outside the gas station near Julie's house where I met Al.

I pulled out Noah's letter. If I understood, he would be staying at his cabin. Really it was his grandfather's cabin, but Noah inherited it while we were in high school after his grandfather overdosed on some lethal narcotic and prescription pill mixture. Noah ends up being important to the story, so I want to make sure you have a good idea of who he is and where he came from. Here's a breakdown of the highlights you need to know.

1 - Noah is nomadic. The only home he keeps is the one inside himself. He sets up a tent just outside of whatever town or city he wants, works odd jobs and sleeps around until he wears out his welcome. Then he moves on to do the same thing somewhere else.

2 - Every few months I would receive collect phone calls or letters keeping me posted on his whereabouts and adventures.

3 - Noah is the sort of person that follows his whims in spurts of enthusiasm, not the kind of existential nomad that rides trains across Europe with a backpack and a pocketful of foreign currency.

4 - He always has a plan and the persuasive ability to accomplish it.

Behind the gas station I saw Al sitting on his overturned bucket reading. He looked up from a thick-spined paperback book with the front cover rolled around over the back cover. He had changed out of his 'Albedo' shirt in favor of one with a picture of a black stallion and the words:

"Horseness is the whatness of allhorse."

"Hurley! Did it work?"

He took his hand out of his pocket, accidently knocked out a tiny twisted bag full of something tan, like light brown sugar but dry. Weird sand.

"Did what work?"

"My advice?"

"Yeah actually it did. Well not at first. Once I stopped looking for it, I found it. Oddly enough."

"That's the trick, isn't it?"

He picked dirt out from underneath his thumbnails.

"Hey, I just wanted to give you something." I reached for my keychain – clipped by a carabiner to my belt loop.

"Oh come on kid, you don't owe me anything."

"No I know. It's a gift, not a payment," I said pulling off my spare apartment key. "This is just in case it rains or something and you want a place to go."

"Hurley, I can't take that."

"I want you to. Please. I bet your ex-old lady has never been there." I pressed the key into his palm. "I don't really want to go back there anyway. Eris – that's the girl – is moving all her stuff out today and I hate the idea of going back to an empty apartment. Anyway I'm gonna be gone for a day or two so you're welcome then or any time you want."

I ripped out an empty page of my notebook, jotted down my address.

"Alright kid, well then I guess I'll see you around some time."

"Let's hope."

We shook hands. Walking away, I updated my categories.

~~Things Eris Has Not Seen~~
~~-Diner~~
~~-The inside of Ryan's apartment~~

Things Al Was Right About.
-You'll find what you want when you stop looking.

Even though my parents lived apart for seven years, they never officially divorced, never legally separated. At first my father flew out once a year to see us, tacked it on to business trips that he had to make in the area. It was always quick, forced, uneasy.

"I don't want to see him, okay?"

"Hurley stop being so melodramatic. He's your father. You have to see him."

"I don't *have* to do anything."

Freshly fourteen, I was always on the defense, easily agitated, struggling to fully own my autonomy.

"Well you have to do this. He'll be here soon."

I mumbled and went up to my room – the walls completely covered with movie posters and abstract artwork some of which I had drawn – and laid out across my gray sheets, the bedspread scrunched up at the bottom where my feet hung over the edge.

why make these tired attempts to have a relationship once a year?
and why try to hold on to something that isn't there?

I turned on my overhead fan and watched it spin, watched the wooden arms speed up and blur, listened as they screamed in whispers.

why would he still come here now that Brody's at college?
and he only ever came to see Brody anyway
and he only ever called to talk to Brody

I rolled off the mattress and turned on Third Eye Blind's *How It's Going to Be*. Even now when I listen to that song, I get that tightness that moves upward from my chest and into my neck when I hear that opening riff. I listened to the song on repeat, let the hot waves move through my chest until I heard my father's truck – a rental – pull into the driveway.

I looked at my hands and wrists, looked at the notes and small sketches scribbled on them in black ink. Most of them smeared, rendered indecipherable.

> *why do i always write on my hands?*
> *and it's just a waste*
> *and it just washes away, drips off*
> *and it's never permanent*
> *and why is he here?*

Even as a teenager I loved getting that feeling of having something urgent in my head, something that had to be recorded immediately by any means necessary, lest it be lost forever. I'd start writing, drawing, letting the idea flow, forming as it solidified. But more often than not, I lost the notes, my ideas dissolving, fading throughout the day. I riffled through my desk, found something more reliable: a small, black notebook that I stuffed in my back pocket. And I pushed up the screen on my window, ducked out onto the roof,[30] and looked out over the edge down to the green grass maybe fifteen or twenty feet below.

> *i can make the jump.*
> *can i make the jump?*
> *i can make the jump.*
> *can i?*

I had heard – I don't remember where – that if you do a forward roll right when you hit the ground that your body can lessen the impact, that the Earth absorbs the brunt of the force, spreads it out. If you land on your feet you're likely to twist an ankle or worse. I visualized my body spinning forward in the air.

> *the roof is a diving board.*
> *the grass is a pool.*

---

[30] My window was the only one in the whole house that offered roof access.

Inside I heard my mom call up to me in my room. I only had a minute, maybe two, before she came up to get me. I rocked back and forth on my feet, ball to toe, weighing whether or not it was worth it.

the roof is a diving board.
the grass is a pool.

→Stay and talk to my father.
   →See something in his eyes that makes me want to hug him.
      →Forgive him pre-emptively.
         →Relationship Mended
         →Grudge Still Held
   →See something in his eyes that makes me resent him more.
      →Get angrier.
         →Relationship Unchanged
         →Grudge^{grudge}
→Avoid my father.
   →See nothing that reminds me of anything.
      →Relationship Unchanged
      →Grudge Still Held
→Avoid my father directly but spy secretly.
   →Allows me to avoid eye contact but gauge his demeanor and level of disappointment in not seeing me.
      →Relationship Dependent On Outcome
      →Grudge Dependent On Outcome

Only one option held room for even the possibility that I could get rid of the grudge, that I could begin to slowly prune back the resentment and self-doubt. So I opted for the high-risk, high-reward uncertainty and jumped off the roof. I tried to spin in the air, to tuck and roll before I landed, but my body didn't cooperate – there wasn't enough time to get the proper position, to nail the angle. So I landed on my shoulder which popped underneath my skin on impact. With my arm hanging lifelessly at my side, feeling like an unpracticed delinquent – which I guess, at least statistically, I was at risk of becoming – I jogged around to the front window outside the living room. The glass was pulled up, the screen down so I could hear the conversation that unfolded after my mom walked downstairs.

"Cliff I think he's gone."

"What do you mean you *think* he's gone? You don't know?"

"Well he was here a little bit ago. And the window in his room is open so I think maybe he snuck out."

"Why would he do that?"

Neither of them answered the question.

is he disappointed?
and does it hurt him to not be wanted?

I searched my father's eyes for some sort of answer but couldn't get a clean look at his face, clouded behind his heavy beard. He rocked in the chair that he always sat in when he came to visit, the one that no one else sat in, avoided eye contact with my mom.

"Does he do this a lot? Is he getting into trouble?"

"Not really. Why do you ask?"

"When I saw him last year something about him just seemed off. He was just really quiet – hardly said anything to me at all."

"That's just his nature."

"I guess. And he had all these numbers and words and sketches written all over his hands and arms. Is he still doing that?"

"Yes. But you know how he loves to draw. Remember how he used to make us little story books with his pictures?"

My father nodded and turned his head towards the window. I ducked down.

"Anyway I think it's just a phase. He'll grow out of it," my mom said.

They both sat across from each other silently until my father chimed back in. "Well no use sitting around here I guess. I've got business to attend to elsewhere anyway."

he's not going to wait to see if i come back?
and he's not going to search for me?

162

I wanted him to seek me out, but he touched my mom's hand and got up to leave while I watched from the bushes outside. When I heard his rental truck pull out of the driveway, I pulled out my notebook and started my first column.

Things I Resent About My Father
-He didn't even try.

I noted his age and the last time that he saw me – my first subject in my ever-growing sample set. Even then, especially then, I was tender, my eyes watering and my throat knotting.

why am i so god-damned sensitive?
and why am i so fucking fragile inside?

I've always had this visible fragility, this weirdly softening skin. This is my theory. I have all this energy, all this pent up recklessness that I turned inward. I don't want to blame your mother or my father or any one person because I'm sure it's more complicated than that. Or maybe it's really simple and it's just a result of my own faults. But whatever the source was, my organs, my ventricles, my ligaments, and underskin have been forced to absorb all that inward energy. And it's shaken and overwhelmed everything inside and created this incredible fragility. But of course I wasn't able to process any of it right then, right as my father was walking out again without seeing me. I leaned up against the brick wall.

--Something about him just seemed off.--
--Seemed off.--
--Seemed off.--
--Seemed off. –
--Seemed off.--

June 23rd 2010

i am unstoppable
and my bicycle is unstoppable
and my tires are made of fucking steel and impenetrable rubber,
new rubber that has so much give,
rubber that the world has never seen
and we are unstoppable together

The bicycle trip gave me something to feel excited about. It's always better, or at least more interesting, to be alive when there's some kind of raison d'être, some kind of purpose, something urgent and flowing through your body, everything heightened, your senses active in new ways. You had been mine, still are mine. I was making decent time on my bicycle largely because I hadn't seen any car traffic since passing Pyramid Hill and turning off SR-128 onto the back roads just past Ross. My finely tuned, efficient bicycle ticked and spun along the pavement. I had never made the trip out to the cabin – located somewhere northeast of New Haven – from my apartment, but I figured it was about a thirty-five mile bike ride. I could easily make it by nightfall.

About thirteen miles into the ride I pulled over in a cornfield on the side of the thin country road for a rest and a stretch. It was about 5:00 p.m. EST so I had about three and a half hours of daylight left and around twenty miles left to bike by my estimation. At this rate I could be at the cabin by seven or eight o'clock, well before the summer sun would fall. I was glad not to have to use my tent attached to the top of my backpack, which I really just brought for show. I owned it more as a symbol of freedom and connection to nature. I had never even put it together. Even if I had been around more, I probably would not have been the kind of father that took you camping on the weekends.

I had already eaten most of the snacks I brought and spilled half my water down my chin. All I had left was a small bag of trail mix. I had slept through breakfast with Mira in my

165

bed and then I napped on the couch through lunch because I was still nursing my hang over. The last thing I actually remembered eating, other than pills, was the three hot dogs in the park the day before. My stomach, triggered by my mind's realization that it should be hungry, burped and gurgled. I drank some of my water, felt it cold and snaky, slither down into my stomach, and even though I was feeling a little dehydrated, I immediately had to urinate.

humans are mostly made of water
and am i dissolving inside,
shrinking slowly into my bladder?

I wanted to do a pH test on my urine to gauge and numerate its acidity, to see if my organs were liquefying. I popped my phone off its post and left my bicycle next to the road while I walked – toes pointing inwards – with my backpack towards a patch of trees.

I was still coming down from my high, still hung over so I was sensitive to sounds, but I remember it being really quiet out. While riding, the wind whistled and whipped in and out of my ears, but on the unmoving ground everything in the air was soft and still. In my haste to leave the apartment, I forgot my iPod which had become a regular companion on most of my lengthy bike rides. Without the constant distraction, the unusual, natural silence of life was amplified and sort of eerie at first. I tried to think of it as refreshing, though my ears itched for some sort of music, something rhythmic and easily interpretable, calculable. And slowly, as I got used to my environment, I started to hear things, industrial, familiar things, even though I was secluded. Plane engines overhead combined with the crickets – their fragile arms and wings rubbing and clanging together – and crunches under my feet. My brain turned the initial noiselessness into a song. My breathing and footsteps provided the percussion while the birds and insects supplied the melodies and auxiliary instrumentation.

♪ ♪ ♪
Step-inhale-chirp-step-crunch-sniffle-tweet-vroom-step-exhale-ribbit-whistle-step.

I tapped my foot in time to the sound of nature, visualized the bars and notations, the measures and doted half-notes while I peed on a tree trunk. Rising in the background of my orchestra, I heard something that didn't match, something unnatural, the faint bump of a stereo and the high whining of an overworked engine. I zipped up and ran back out to the roadside just in time to see a middle-aged man in overalls loading my bicycle into his truck bed. I yelled and waved my arms unabashedly, but he drove off without noticing, probably pleased to have such a valuable item to sell to the pawn shop. I stomped, even pouted briefly over the senseless thievery. But the man's blaring country music drowned out my protestations as he drove away, probably flashing a smile that was all lips and hot red gums with cartoonish mustardy wisps spilling out between the few teeth – stained yellow and chipped – that he did have. Left standing by the side of a deserted country road with only a backpack and tent, I forced my thoughts onto positives.

> *at least i still have my drugs*
> *and i can create new edges*
> *and then dull them,*
> *soften their razors.*

I know that doesn't sound good, but I'm just being honest with you. I pulled out the joint that was tucked behind my ear, lit the end and took out my velvet bag of pills, dry swallowed another yellow one. I flicked my gray lighter on and off.

> *at least i still have my phone*
> *and i can just call someone*
> *and have them pick me up*

But I didn't have any signal. Even if I did, I had no one to call, no one to lean on, nothing permanent. And so on the topic of burned bridges I thought, naturally, of my father. From what I remember and heard he was a nature guy, believed that out of nature, through labor, we create culture; that nature, when sketched, looks like a human. He would have purely on instinct had the landscape mapped out and know which direction to travel, would know which berries were edible and which plants were poisonous. Of all the things from him that I *had* inherited, his intrinsic resourcefulness, his outdoorsy acumen was not among them. Lost in the back country of Ohio I could hear – via the residual effect of some sort of unwanted, latent psychological indoctrination – his disapproving voice chastising me for not having the same intuitions and decisiveness that he had always possessed but withheld genetically.

I was left with two options: either travel the seventeen miles by foot or hitchhike. I had always been intrigued by the idea of hitchhiking but had never actually tried it. Noah had told me stories about his hitchhiking adventures but it was the type of thing that I preferred to experience vicariously not directly. I put my hands to my face and tried to picture how others would perceive me.

→Beard growth
  →Scraggly, patchy at best
→Hair growth
  →Shaggy around the ears, matted and wind-blown
→Facial Complexion
  →Droopy skin around eyes from recent intermittent sleep
  patterns
→Eye Pigmentation
  →Doubtlessly blood shot, possibly even visible patches of
  burst vessels
→Skin Pigmentation
  →Burnt red in most visible places from the increase in outdoor
  activity
→Clothes
  →Jeans with the right pant leg rolled up, gray t-shirt with dark
  circular armpit stains
→Visible Items
  →Dark green cloth backpack
  →Tent

I sifted down through the mental inventory and saw the probability of getting picked up – if a car actually drove by – was slim.

can i run the distance?
i can run the distance!

Seventeen miles: a little more than a mini-marathon, not as far as a full marathon. I was in decent shape. I ran on the weekends, ran in the rain sometimes. I could push through. I jumped up and down to test the weight of my backpack.

i can do this
and i can run seventeen miles to Noah's cabin
and this is good
and this is right!

Just the thought of shaking the rigidity out of my bones, of recapturing my youthful enthusiasm empowered me, filled me up. I started jogging lightly at first, tried to find a comfortable pace, but I sped up as I got more excited.

yes, i will run
and this will change everything
and i will burn adrenaline as my fuel
and i will sweat all over the bushes
and the bushes will drink in my sweat
and love it!

My backpack bumped up against my neck, pinching my nerves.
"I'm going to run seventeen miles! Seven-teen-miles."
I was yelling. I was smiling and yelling. And then I was clapping and smiling and yelling.

why did i ever stop running?
and why does anyone ever stop running?
and why do birds ever walk on those fragile little legs –
those legs made of frozen strings – when they have wings?

169

they have fucking wings, wings like soft swords
and we have been missing it this whole time!
and my body's capabilities are staggering, unearthly
and the connection between my muscles and bones
is a melodramatic mystery!

I clapped my hands together as I sang and ran and yelled and grinned.

"Seven-*clap*-teen-*clap*-miles-*clap*-to-Noah's-*clap*-cabin."

I sang my new mantra, keeping my steady pace until I couldn't catch my breath. I stopped yelling and said the words in my head, though I maintained the clapping and the grinning.

Seven-clap-teen-clap-miles-clap-to-Noah's-clap-cabin.

Al was right. I felt loose. I felt unstoppable. Though looking back on it now I probably looked like a drunken caveman jogging on the gravel shoulder of a brown-tinted Ohio country road. But it felt right.

Like I said before, I've always thought that we each have tiny strings – not like a spiritual thing though – inside us. And everyone's strings are tuned with a different tightness or slack. And it sounds dumb when just one person's strings are playing or when you just hear a few notes, but when we listen to everyone's strings playing it turns into a universal song. That's how I felt while I was running, like my note mattered in the big picture, like it had found a niche, like I was provided integral harmonies to foreign bodies.

But my fervor was soon shattered by a sharp pain in my lower left abdomen again – a cramp, an internal pop and a snap. And then my saliva started to thicken and became difficult to swallow. I felt a welt developing between my shoulder blades, just below my neckline from the incessant bouncing of the pack. My body was pushing back, creating boundaries, setting limitations. My pace eventually funneled all the way down to a walk slower than before. With my hands balanced on the top of my head to stretch my aching abdomen, I turned around and could still see, just below the horizon line, the same copse where I felt new life just minutes before.

Out of other viable choices, I walked with the hope of covering as much ground as possible before dark. I hoisted my backpack a little higher up onto my shoulders and headed what I believed to be northeast on foot, resigned to the fact that there is a tangible limit to what a body can do, governed by physics and carbon composition and all that.

The schism with my father, rooted in childlike resentment, lingered on much longer than the transgression(s) warranted. So maybe you're wondering why I let it go on so long.[31] The explanation is just simple math.

$$E = mc^2$$

Einstein proved that the more energy (E) something has, the more massive (m) it becomes. It was the same thing with my father: a battle of wills – him insisting on reconciliation, me insisting on him not getting that satisfaction – each of us racking up the score, balancing the equation. The real turning point was my sophomore year of college.

When I first got to college I was interested – among other things – in art or at least the idea of being an artist or looking like an artist. I was desperate to be interesting, to have exclusive experiences that people would want to hear, would need to hear. In my imagination, when I spoke, people would be compelled to listen by the tonal qualities of my voice and mesmerized by the content of my words, by my vast lexicon. They would gather around, sit in a semi-circle with their necks craned up at me – because of course I would be sitting up above them – waiting for me to throw and sprinkle the lessons from my deeply moving experiences across their smooth heads, into their glossy eyes and waxy ears. But, naturally, I kept mostly to myself and had little to offer in terms of advice or life lessons.

While I adjusted to life at school my father ditched his California girlfriend and moved back to Urbana to try to work things out with my mother. Somewhere along that timeline he also made amends with Brody, who was fresh out of college.[32] Brody was still old enough when our father left to have already built a solid base which made salvaging the wreckage more

---

[31] Or maybe you're nodding your head in complete agreement.
[32] I still haven't gotten the full story.

plausible and at least somewhat desirable. I, on the other hand, knew little of my father. And since I effectively did not have one single father, I had many – an ever-changing, surely distorted, image of him that constantly morphed. My father was anything I wanted him to be. He was a chameleon.

So when he showed up outside my dormitory when I was nineteen, I obviously – and I'm sure you can understand this after all the times I've tried, out of turn, to show up to see you – had mixed feelings. I hadn't seen or talked to him in person in five years, not since that night that I snuck out of the house. I was sitting on my thin, twin sized, dorm bed working on my art portfolio when my phone buzzed on my desk. I didn't recognize the area code.

"Hello."

"Cetus?"

I knew right away that it was my father.

"How did you get my number?"

"Brody gave it to me."

> *i made him promise and he did it anyway*
> *and he can't be trusted*
> *and no one can ever be trusted*
> *and this can't be won*

"Look, I really have nothing to say to you, okay?"

"Please don't hang up. I know you don't want anything to do with me and I totally understand, but I just have a couple things to say to you. Can we meet for just a few minutes?"

Though I knew little of my father, I knew to expect him to not go through on his word. I agreed to meet him assuming that he would never actually make the effort to fly out from California just to meet with me. But at this point I didn't know he had moved back permanently.

"When do you think you'll be in town?"

"Well, actually I'm in town right now. When Brody gave me your number he also told me which dorm you lived in. I'm outside your quad."

I peeled back the paper thin curtains and saw my father standing in the common outdoor area outside my quad, his back turned to me. He was wearing a black suit and tie with his thick brown hair waving in the breeze. His tie was thrown up over his shoulder, the tip flapping in the air.

"Which building are you in?"

"I'll be right out."

I had envisioned this moment so many times with so many different outcomes. Sometimes he would boldly apologize and I would melt into his massive arms. In other scenarios it would turn into a verbal boxing match ending in a few landed punches, possibly with thrown chairs and Indian rug burns. In one recurring scenario my father and I wore white robes with gold belts and had a chariot race in an empty half-dome coliseum. The winner had to take responsibility for everything. Walking down the corridor of my dormitory – the glass-covered fluorescent lights lined along the carpeted ceiling – I was still not sure how it would go, how I would react. He turned around when I opened the door behind him.

"Cetus?"

"Yeah it's me."

His face – annoyingly smug – was tan with wrinkles visibly forming on his forehead and cheekbones, which were still square and defined like I remembered them. He was clean-shaven, young and smooth skinned.

> *what gives him the right to be tan, to sit out and enjoy the sun?*
> *on what grounds could he allow himself to be firm-jawed,*
> *in top shape?*
> *he should be overweight.*
> *underslept.*
> *overworked.*
> *depressed and frantic*
> *and gasping for new air*

"God, you just look so much different than I expected. You're almost as tall as me now."

He moved towards me clearly unsure of whether to extend his hand or to attempt an embrace.

"What exactly were you expecting? A short, fat social cripple?"

It was an instinctively harsh response that came out unplanned. I took a step back.

"Look I know you're angry that I haven't been there for you."

"Haven't been there for me?"

"Okay I know you're not sure how to deal with me being here now, but just listen to me. I've been through a lot these last few years and me not fighting to see you boys more is the biggest regret of my life."

He stepped towards me with his hand held out, testing to see whether or not I would let him put it on my shoulder, which he eventually did.

"I just want you to know..."

"Look you have absolutely nothing to say to me." I said shrugging his arm off my shoulder. "Seriously. You've had five years to say something."

I was stepping towards him. I was in a chariot. My tongue was on fire. My teeth and hands buzzed, vibrations running through all my limbs. Every muscle trembled and shook under the oscillations. I lost control of my body. I was outside my body. I didn't have a body. I floated forward and punched my father in the jaw. I'd never punched anyone before and it felt much different than I expected. I thought it would feel like hitting a brick wall, but instead it was more like hitting a piece of soft wood covered in solid, dry dough. I held the inside of my forearm in front of me, wiggling my fingers, watching my tendons crawl under the skin while my father stumbled backwards from the impact.

"It's easier to think of me that way isn't it?" he said dabbing his lip on the sleeve of his suit jacket.

A handful of watchful students walked, heads turned, on either side of the grassy knoll that had become our ring, our stadium. I funneled back into my skin and the full-body pulsations slowed down.

"You should go," I said, breathing heavily, shoulders shrugging.

"Cetus…"

"Look, we're done here. Okay? Just go."

"One day you'll wish that this went differently."

"We both will."

I turned towards my dorm. Just inside the door, I backed up against the wall and slid down to the ground. My arms and legs were still shaking, still reverberating. I closed my eyes and slowed everything in my body down, bringing it all back to equilibrium. My father tried to contact me several times after that incident but I never returned any of his calls or letters.

Walking down the gravely side of that empty, poorly paved road, the tiny drummers inside my head awoke and shifted. Apparently the jogging and jostling had disturbed their slumber. I pictured each tiny person rolling off a tiny cot, grabbing a tiny drum stick, standing, confused but waiting to run through the rudiments – paradiddles and flams.

I took out my last bit of food, the bag of trail mix, and funneled it into mouth. My side and chest were still cramping, still reeling me back in any time I breathed deeply. I pulled out my notebook, caught up on some notes.

-Bananas relieve cramps. Always carry an almost-yellow banana.

I ran a quick scan of the rest of my body, felt the itch of blisters forming on the sides of my feet, felt the chafing and reddening of skin. The thin cloth on the inside of my ragged chucks was clearly not conducive to extended periods of biking and jogging.

I don't want it to come off like I was hopeless or desperate but I had more hours of daylight left than I had energy, so when I heard a car coming I quickly shed my cloth backpack – still covered in circular pins from causes I supported in college.

-Slow Food Revolution!
-A Factory Is Not a Farm!
-Fuck the Chads!
-Marriage is Gay.

what do i do?
just hold my thumb out?
look casual.
breezy.
but stand up straight!

SMILE!
should i wave too?
comb my hair?
i should make a sign with my credentials.
"I am safe to pick up!"
"I am like you!"

My thumb was out casually – but with a confident fervor – to my side, waist high, as the car approached. As soon as it crested the hill, the car signaled and switched into the opposite lane to avoid me, my toes flesh against the cracked white shoulder line. The driver, a young corporate looking woman with her dark hair pulled taut – pulling at the skin along her hairline – and large shades concealing most of her face didn't even turn her head a half inch in my direction. She just blazed past, stirring up a rush of dust and wind in my face.

I yelled a string of obscenities that circled into a vortex and funneled up into the ash-colored clouds. I jumped and screamed and pawed at my eyes speckled with dust. I waited – seething, pacing, cursing – at the side of the road for another car.

i'll jump out in front of it
and i'll dance a bird's mating dance until it stops
and i'll dive into the open window and demand a ride
and i will not be denied!

But, of course, a car never came and my energy slowly faded, my body suddenly aged and unproductive. I wasn't sure how much farther I had before I got to Noah's cabin – at least fourteen or fifteen miles I figured – but whatever the number might have been, I knew that I wouldn't be able to make it in one night. I needed to conserve my energy and resources. Since I'd already eaten all of my food, the only thing I had was water to hold me over until I either got to his cabin or blew away in the wind.[33] Dizzy and unable to read the landscape as a text, I sat down in the thick grass to try to compose my thoughts and to devise some kind of plan.

---

[33] Melodramatic, I know. But that's how I felt at the time. It was life or death!

i just need a safe place to rest and refuel
and there has to be something, somewhere,
a memory, something deep down that i've forgotten
and i know there's something
and i remember this place

I blinked dust out of my watery eyes, my head suddenly hot, my skin strangely sensitive.

there's something hot in my head, something buzzing, sizzling
and it's too warm
and is it a fever?
and it's new ideas splicing
and it's new ideas and it's old ideas,
searing themselves together,
finding new contexts
and new bodies
and
THE GAS STATION!

A new memory settled in. One night my senior year, a group of friends was partying at Noah's cabin when he told us a story about this abandoned gas station out in the woods a few miles behind the cabin. He said it was called "Stinky's Gas" which of course none of us believed so we wanted to see it for ourselves. Noah led us all stumbling – fondling each other in drunken pairs – through the brush and wild grass until we reached an abandoned building on a gravel road. Just like Noah said we found four old gas pumps and a tall white sign, "Stinky's" written in bold. Apparently some kind of problem with the underground pipes prevented the gas station from ever opening, so it just rotted out in the middle of nowhere right after it was built.

The abandoned gas station looked the same, heavy and rotted, as it had that drunken night my senior year. But the peeling white sign with Stinky's name etched in cracked red letters had fallen off its poll, armed shrubberies gripping and holding the sign down, weeds growing over its corners. On the building itself the white paint had flaked away exposing the molded-wood frames of the structure. The stench curling out of the jagged windows initially dissuaded me from seeking shelter inside but my curiosity over-ruled. The front door had been removed but a 'CLOSED' sign was nailed over head. Inside it smelled familiar, though at first I couldn't think of what it was.

ammonia?

It was definitely acidic. I took another big whiff of the room before it clicked. It smelled like cat piss. In a much stronger way, it smelled like I had come back to the apartment after having left Tails alone for a day or two and he had pissed everywhere, soaking it into the upholsteries and bed sheets. Against each side wall, there were two stained collapsible tables each covered with some kind of chemistry set of tunnels and pipes. Hollowed out light bulbs and empty soda bottles were littered across the floor – missing chunks in key places. A half dozen brown glass jugs – several tipped over – were under each table. The acidic litter box smell was burning my eyes and throat so I quickly went back outside. With the idea of sleeping inside ruled out, I unpocketed my notebook, created a new category.

Things That Look Sketchy
-Stinky's Gas Station

My lips were chapped, tender and cracked from wind exposure, and my sinuses were dried out – thick sandpaper in my throat – sending itchy waves down into my ear canals. I tried to spit but my saliva thickened – caked like old mud to my teeth – accreted and dribbled down my chin.

I mumbled something to myself for no other reason than to loosen my throat phlegm and to verify that this was all real and that I still existed. Sometimes I, and maybe you do this too, lose track of the idea that the sum of what I do each day, the sum of each moment, equals my life. And if I constantly remind myself of that, it makes everything, every experience, every encounter more urgent and essential. So I stamped my feet hard against the ground, sending forced vibrations up in my knees, to try to reconnect my mind with my body, to remind myself that my soul was still encased in my flesh, to remind myself that my body was still my home. --*I exist! I endure!*-- My stomach had accepted its emptiness, quietly resigned to the fact that it wasn't going to be fed.

I pulled the joint out from behind my ear, lit and pulled out everything that was left, then reached for my backpack to take a closer look at what else I had: two round blue pills, another small round white pill, three elongated yellow ones, and an orange one. I took the orange.

> *is there any nutritional value in a pill?*
> *any calories in narcotics?*

I didn't feel any fuller after swallowing it. Leaning my back up against the molded wood walls on the backside of the building, I flicked my lighter on and off, holding it up to the sky to check the liquid level – almost out. The soft sun was falling below the tree line, filling the sky with its hot colors – pale-yellows and gold-oranges – as it spun to the other side of the world where it would continue its cosmic restlessness. People often say – so often that it's become a cliché now – that the sunset is beautiful, that it's one of life's great pleasures, a gift from nature. And maybe that's partially true, but while I was sitting outside that run-down gas station, deliriously tired, the orange pill dissolving inside me, I saw the selfish flaw in that kind of comforting logic. The sunset doesn't need me or you or anybody in order to be beautiful. It doesn't require anything of us. It's not contingent upon us. The cosmos are not producing clean images, spaces and timeframes for my own benefit, for my viewing pleasure. It doesn't require a measurement or some kind of assessment to exist. The reality of the universe doesn't require us to open our eyes. I know that idea is debated among physicists but it felt so true in that sinking moment. Whether or not I was watching it, the sunset would have still looked the same that night. The sun will always swirl and paint and go on living and burning with nuclear fusion regardless of what we do. Always remember that, Luna.

My eyes watered and burned, my eyelids had tiny anchors pulling them shut, but they refused to close.

> *how can i sleep when things are like this?*
> *and how can i sleep with all this energy twisting*
> *and furling inside me,*
> *re-aiming, re-vectoring?*
> *and how can anyone ever sleep?*
> *and how can people sleep?*
> *and how do…*

June 24th 2010

Before the sun even rose, I woke up abruptly to the pop of gunshots and the unmistakably sour smell of cat piss. I stood up and stretched, shook the dew droplets off my shoe tops, brushed them off my backpack. It had gotten surprisingly cold overnight, probably touching the forties, though it had easily been in the nineties at the sun's peak the day before. In the deep parts of the night, when the sky is made of black tar, of dried syrup and molasses, I had woken up shivering against the wall and put on every piece of clothing that I brought with me, and I still had everything on when the gunshots awoke me.

In my nightly shivers, I tried – without success – to assemble the tent in the dark to provide some protection against the wind and to block some of the fumes that I was inhaling from the building. Again, I know you don't know that much about me but my chances of successfully assembling the tent in comfortable temperatures with daylight and a clear head were slim enough, so in the dark I gave up and used the softer tent parts as a pillow instead, used the nylon fabric as a sheet. I pulled out my notebook.

Unmasculine
-Peeing in stalls
-Sneaking around outside an acquaintance's house
-Identifying rhododendrons
-Not knowing how to assemble a tent

As I had drifted back to sleep after the tent failure, I remember looking up at the stars – sheets of clear colored holiday lights draped across spacetime, tiny cosmic porch lamps left on overnight. My bones were stars, my muscles constellations connecting the dots to hold the sky together, supplying wholeness and purpose to my body.

isn't it crazy that the same force that keeps me on the ground,

keeps the sun and the stars together?
and isn't it crazy that stars are just dead balls of energy
lifelessly sending their signals from the grave,
transcending time as they expand further and further out into space?
and isn't it crazy that people are made up of the same components
as the universe which is rapidly expanding outward?
and water vapor unites us all
and dark energy is pulling our universe apart
and are people expanding apart inside
and is the darkness inside, the dark energy,
the black water slowly pulling our bodies apart
until our strings snap and

I heard another gunshot, this time closer and followed by barks. I stood up too quickly, got light headed, everything briefly going dark in front of my eyes, my brain tingling, quickly aware of how hungry I was, how weak I was getting. Staggering up against the building to regain my balance, my vision slowly returned, gray specks dissolving over my eyelids almost like I was waking up again. The quiet sun was still rising from its bed as well, stretching and flashing its warm colored lights over the tree line. It took a moment for my eyes to adjust to the dimness, my eyes still shaking off the film of sleep.

Parked on a gravel path that I hadn't noticed the night before was a pick-up truck – assembled from the metal bodies of dead trucks, each panel a different color – with half a dozen large brown jars in the bed. There were also three solid black – a black that looked like rusted orange in the right light, at the right angle – German Shepherds tied in the back. Sitting on the hood of the truck was a frail, scraggly white man, his age impossible to guess. He was thin enough for the wind to scoop him up at any moment, but he had a gun and three dogs that appeared to be hungry and maladjusted, so I didn't move or say anything. He had on a baggy white t-shirt that said "Go Big or Go Home" with a picture of a dirt bike and a dusty cap, the bill curled down, pointing towards the outer edges of his eyes.

"You a cop, son?"

"No."

"What you doin' out here?"

"I was just passing through, looking for my friend actually."

"Ain't nobody livin' out here, son."

"Well good to know. I guess I'll be on my way then. Sorry for the bother."

I reached down for my backpack and started picking up the tent supplies scattered along the gravel.

"I can't let you just walk on outta here after what you seen."

His voice was shaky and high pitched, like he was always on the verge of bursting into tears. As he jumped down from the hood of his truck holding his rifle, the dogs barked in the truck bed.

It's probably not even worth mentioning this, but I took karate briefly – my father pressured me into it – when I was in elementary school. And for some reason that was the first thing I thought of when he came towards me. I guess I was racking my brain, trying to think of some moves that I could pull. But all I could recall were some useless routines with forward kicks and weak punches. We never actually learned anything useful. The only real punch I'd ever thrown was at my father and it had been the product of an organic-inner-overflow-of-anger. I couldn't reproduce it.

> *i should have signed up for a self-defense course,*
> *something practical.*
> *krav maga.*

The frail man moved around to the back of the truck, letting his three dogs out to run wild. Another vibration shot up my back and down through my arms, weaved in and out of my bones, mapping out its own route underneath my skin.

I was raised to think that real men like dogs, know how to tame them, but I had never grown accustomed, especially to big ones, wild ones. Almost as soon as you started talking, Luna, you wanted a puppy, something small and soft, flaps of skin folding everywhere. But I knew it would grow into something ugly, something dangerous. And to me even tiny nascent dogs look like little wild horses, their muscles ready to break through the skin. So we never got you one.

Anyway, the panic vibration as the frail man released his dogs was two-fold: a gut-wrenching reminder of my male inadequacies and a legitimate fear for the immediate safety of my disengaged body.

The dogs, black and fanged, circled around the building, barking and nipping at each other's tails. But it was like there was an invisible fence, a safety threshold around the building; they wouldn't get close, I guess because of the smell. So I backed up all the way against the sour smelling wood of the gas station, hoping to keep the beasts at bay.

The frail man walked – spine crooked, knees shaking – towards me with his rifle at his side. It was too early for there to be much natural light – the waking sun still hidden behind the tree line – but I could still see open facial scabs on his cheeks and forehead, sweat collecting in the folds under his curved camouflage hat, the edges of the bill whitened and faded. In the chest pocket of his flannel shirt there was an imprinted outline of a cigarette box. As he got closer, I saw an unmistakable paranoia in his eyes darting around inside his sockets, unable to focus – a fear of what he might lose, a raising of the stakes.

is it possible to have two lazy eyes?
and is it possible to die when you don't fully have a body yet?
and no one will ever find me
and my bones will turn into rocks
and Luna will never know

He shoved the barrel of the gun against my sternum, pressing me hard against the back wall of the old gas station. Though his hands were shaking and my cocoon of shirts softened it a little, the blow to my chest was solid. I collapsed to the ground and my notebook fell out of my back pocket. He cocked his rifle and fired it straight up into the air inciting all his dogs into a frenzy of barking again.

I had always been amazed that in light of my litany of deficiencies, in a life backlit by weaknesses, that natural selection had not eliminated me yet. So this moment felt logical,

190

inevitable, required by nature. Sitting on the ground, I reached my hand into my front right pocket to feel your brown button. I felt my back left pocket for the origami fortune teller and patted my left pocket for the shape of my lighter. The frail man whacked me over the head with the barrel again and pointed the gun at my blistered feet. I don't think he wanted to kill me, just maim me.

> *this is it and this is right*
> *and i had this coming*
> *and she will never know*
> *and that will be better*
> *and easier for her to handle when she gets older*
> *and i won't have to sign anything*
> *and be held accountable for anything*
> *and this is right and this is good*
> *but this is not how it is supposed to happen and*

At what seemed like the fulcrum of the attack, a motorcycle skidded – constantly on the cusp of crashing – down the gravel path, sliding its way up towards the old gas station. A full-bearded man parked his motorcycle and strutted over towards the two of us. I didn't recognize him at first.

"What are you doing here, Frank?" said the bearded man.

"This guy was trespassing on my property."

"*Your* property?"

"You know what I mean."

"Look, I'm only going to tell you this once because you and I both know that I'll blow the whistle on this whole thing and lock you up if you make one wrong move. So round up your dogs and get the fuck out of here. Got it?"

The two men had a brief stare down before the frail man, twitching and wheezing, whistled for his dogs. They all jumped back up into the truck and the frail man drove away, looking over his shoulder through the broken back window. After he disappeared down the gravel path, the full-but-kempt-bearded man came over to help me up.

"I was wondering when you would be out to see me you dirty motherfucker," he said helping me up.

"Noah? Man, am I glad to see you. I seriously thought that guy was gonna kill me."

"Nah I don't think he would have. He barks loud but he's really just a fucking pussy when push comes to shove. Nothing to worry about."

He raised his hand up into the air, palm facing down and squatted ready for our secret handshake that we created in high school. It involved several spins and slaps, some fist pounds and intricate finger interlocking, but I couldn't remember the details or chronology. I looked blankly at his hand.

"Shit. Did you forget already? Jesus Christ, Gumby. Here I am doing this, you know, laudable thing for you and you've gone and forgotten our handshake."

"Well, okay, come on. Let's give it a try. It starts with me doing some kind of bear claw gesture right?" I curled my fingers like rose petals.

"Nah forget it man. I'm just fucking with you. Namaste." He put his hands together in front of his chest and bowed before wrapping his arms all the way around me. "So how the hell did you get out here?" He looked around. "And what the fuck are you wearing?"

"Long story," I said laughing, peeling off my overshirts in the warmth of the rising morning.

"Why would you come *here*?"

"I don't know. I was running out of daylight when I remembered the gas station from when we came out here in high school so I figured I'd use it as shelter."

"Bad idea, Gumby. I have an unspoken agreement with Frank and his compadres in the area. They get to use the building for their own purposes and I let them without blowing the whistle on anything."

"What do you get out of the exchange?"

He clapped me on the back with his hand, ignoring my question. I hunched over, the muscles holding my shoulder blades together coiled like a spring from the tent pulsations, my back sore from sleeping on gravel. Even hunched over, Noah was much smaller next to me, more compact, more efficient.

"Let's get you up to the cabin."

Walking towards his motorcycle his body was fluid, no straight lines anywhere, everything bending and leaning, flowing into everything else. I dusted off my notebook – stubborn flakes of semi-liquid mud clinging to the spiral wires – before placing it into my back pocket again. With a concerted effort to stay upright, to keep from curling in on myself, I shuffled over to Noah's motorcycle and we rode up to his cabin without saying anything else.

Sometimes on breezy Sunday mornings my father would take me out to the country back roads for a ride on his motorcycle. We wouldn't say anything to each other but those mini-trips were some of the only times I remember feeling connected to my father.[34] I would grab tightly around his firm waist, would hold onto his pointy hip bones because I couldn't get my arms around him, and I would squeeze the side of my helmet up against his solid back. I was too afraid to look straight ahead, so I would just watch the white-wooded fences, the dead brown, wilt-topped corn stalks whiz by at the road side. With Noah, I turned to watch the still pines and steep sloping hills flash by, kicking up dust in our wake.

---

[34] I'm hoping that this story is making you remember some of those moments with me.

At the intersection of a gravel road and a clay-dirt driveway there was a plastic garbage container – 314 Pi Road spray painted in bright orange across the side – anchored to the ground with chipped cement blocks. Tied across the top of the can was a plastic crate tethered with some kind of hammock-like contraption made of frayed rope and bailing wire. We turned left in front of the can.

"Do they actually deliver your mail in that?"

"They would if I ever got any. I registered the address anyway."

The cabin, surrounded by massive Sawtooth Oaks and Spicebushes, had a thin trickling rivulet running audibly behind it on the northern side. When I came to the cabin in high school I would dip my fingers in the dark water and imagine that the rivulet spilled out of a stream and that the stream connected to a river that came out of a lake and that the lake was not man-made, that it was connected to the ocean which touched foreign lands. That way when I touched the black water, I was touching something real, something of universal value. I wanted to taste the spilled oil in that rivulet, wanted my belly to swell from that water.

Carved deep into the wood of the front door was the ligature that I created in high school for our band. I had outlined it on the door and we all spent time carving and smoothing out the shape with pocket knives.

Inside there were four rooms above a full basement: a kitchen, bedroom, a bathroom, and a community room, as Noah called it. The only piece of furniture anywhere was an old glass coffee table with a clear spray bottle, a rag, a bag of colored straws, and three bottles of eye drops on the edge. The walls were covered with mis-matched needlepoints. Noah's mother had an obsession with sewing and finished more needlepoints – of kittens, flower pots, Chinese calligraphy, square-headed babies, anything imaginable – than she knew what to do with.

195

So the cabin had become her storage zone for the ones she couldn't pawn off on someone else. Her sewing enthusiasm had clearly continued unbridled since I had last been there.

I sat down on the floor next to a stack of framed needlepoint pictures, tightly packed hand-sewn pillows, and decorative bolsters in the community room while Noah worked on something in the kitchen – the counter littered with more straws, halved and then re-halved, and hollowed out ink pens split in two. Noah slipped a small tin wrapped in a rubber band into his pocket, sweeping the straws into a drawer.

The pain from my blisters had actually subsided – or numbed anyway – but I was afraid to actually find what was inside. Shapeless patches of red soaked into the white cotton sock. Once my shoes were off, the pain returned and I could almost visibly see my feet start to swell. I was relieved when Noah brought in a plate of food of what looked like some sort of Asian rice and vegetable mixture. I had almost forgotten how hungry I was.

"Whoa, Gumby, those blisters look awful."

"Yeah, I guess so."

"Tell you what. The overhead shower doesn't work, but go hop in the tub with your socks on and just let the water break the blood coagulation. It'll hurt at first because the blisters might open up and start to bleed a little again. But otherwise it's gonna hurt like a motherfucker trying to peel cotton socks off a wound that's a day old like that."

I quickly ate the warm plate of food and went to the bathroom. The light switch illuminated a single exposed bulb overhead, throwing the light across the white walls wildly, nothing covered and dimmed through a glass fixture. On the cracked ceramic sink were two metal spoons caked with a dirty-brown semi-liquid on top and singed on the bottom, a tangled leather belt, and a lighter. Lining the walls of the sink in a v-shape pointed in the back left corner were dozens of orange, transparent pill bottles with white twisty lids.

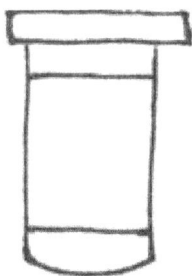

I picked up a few which had unfamiliar names and scientific nomenclature laminated onto the sides, took a pill out of each container and put them in my velvet pouch. I balanced my gray lighter across one of the lids, undressed – except for my blood-sticky socks – and popped one of the pills – an egg-shaped white one, hoping it was a painkiller.

Standing naked at the edge of the empty tub, I ran my hands across my skin, smooth and hairless. I had never been a hairy person. I remember my father looking like a Wookie when we would go to the pool when I was young, so I assumed I would someday grow into that same hairy skin. But like many things I had expected, it never happened. I just had a few unusually long hairs on my chest, my body allocating all its hair-growing resources into these few sickly-looking hairs, leaving the rest of my skin the fuzzy texture of healthy leaves.[35]

My knees – knobby, made of sugary brittle – had some scraps from the scuffle, and the pale-gold tone of bruise was sinking in around my shins. I twisted my upper body, tried – though unsuccessfully – to look at my back, checking for potential bruises or early stage carbuncles around the tip of my spine where the tent pounded during my short-lived marathon. I ran my fingers across my face – surely gaunt – and felt several small open cuts, not the kind that required sutures but the kind just deep enough to itch as they scabbed.

I stepped into the brown stained acrylic bathtub – no shower curtain attached – and instinctively turned the hot nozzle all the way to the left but nothing came out, so I turned the cold knob. The faucet made a coughing noise, spitting out air followed by a weak stream of water, freezing cold and tinted tan. The tub looked too dirty to sit in and since the overhead shower didn't work, I bent over to peel my socks off, starting from just above my ankle line, rolling them down to the base of my heel where the blisters started. I ran the cold water directly over my foot which opened the wounds but also released the fabric, though it left tiny bits of fuzz behind.

My upper half still filthy, I dried my feet off, dressed in my old clothes and went back out to the community room where Noah was crouched – next to a knee-high narghile pipe – on the floor doing some sort of leg stretches. He wore a dingy orange t-shirt with the pi symbol and a thought bubble that said:

"Rationality is Overrated"

On the back, at the bottom corner the anarchy symbol was ironed on. Noah had never been into fashion, which I think people found sort of fashionable.

"So how did you know I was out there?"

He shifted from his crouching position and rolled with his hands into a full head stand. His toes pointed directly up at the ceiling then wiggled. With the palms of his hands on the ground he slowly, with control, brought his knees down to the

---

[35] I was once asked in college by a one-night stand if I shaved my body.

floor and lay flat on his back stretching his arms and legs in the opposite direction. He sat up in the lotus position.

"Holy shit. That was awesome. Where'd you learn to do that?" He didn't respond for a few seconds, though his eyes were open wide. I pulled out my notebook to catch up on what had been happening.

Things That Look Sketchy
-Stinky's Gas Station
-Noah's mailbox
-The paraphernalia scattered around here.
-My foot blisters

Unmasculine
-Peeing in stalls
-Sneaking around outside an acquaintance's house
-Identifying rhododendrons
-Not knowing how to assemble a tent
-Complaining about foot blisters

"Sorry Cetus," Noah said. I clapped shut and repocketed my notebook. "When I'm in lotus, I have to stare at an invisible plane of existence that stops at the tip of my nose. So you were invisible for a moment." He fanned his fingers in front of his nose, smelling them before he continued.

"What's in the notebook?"

"Nothing."

"Fair enough. To answer your first question, I heard the gunshots and was afraid that dumbass Frank was going to blow-up his own meth lab. Coincidently you were there too. As for your second question, I learned to do my morning stretches while I was living outside of Los Angeles. I met a girl, a silkworm breeder, who was studying Buddhism at The University of the West, and she was a firm believer in morning stretches that pushed the limits of your physical capacity. She taught me all sorts of yoga exercises and we each sort of created our own variations. Best lover I ever had. So flexible."

The skin on his forehead – all rubber and velvet – creased and rippled. I think he was picturing the bendy silkworm breeder.

Every time I saw Noah – only a handful of times a year at best – I felt like I was meeting a newer version, all the older versions wrapped and tucked up underneath, peaking out through his eyes or gestures. It wasn't like he was ashamed and hiding who he had been, he was just always building something different with the same blocks. And so it always took some time for me to get comfortable, to figure out who he was and what had been moved to his center. But Noah, in typical fashion, dove in, held nothing back.

"Well, anyway, thanks for saving me back there."

"No problem, man. I'm just glad that fucker didn't blow the lid off that whole place. That dude is *crazy*."

He bulged his eyes, emphasizing the last word.

"How long have you been back out here?" I looked around at the all the stacked needlepoints.

"Well it's an interesting story. I was doing my typical routine, you know, camping outside of a town, working odd jobs, until I wooed the wrong woman and wore out my welcome. Eventually I ended up outside an Indian Reservation in South Dakota trying to launch a campaign to stop bison hunting. And I know what you're going to say: Isn't that a Native American tradition? What gives you any right to take a stand against that? But what you probably don't know is that it's so much bigger than that now. People are just waiting outside of national parks where the bison are protected, waiting until they pass the boundary into common forest land where they're not technically protected. And maybe you're thinking – hey, would people actually do that? And yes there are tons of poachers out there. It's crazy what people will do to make a buck. Pass me that towel?" he said pointing to a hand towel on the floor. I passed it over and he wiped the sweat off his temples.

"Anyway," he segued. "It was a lost cause so I started hitchhiking back down this way. Long story short, I ended up catching a nasty cold, something wicked in my chest. So that landed me in a hospital outside Topeka. Great state, Kansas."

He folded his hands, tapping his fingertips on his knuckles while he caught his breath.

"But unfortunately that particular hospital was total shit, not very accommodating to outside opinions and untraditional medicinal usages. So I ended up having to shimmy down the fire escape. I laid low in Kansas for a while but I was still pretty weak from my illness so I decided to take a bus back to Ohio and recuperate here. I had been renting the basement of this place out and since my renters are out of the country indefinitely I figured I'd stay here for a while."

"Wow. So you've been here how long now?"

"Right, I've gotten off track from your questions. I guess just over a month and I just haven't worn out my welcome yet so I'm gonna give it a try and just sort of see what happens."

I was jealous of Noah's capacity to experience life at a higher voltage than I could handle. He lived fast and strong, followed his convictions and learned what he needed along the way.

"You're a crazy son-of-a-bitch, man."

"Nah, you're the hero. Teaching? Now that's noble. I mean, you know me, I always hated formal education because it just showed me how ignorant I was. And no one likes that right? And as if teaching isn't enough, on top of that you're raising a daughter and a family. That's more admirable than anything I've ever done."

When Noah and I were in high school we bonded over our kindred spirit for travel, an insatiable desire for constant displacement. So I felt sort of embarrassed to admit that I had become more planted, to admit that I wasn't as rugged as I had set out to become. But hearing him say that he admired me for being there for you made my chest swell – but it soon deflated and ached.

she's gone and i'm gone
and this is the real edge
and the water,
the cold black fucking water is somewhere down there

No longer hungry and the pills slowly dissolving, I felt a series of familiar circular vibrations swirl in my chest while I debated whether or not to bring it up that Eris had left. I hadn't told anyone yet, at least not sober and in control, so I wasn't even sure how to approach the subject, wasn't sure which angle made sense and even what angle was the real one, wasn't sure I even wanted to know how the words would taste on my tongue without being diluted by chemicals. My body had spent the last seventy-two hours trying to harness and hush all the wild vibrations shaking it inside and out, loosening the clots. It might not make any sense to you, but I just wasn't ready to feel everything yet. All the vibrations might have crushed me, ground me down to a fine white powder and rumbled me into the cracks in the Earth. Feeling dizzy, I pulled out my gray velvet pouch and dry-swallowed a Coumadin that had sunk unnoticed to the bottom.

"How are they anyway? How old is Luna now?"

"She just turned three this past March."

"Uh-oh, you answered my second question first. What's that mean? Sexual problems? Like I always say, good sex is like making macaroni – you have to warm up the water before you put the noodles in. Do you warm her up first?"

He scooted closer to me and crossed his legs back into the lotus position, this time looking right at me.

"Look it's not that. It's nothing."

"She left you didn't she?"

"What? No, absolutely not."

"First of all, don't say 'absolutely'. Come on, that's something you taught me. There are no absolutes, only probabilities right? Words like 'smallest' and 'biggest' and 'finished' are meaningless, as I believe you said. Or did you say irrelevant?"

→Absolute
    →Middle English: Absolut
       →From Latin: Absolutus
         →From Past Participle of Absolvere
           →To set free, absolve

"Irrelevant."

"Right. And secondly, are you fucking serious? I save your life and you're going to sit here and lie to me?"

"Okay, fine, you're right," I said opening my fingers like flower petals out of my fist. "Eris left me and she took Luna with her. And she wants to take sole custody. And I have no idea how to fight it. I can't lose Luna. But I don't know how not to lose her at this point."

It sounded selfish coming out – all about my loss, about what I would be missing, not about the effect it would have on you. But you have to understand that it was all still so fresh then and it was hard to get any kind of rounded perspective, but as I started talking about it, I had a sudden urge to run again, to run to Hamilton and storm into Julie's house and seize you back instead of hiding.

"That's terrible," he said with surprising empathy before returning to his normal diagnostic demeanor, his self-made perch. "But I knew something was up. You seemed weirdly static, nothing rattling around in there," he said putting his palm over my heart.

"Yeah I guess."

"So why'd you come up here then? Catharsis?"

"No it's not just that."

"Come on Gumby. Be real with me."

I paused, pictured your mother flipping over furniture, pictured her searching for evidence at the apartment.

"Well really I just had to get out of the house because Eris was coming to pick up her stuff. And I got that letter from you and figured this might be a good place to…" I shrugged. "Yeah, I guess find some kind of cathartic release, clear my head, whatever you want to call it."

i came to hide
and i came because i'm lost
and i came to hide
and i came to hide
to hide

"See that wasn't so hard was it."

I shifted positions, wrapping my ankles together in front of me.

"Alright so here's what we're going to do. We've got to get you out of this static funk. We've got to get your heart screaming again. Can you even feel your heart in there! I mean this is no way to live," he said darting his eyes up and down. "Life is supposed to be lived kinetically. Frenetically!"

He stood up and then crouched back down.

"So what? You're going to hook me up to an EMD or something?" I asked loosening up.

"Maybe. Figuratively at least. Tell me a little bit more about what's been going on while I think of a game plan."

"Okay. Well, like I said the worst part of this whole thing is losing Luna. But I'm sure there's some kind of loophole that would keep Eris from taking her away completely. But I don't really know much about the legal system and custody rights, so maybe we should look into that? Maybe find some legal counsel?"

Noah had his eyes closed and gently swung his upper half in a small circle, still crouching on the floor.

"And then everything is boiling over with Mira. But I think that'll just complicate things. And I guess I just want everything to be in balance again. And…"

"Okay Gumby, I think I've got an idea. So you came here as a sort of pilgrimage, looking for an emotional release, hoping to open up some new vistas. But I think I see the problem. And this is going to sound out of left field, but stick with me here." He lowered his head dramatically and raised it slowly. "Since your father left you at a young age, you never had any proper rite of passage into adulthood. So you're maturationally stunted."

He poked his finger into my chest.

"I don't think that's it."

"Of course *you* don't. But here's what I want you to do. Stay here for a few days and clear your head."

"What does this have to do with Luna?"

"It has everything to do with Luna! Don't you see it? You can only stay on two conditions though, okay?"

"What conditions?"

"Okay, first you have to do whatever I ask of you. I promise I can get you rattling around on the inside again and on to bigger and better things if you just do what I say. Deal?"

"I don't know."

"What do you have to lose?"

Luna
and i'll try anything to keep her

"Fine. What's the second part?"

"Second, it's better that you're a little in the dark so you can't have any expectations. Because if you come into the experience expecting to gain something specific, it won't happen. You'll try to force it. And then if it doesn't happen, it's anti-climactic anyway. Do we have an agreement?"

→This would keep me from having to think about things.

→Not thinking about things might help me to mentally relax.

→Relaxing might help me figure out how to control the vibrations on my own, without the softening of the edges.

→Which might allow me – at least legally – to see Luna consistently.

→**Approved.**

"Yeah. Sure."

"Great," he said unfolding his legs. "I think we can get you to learn to just let go and live." He twisted his hands into the shape of bird wings which he started to flap in the air. "I'm glad you're here Cetus. Now you should get some rest. You look like hell."

He showed me to the bedroom which, like the rest of the cabin, contained no proper furniture. The only thing in the room was a green, foldable cot in one corner that looked more like a cheap, unstable gurney, no sheets or pillows.

"Take a nap. You'll feel better," he said pointing towards the cot.

I woke up of my own accord to a quiet cabin, the dirty glass windows thrown open, the dusty screens pulled down tight. I rolled off the cot – not much more comfortable than the gravel outside the meth lab – and tried to straighten my spine. But my muscles, cowering in abusive timidity, huddled and tightened, refusing my back's normal alignment. On the kitchen counter next to a translucent orange carafe filled with a clear liquid, Noah had left a hand-carved Russian nesting doll with his face painted in striking accuracy on the front. I opened it up and saw an identical, tinier doll, which I opened to find yet another smaller wooden doll. There were seven of these concentric dolls before I got to the smallest one, which when opened had a note from Noah inside – significantly more pleasant than the last note I received, the one from your mother.

"Gone to work. Back later. Today's Proverb: If you live in the present the past will make more sense. Be ready to kick it tonight!"

It was hard for me to picture Noah working a steady job, and I didn't feel, either physically or emotionally, up for going out to "kick it." But I had agreed to follow his lead so I was left choice-less, which was actually a huge relief.

I called Brody to tell him that I might be gone longer than I expected. Someone would need to check on Tails and water my garden. My cell phone wasn't getting a signal, but Noah had a landline on the wall in the kitchen that looked like it was straight out of the 1970s. I spun the dial seven times to ring him up. Bailey answered.

"Hey is Brody around?"

"Hurley?

"Yeah."

"Well he's in his office working and you know how he doesn't like to be bothered while he's working. Do you want me to give him a message?"

"Well I guess you can help me too. I'm wondering if you guys can swing by my apartment tomorrow afternoon to check on Tails and water my garden. I...well I had to leave kind of abruptly and I thought I would be back tonight but it looks like I'll be gone a little bit longer. So I just want someone to make sure everything's okay over there. Brody should have a key to get in."

I stretched the cord, fiddled with the deadbolt on the cabin door.

"Sure we can do that. Is Eris out of town too?"

I had again forgotten that nobody knew that she had left me. It caught me off guard, left me without a scripted response.

"Yeah she's, you know, she took Luna to see...," I trailed off and made an inaudible syllabic grunting noise. "So you guys can stop by?"

"Sure."

Bailey's voice inflected higher with her response, a question mark left hanging in the airwaves between us.

"Okay. Thanks. Bye."

"One last thing Hurley."

"Yeah," I said it hard, quicker than was necessary.

"Are you still planning on meeting with your father this Thanksgiving? We were thinking about hosting it at our house this year and we just want to make sure that we set enough plates and have enough food if you'll be joining us."

"Yes I'll be there. Anything else?"

"Hurley, is everything...?"

I hung up the phone before she started probing. I wasn't ready to address questions yet, wasn't ready to think about the real answers.

Though I had agreed to meet my father at Thanksgiving, I was still not sure I was ready. I think I mentioned earlier that I would explain a little more about the notebook and all the probability and statistics, the tallying and counting. I think we've finally gotten through enough that it'll be relevant and make sense. When I started experiencing heart palpitations, the weird vibrations in my chest, I had the overwhelming feeling that it was related to my father, that the resentment had become a caustic poison in my vessels, a clogging calcification. And since my father had been having health problems related to his heart as well, my mom convinced me it was time for us to at least talk, that because of my "pent up resentment which I had no business holding on to anymore", I was depriving you of your grandfather which wasn't right, especially since you were getting older. But even though my father and I were both undergoing varying levels of vascular degeneration, I still felt like I wasn't ready, that my data – my sample size – was insufficient. The numbers told me I still wasn't ready. I needed to ask more questions, needed the tallies to spill off my notebook pages and onto my body. I wanted to fashion a graph with intricate charts, cite precise mathematical bylaws, possibly develop a slide show with pictorial bell curves illustrating that he, in fact, was a statistical anomaly, that he was unusual and therefore wrong – solely to blame. My presentation – thorough and trenchant – would prove this, would prove with overwhelming evidence that my father's choice to leave was historically not natural and as such, all the more reprehensible. But like I said, I knew I wasn't ready.

Actually I knew that what I was trying to do was impossible. All I had was a number, a percentage, a possible likelihood, a partiality. But I kept collecting data in my notebook, kept asking questions sure that I would find a loop-hole. But the longer I went without seeing my father and the longer I postponed the presentation on grounds of insufficient data, the harder it was to visualize a reunion with him. I blamed it on the numbers, but at the core I think I was just scared to forgive him, scared of what that would say about me. And I didn't want him to win. So anyway, that's the story there. Maybe you can relate.

The inside skeleton of Noah's cabin looked exactly like it had in high school. In the main room I lit and took a few hits off whatever was left in Noah's narghile pipe, something smooth, sweet. On the side of the living room there was a swinging door that led down into the basement which we had turned into a make-shift recording studio for our band, complete with a full sound room. Noah had mentioned that he rented that room out, but he also said the renters were gone so I went down to see what it looked like, to see if any of our musical instruments or recording gear were still down there, to search the room for memories and relevance, maybe bang out some jams on the keyboard. At the top of the tightly wound spiral staircase there was a string hanging from the ceiling that, when pulled, turned on the overhead lights. It felt like it might break when I pulled it, and the wooden stairs wobbled underneath me.

The room was completely different than I remembered. It had been split, with a crooked row of carpeted office partitions reaching halfway towards the ceiling, into two halves. On the side where the stairs ended one wall was covered with mounted plastic shelving filled with dozens of shoes: heals of all colors and heights, sneakers at various levels of decay, boots – both workman and fancy. In fact that entire half of the room was covered in junk: several types of doors[36] propped against the wall, chairs of all shapes and sizes, garden tools, pipes, an old-style bathtub. And then there was a fold-out table covered in plastic storage crates that held smaller junk: a staple gun, several walking canes, piles of gloves – things like that.

The other side of the partitions was clean and sectioned off into several different floorings – one section hard wood done in parquetry, one stone, one carpet – all surrounding a pit maybe three feet deep, covered at the bottom in sections of dry light brown dirt, straw, and jagged gravel, lined with wooden planks. Mounted along the front wall was a massive white projector screen, the sound-proof booth we set up for recording in high school on the opposite wall. Microphones and boom stands were set up all across the room which I couldn't imagine anyone actually living in. I'm not sure how long I was down there, but when I made my way back upstairs scribbling in my notebook, Noah – covered in what appeared to be sawdust, his deep brown beard speckled with plaster – stood in the kitchen at the top of the helix staircase.

---

[36] They were made of wood, metal, plastic – all different textures.

"Hey, there you are Gumby. Get a good nap?"

"Yeah thanks. Hey what the hell goes on down there?"

"Oh yeah. Like I said, I rent that out to some people."

"People live down there?"

"Oh no. It's just these two foley artists. It's ideal for them because it had already been converted into a sound studio. They just had to install a projector screen and haul in all their sound tools and they were good to go."

"What the hell is a foley artist?"

"They do all the real life sound effects for movies. Like, for example, when you hear a guy scratching his scalp or crunching his feet when he walks, that's not actually recorded in live action. That's a foley artist creating the sounds for us."

"No way."

"Sure. Anyway the people I rent it out to do mostly foreign films so they're overseas a lot. When they get back to the country they just show up here and do their work. I think I scared the shit out of them when I showed up here last month because they weren't expecting me. Check this: when I first got here I walked down stairs and one of the guys – and I mean he's a grown ass man – was wearing red high heels, running in place on the hard wood floor while rubbing jeans together in his hands and staring up at the projector. I guess he was recording the sounds for a woman walking down a hallway or something. But it was fucked up looking. And then they both shit their pants when they looked up and saw me."

"That's messed up."

"Yeah but I explained who I was because they'd never actually met me before, and they just went back to work. But they left the next day. Said they were flying to Europe to get some more films and would be back in about a month. Haven't seen them since though. Weird dudes."

"Sounds like it."

"I've done a little bit of recording with their stuff in absentia. Pretty cool work they do actually. Anyway, get ready for tonight buddy," he said slapping me on the back which was still tender and ached under the skin. "We've got big plans."

I pulled out my gray velvet pouch of pills, hoping for some sort of detachment before we left but it was noticeably lighter, only a few pills left. I took another and flicked my lighter on and off, while you floated further, the string between us fraying.

Noah and I rode down back roads to Hamilton and parked his motorcycle in a twenty-four hour shopping lot. He said he hated finding parking downtown so we took the Metro bus from Hamilton down to Cincinnati. The heavy sun was just starting its descent into the ground, towards the other side of the world, and it was cool and cloudy out, everything covered in a salty gray film.

"You're gonna love this place. I'm meeting my girl there and I told her to have a friend for you too." I looked away, looked up into the clouds, strangely low, hovering at arm's length. "Come on man, it'll be fun. It'll get your mind off things."

He slapped my back again, knocked me onto my toes.

"It's just that I've got this person back in Hamilton, this girl Mira and I haven't even figured out what's happening with Eris and…"

"Right, yeah, of course. It doesn't have to be like that. It's whatever you want. It will be a good night no matter what. Plus these bus rides are always an adventure. Last time I rode this thing there was this crazy lady. And I'm talking like *legit* crazy. Her face looked like a demon. An ugly one. It was all bruised up and there were these open cuts on her cheeks. She was in the front seat, right behind the driver too so everyone had to look at her when they got on the bus. But the whole time she was mumbling something to herself over and over again. And she had her hand in her purse too which was weird, right?"

He paused just long enough to take a breath. When Noah starts telling a story, there's no stopping him or getting a word in, even if he asks rhetorical questions, which he would usually pose before sucking in another deep breath of preparation.

"So I'm already on the bus and kind of eyeing her 'cause she seems weird. But then this mentally handicapped guy in his early forties gets on the bus and all the seats are taken so he sits

213

right across from her. And this guy doesn't know any better so he starts trying to talk to the crazy lady, who remember still has her hand in her purse, so we don't know what's in there, right?"

We were standing at the bus stop on Hamilton Avenue. Sensing the direction of his story, the bus, which I had never ridden, was starting to seem like a bad idea.

"So he's asking her all these questions about where she lives and what she likes to do and she's just totally ignoring the guy. And he's just not catching on that she's crazy and isn't going to respond. But this guy starts getting upset. He starts talking really loud because he thinks that maybe she can't hear him or something. So the crazy lady finally looks up at him. And about this time the driver pulls up to his next stop and the crazy lady gets up. And everyone on the bus is, you know, thinking 'Thank God' because we all thought there was gonna be a showdown between the retard and the loon, right?"

Another man was standing at the bus stop with us, scraggly bearded and smiling toothlessly, wearing a t-shirt with a picture of a rainbow colored unicorn.

"But then when the crazy lady stands up she pulls her hand out of her purse. Apparently she was holding a dead bat because she threw it at that poor slow guy and then ran off the bus. No one really knew what to do. We were all just sitting there like, 'Fuck did that lady just throw a dead bat at that retard, Jesus.' The bus driver gets up grabs his broom and sweeps the thing off the bus and into the street and then drives off."

He laughed in a guttural high pitch. I could hear the bus rumbling towards us and had to resist the sudden urge to run away.

"Anyway man, we're gonna have some fun tonight, right? This is Stage One."

"How many stages are there?"

"Depends."

The bus was painted lime green and white with a massive cerulean blue asterisk on the back and a smaller one on the front. Once we got on the bus I did a quick scan. Thankfully there were only a few people on board, none of whom had their hands in their purses. Noah and I took two seats next to each other near the middle. It was almost eight o'clock and my stomach started growling again.

"How far is this place?"

"Not too far. We've gotta make a quick stop though before we get there."

I really didn't even want to ask where we might be going first. My goal at this point was just to make it out of the night without getting a dead animal thrown on me. We seemed to be moving further and further into the underbelly of Cincinnati, the buildings older, everything covered with graffiti, the turns getting sharper, harder to maneuver, the roads narrow. Everything flashed by quickly outside my window, but I'm almost positive that I saw someone get stabbed in the gut with a switchblade, saw a body crumple and collapse on the pavement.

"This is us."

The bus came to a quick halt, everyone's head bobbing without thought . Noah and I stepped off and he immediately started walking. I think we were somewhere south of Forest Park but I didn't recognize any of the street signs or landmarks. Noah – several steps in front of me – took a sharp right turn down a side alley in front of a bodega and pulled me aside.

"Wait here. I'll be back in a few."

I looked around the alley and didn't see anyone, unsure if this was good or bad. But I didn't really have any choice other than to assume that Noah knew what he was doing. He turned out of the alley and jogged across the street towards a brown-stained brick building. A low-hatted, baggy panted man let him in, and I dropped my head, started pacing around as the man who opened the door did a quick street scan with his eyes. I got the sense that the low-hatted man wouldn't have been happy to see someone loitering outside of the building. It was darker, everything blanketed in soot, the clouds hanging low with moisture, threatening with rain, the only visible streetlight flickering on and off.

> *there's no light and no one can see*
> *and we can't believe that the shadows are real*

215

and we're all just swimming in the black water
and we're all just reaching and feeling the walls
and tripping and cutting our knees and slicing our tender palms
and we all just want success even if ill-gotten
and all i want is Luna
and i shouldn't be here
and this will never work

The echoes of a car backfire rattled across the brick walls on each side of me when a bag lady pushing a wobbly grocery cart crossed in front of the alleyway. She had on a clear shower cap, an oversized red sweatshirt that said YMCA and black swishy pants. In the flickering light I saw her face, spotted with dirt and a heavy layer of blush. Her cheeks were sunken deep into her thin jaw and the skin underneath her deep-set eyes sagged. In the lower basket of her cart she had a trash bag full of something lumpy.

it's just clothes.
clumps of them
and oh god it smells so bad

There was also an old blender, a jumbled mess of extension cords that poked out the sides of the cart, and two mop buckets – one filled with recyclable plastics, one with glass. In the upper basket I saw a broken recorder and something metal that flashed in the flickering street light. She stopped pushing her squeaky cart and peered down the alley towards me. The woman looked lonely and for a brief moment I felt close to her.

→This woman is like me; she is searching.
　　→Maybe she has small children, estranged.
　　→We can search together.
　　　　→She can teach me the ways of the streets.
　　　　　→The ways of the wayward.
　　　　→I can make her learned on the suburbs.
　　　　　　→**We are the same.**
　　　　　　→**We are perfect.**

216

An irresistible urge to give her my last apartment key or to hug her itched in my heart and shoulders. So I took a step towards her, my elbows loose. She immediately reached for the shiny object in her upper basket.

"Blasphemer!" she shrieked, revealing a rusted hatchet. Her voice was shrill and coated in phlegm, harsh and wet. My cochlea vibrated and contracted.

"But I didn't even say anything. I just wanted..." I stumbled back as she took a step towards me with her hatchet. Thankfully Noah came jogging back across the street and shooed the bag lady away.

"Yeah you gotta watch the crazies around here. You ready to go?"

"Yes, please."

We got back to the bus stop just in time to hop on again. The bus was more crowded this time. All the seats were taken so we stood towards the back. I held the bottom of my shirt between my hand and the smudged-silver balance rail to cover what appeared to be blood stains. A young mother had her toddler son in her lap who happened to be sitting right at my crotch level. I smile apologetically.

"Fuckin' pervert," she said.

I tried to adjust positions to face the other side, but a thick-chested man grumbled at me as shifted to move my crotch out of the eye line of the child. So I turned again getting an unwelcome whiff of his breath – an equal combination of sour milk and mucus mixing with the overall salty sweat stench of the whole bus. An overhead light flashed and we stopped suddenly. Another group of stragglers filed on, but only one got off so Noah and I were pressed further towards the back of the bus. With my elbows tucked in at my sides, I tried to pull out my notebook to categorize all the visual input and to possibly conduct interviews. Though no one looked willing to answer any questions, I had been slacking and desperately needed the data for my upcoming meeting with my father.

the data is here
and it just needs to be collected

217

and it's everywhere all the time
but i can't hold it all
and i can't hold everything
and i can't hold anything

I was pressed further into the back, forced to turn sideways and found myself crotch to face with a mumbling lady with a hand in her purse. Her face had some faded yellow patches and several scabs. She wore a huge black t-shirt covered in stars with words printed in cursive along the bottom seam.

"The contents of the constellations are transient."

I looked at Noah who confirmed with his wide eyes that this was the same Bat Lady from his story. Her eyeballs twitched back and forth.

"Hey this is our stop."

I put my notebook away, hooked my knuckle on his belt-loop and followed as he shouldered his way back onto the street. Noah and I found ourselves in a well-lit bustling area that I still didn't recognize – somewhere on the southeast side of Cincinnati, near Batavia I think. I did another quick scan of the area: no bag ladies with hatchets, no people talking to themselves, and no one hovering around my crotch. I caught the burnt-breading scent of fried potatoes and my stomach growled. As the bus pulled away, the Bat Lady watched me out the back window, her lips opening and closing like a fish.

"Come on man, another alley? Can we get some food soon? What are we doing?"

"Yeah, sure. This place has the best burgers you'll ever have. Trust me. We're almost there."

Maybe I'm coming off as annoyingly passive, as weak and callow. Those things are probably true, but just remember, Luna, that I was trying, that I was only going along with the plan because I was desperate. I was looking for some kind of healing elixir that I knew I couldn't find on my own. I was misguided at worst, but never mal-intentioned. And despite everything you're about to read, I was always thinking about you, about how I could keep us together without resorting to thievery and moving to the lower coast of Antarctica. I know it doesn't look good, but this was all I had, this was all I knew – the fucking edges, the blades self-sharpened.

On the side of the building in the alley, obscured by the darkness, there was a small case of four black stairs leading down to a metal door I hadn't noticed. Noah knocked. I skepticized. A large black man with arms the size of my thighs opened the door.

"Noah! 'Bout time you got your ass back here."

His deep voice boomed and echoed down the alley, bounced wildly off the brick walls. Apparently Noah was like a rock star among band geeks at his place, so I slipped in behind him hoping that the bouncer wouldn't see me. He stepped in front as I tried to pass.

"He's with me, Walrus."

Walrus, as I could see why he was affectionately called, stepped aside and let me in, eyeballing me. He had a drooping mouth that exposed two fang-like teeth underneath a prickly mustache. Noah and I passed through a small, dimly lit hallway – more of a tunnel whose walls were shaking with stereo rumbles – that ramped downward. At the end of the tunnel there was another staircase, lined with swinging kerosene lanterns, leading down, this one wooden and creaking unappreciatively. The rumbling stereo was getting more and more muffled as we descended, the sour smell of sulfur constricting my nostrils, shrinking everything.

"Where the hell are we going? Seriously."

"Just relax."

At the end of the staircase Noah opened a wooden door that led into a room bursting with fluorescent lights. I blinked and squinted before I saw several chipped wooden tables jutting like jetties out of the walls. In the center was a bar, whose tender was a slender young woman. She had huge, fluffy black hair seemingly held together by a neon orange bandana wrapped around her forehead and tied off at the nape of her neck. I was still blinking and shaking my head, trying to figure out where we were and how we got there.

"Hey baby!" The gorgeous woman was talking, she was leaning across the bar and giving Noah a wet, tongued kiss on the lips. Then another. Her hands were moving across the cracked table. She sucked his bottom lip and pulled away, eyes wide, unfocused.

"Babe, this is my buddy, Cetus. Cetus, this is Korie."

She leaned across the table again and hugged me. She was magic, made of sugar and cream, smelled of warm tea and lavender. I couldn't stop looking at her, kept stealing glances at her wide, brown eyes, her soft lips and clear cocoa skin. I reached into my pockets.

"It's great to meet you finally," she said. "Noah has told me a lot about you."

I don't know if she was just being polite or if Noah had actually mentioned me to her. I looked at him for confirmation but he was staring at her ass that was popped up in the air as she was leaning over the counter giving me another side-hug.

surely she is on stilts
and her legs are unending
and her legs are deserts

"What do you guys want to drink?"

220

"Two of your specialties."

"You got it."

I watched unblinkingly as she moved around behind the bar. Her head didn't bob up and down like a normal person. She walked with a glide, moved on a conveyor belt. She balanced a porous, triangulated spoon over a thick-rimmed glass and poured a faint green liquid through it. Looking around the room, I saw a few women in bikini tops sitting at tables with empty pitchers. Some kind of bass heavy, snare-snappy music played quietly over the speakers. I got the feeling that this room was a staging area for something else, everyone half-dressed and rushing to the crowded corners. Korie placed a sugar cube on top of the porous spoon, poured another shot of the green liquid over it

"Anyone got a lighter?" she asked.

"Yes!" I reached into my pocket and pulled mine out.

She flicked it several times, but the lighter fluid wouldn't spark, wouldn't catch.

"I think yours is dry Gumby," Noah said, pulling one out of his pocket.

Korie moved to throw my lighter away.

"No! I'll take it!"

"Alright. Calm down."

"Sorry. It's just that I've had it for a long time."

She handed it back and I repocketed it. With Noah's lighter, Korie set the doused sugar cube on fire, and as it caramelized, tiny tear drops of fire percolated down into the green liquid, clouding the whole drink into a strange haze. After the sugar was mostly mush, she dripped a clear liquid over top. She swirled the spoon through the liquid sending tiny pockets of fog eddying around the glass. Noah took the drink, sipped it casually as she proceeded to make the same drink again, presumably for me.

"So that's your girlfriend, huh?"

He looked away, clearly ignoring my question. Noah hated that term, hated its permanence, too much of an absolute.

"Do you think she'd mind if I asked her some questions?"

221

the numbers don't matter
and will never say what i want them to say
and even the biggest numbers can be halved
and even the smallest numbers can look so big on the page
and it's so god-damn bright
and how can anyone ever stand the light

"Let's get you some food," he said slapping my back again. "Hey, can we get two Gutter Burgers over here?"

Korie pushed some kind of intercom button and yelled, "Gutter Burgers Dos."

I didn't want to see the receiving end or what exactly was on a Gutter Burger. Korie placed another mysteriously muted, strangely clouded green drink in front of me.

"Now you have to promise not to cut your ear off if I give you this, okay?"

"Sure," I said confused. "So how is any of this supposed to help me get Luna back?" I asked turning back towards Noah.

"Cheers!" he said raising his glass.

We clinked our cups and each took a swig. The drink was palatable – tasted of anise and mint – though not that pleasant to be swallowed fast, meant to be sipped. As the liquid hit my stomach, it whined loudly, a clarion call. A young boy – too young to be wherever it was Noah brought me – appeared with two plates. I'm not sure where he came from or where he returned to, but the plate he brought contained a massively messy burger that covered the whole dish. I was too hungry to be concerned with the quality of the meat or its preparation, to think about how the animal was cared for, to think if anyone had honored its life. Watery-red and rusted-orange juices dripped down my hands and arms and onto my notebook, fittingly under the Sketchy category while I took a huge bite.

"Best burger you've ever had, isn't it?"

Noah spoke with his mouth full, crumbs stuck in the corners of his heavy beard. I intentionally ignored his question, focusing all my attention on the contents of the plate in front of me, my stomach protesting with each greasy swallow. Korie brought us two more drinks, these different in temperature, texture, and color scheme. I don't know what either drink was but the second was sour, though easier on the palate and more effective at washing down my Gutter Burger. I switched back and forth between beverages while I ate, running my hands over my gray lighter.

"I'll be right back, Gumby."

Noah took another bite of his burger before he and Korie disappeared down a side hallway. I sipped on my beverages until Noah and Korie returned, both sniffling, rubbing their fingers under their noses, another girl – a carbon copy of Korie – with them. She was tall, long-legged and dressed in pink sweat pants and a white tank top.

> is this some kind of pajama party?
> and am i over dressed?
> and i could strip down.
> level the field.

The girl's eyes, though long and narrow, were dreary, heavy, a strong scent of must and coconut surrounding her. She also had a noticeable facial tic with her right eye. I wasn't sure if she had some mild form of Tourette's or if she was just wasted. My gums started to vibrate and itch under my lips, and the enamel in my teeth buzzed, my tongue and jaw alive.

"This is my friend Jasmine," Korie said.

Jasmine immediately gave me a hug, wrapped her thin arms around the back of my neck. I kept my hands, still dripping with grease and burger juice, at my sides, unwilling to fully participate but unable to comfortably leave, unsure of how to get anywhere different, anywhere safe or productive.

"Jasmine has to go get ready for her performance, but we'll all hang out when she's done."

"Oh are you a singer?"

Everyone laughed except for me.

"Come on, let's go."

"But I want to finish my burger."

"We'll come back for it." Noah and Korie headed back down the hallway. Jasmine was already gone.

I wiped the greasy notebook page on my pant leg and followed. My eyes slowly adjusted as we moved through the dark hallway. There was a ramp, this one tilting us upward, which quickly turned into another creaky wooden staircase at the end of the hall. Noah opened a door that led us into a large, dark room accented with colorful flashing lights and cigarette smoke. Louder bass heavy music thumped over the speakers, but even louder bass beats still shook the roof.

Around the room, set in carved wall cubbies were large electric lava lamps with warm colored globs, blood-oranges and mint-yellows, floating around inside. Directly to the right when we walked in – which I think was actually the back of the club – was a topless woman dancing between two silver polls on an elevated, slick-floored platform lined with white lights. The bounce-busty woman grabbed hold of one poll and, hanging upside down, started grinding slowly and seductively to the music. Several young-looking, baby-faced drunken men – boys really – sat in rounded, red velvet chairs around the stage, placing singles on the floor around her, staring with glassy eyes, eyes made of silk. Along the perimeter, I saw several side rooms behind thin white curtains tied off at the bottom, topless women briefly visible as the curtains fluttered.

> *all these girls are daughters*
> *and all these men are fathers*
> *and i shouldn't be here, not now*
> *and this isn't helping*
> *and she's floating away, floating on a string,*
> *and the string is thinning and soon to break*

The girl on the main stage did a flip off her pole, grabbed her string-like bra off the floor and walked down side-stairs and out the door through which we entered. The crowd around the stage dispersed as they watched her walk – spine bowed like a 'c' – away. Walrus then came through the door and collected all the cash that was left on the outskirts of the stage.

"What exactly is this place?" I asked, jogging to try to keep up with Noah and Korie

"What, you've never been to a strip club before?"

→"Of course I have! I love these places!"
>→Pull a thick roll of singles out of my pocket and proceed to 'make it rain' on stage.
>>→I don't have enough singles.
→"Never!"
>→Noah would respond: "You've never been to a titty bar before? Oh buddy, we've got to get you a lap dance ASAP!"
>>→He would pay for a lap dance.
>>>→Which, given the context would be distasteful.
→"Of course I've been to one but it's been awhile. I've just never been to this particular location before, specifically coming through the back door and all which provided an unfamiliar angle to the whole scenario."
>→Too verbose
>>→**Paraphrase.**

"Yeah it's just been awhile I guess. Look, how is all this supposed to help?"

Another girl walked out through the side door and the crowd of smooth-chinned younglings reconvened. This girl I recognized: Jasmine. Somehow she had already disrobed, made it up stage and was standing in front of everyone in a black thong and nipple covers.

"Just give it time. You sit here and enjoy. We'll be right back."

Noah led Korie into a curtained room where a massive bald man nodded and released the curtains to conceal the room after they entered. He stood, tattooed-arms crossed, head on a swivel, in front of the room. Left alone and feeling increasingly uncomfortable and fucked up – my brain addled – I looked around the room for a secluded spot to jot down some notes. I saw topless waitresses going from table to table whispering things into patron's ears. There was an empty table for two near the middle of the room, away from the stage and the curtains, so I walked over and pulled out the chair using the edge of my shirt as a glove. My shoes got harder to lift because the floor around me was sticky.

--someone spilled a drink!--
--can someone come wipe up this old smelly beverage off the floor?--
--excuse me!--

When I sat down at my table a topless waitress – pale and wearing plastic vampire teeth – came by and asked me what I wanted to drink. She talked casually, like her breasts weren't visible, like her skin wasn't made of cream, like she wasn't a ghost. I ordered a beer. Despite what you've probably heard about me, I honestly had never been to a strip club so I didn't have much frame of reference but on a first glance, Jasmine was not as good on the pole as the last girl, not as lithe and free. She looked like she was trying too hard, but no one seemed to really care. Her facial twitch became more pronounced as she moved her body for the boys in the front row who pulled dollar bills out of their sleeves like colored scarves, tucking the endless supply into her bikini strings. It all seemed so cliché, but it looked like she was actually making good money and was enjoying all the attention. She saw me sitting away from the stage and blew me a kiss. I bobbed my head, raised my beer in obligatory acknowledgment.

She finished her routine, went back through the side door, and I stared down into the neck of my beer bottle, which I held onto closely like some sort of security blanket, a way to ward off conversation while I sat alone.

I took a yellow pill with the square root sign out and washed it down with my beer before Jasmine came back out fully dressed.

"What'd you think?"

"Very sexy."

The alcohol had definitely reached my extremities. Drunkenness, in addition to either intense feelings of euphoria or loneliness, always makes me feel like a child learning to control my muscles. I stood up to flag down our topless porcelain waitress, knocking over our tiny round table with my gangly knees in the process. Jasmine giggled politely while I stumbled to pick it back up and ordered us two more drinks.

I drained the beverage and looked at my wavy face reflecting back at me at the bottom of the blue glass, the image blurry and distorted. I slapped my lips together trying to get the bitter taste off my lips and tongue, rubbed my hands against my pants feeling for my lighter.

Jasmine talked the whole time but I couldn't catch any of it, couldn't register her rapid-fire words. Noah and Korie eventually emerged from behind their curtain, Korie's large fluffy hair matted down in the back, Noah's shirt turned inside out. They were both sniffling and rubbing their noses. Behind Noah's ear he had tucked a hollowed out ink pen. He slipped it into his front shirt pocket, the outline of a tin dish visible.

"So what'd you think of Jasmine's show?" Korie asked.

I nodded my head in approval, afraid that I wouldn't be able to get any words out. Things were spinning wildly making it nearly impossible for me to reliably process any sort of visual input. My lips felt inflated, all cartilage and collagen. Floatation devices.

> *yellow floaties and green duckies*
> *and this isn't how it was supposed to be*

"What do you we say we move this party upstairs," Noah said.

I don't know if you're familiar with the feeling yet or not, but the numbing buzz – the full body vibrations that cancel out all the other ones – made it easier to live life in the passenger seat, to just enjoy the scenery rather than guide the car. So I followed the group of three towards another stair case, this one metal and slippery, not wooden and creaky like the previous one, the music getting louder, deeper. At the top of the staircase was another man, this one long-haired and disinterested wearing a curiously dark pair of shades, given the time of night.

> *maybe he is missing an eye*
> *and morally against wearing an eye patch.*
> *he is a reformed one-eyed pirate!*

227

The reformed pirate saw Noah and waved us through, though he glared at me with his one eye as I passed.

"Argh…" I mumbled.

He stepped in front of me and I nodded to indicate that I was with the apparently familiar trio. Noah whispered something in the pirate's ear and he let me through. On the other side there was a more traditional bar where the elusive bass beat originated. My vital viscera rattled around in my rib cage as we pushed our way through the crowd. Somewhere inside me, everything that I had been pouring into my body – lead by the cloudy green drink – battled for positioning, boxing out and throwing intentional elbows.

flagrant!
double technical!
toss him out!

I ducked down between two people and leaned over against the wall, certain that I would either throw up or pass out. All around me the voices and screeches created a collective nonsense. Through a window next to where I was doubled over I saw we had finally reached the ground level again, finally un-catacombed. But it was raining so hard out that I thought I was still underground, somehow underwater. I could barely see outside, the window like an empty aquarium.

black water and no one is breathing
and we're all just loose sprigs
floating in tiny bowls of glass that's ready to break,
glass that's been cracked since it was shaped
and she won't even know that the bowl is broken

Time sped up both visually in the moment and in my memory, and I realized that I had lost my group of three. I stumbled around the bar, swinging my hand from stranger's shoulder to shoulder trying to keep myself afloat.

did he leave me here?

228

and did he move on to another life
and leave me alone to finish mine?
and did he forget that i am still contractually bound
to follow his instructions?
and does he even know what he is doing?
and does anyone even ever really know what's happening?

None of the faces I saw were right. Everyone's skin was too loose, creating all kinds of unnatural folds and creases. Everyone was a Halloween mask. My steps slowed and I accepted being lost, accepted that my ligaments would just atrophy away as I staggered around looking for the one that was to tell me what to do next. The buzzing noises around me got louder and louder – the volume knob stuck all the way to the right – got more and more indecipherable and I began to sweat uncontrollably.

"Turn the fucking...buzz down. Jesus..."

it's so dark and the water is black outside
and it's leaking in under the windows
and it's all wrong
and Luna will never know
and there's so much data going uncollected here
and fuck it
and fuck,
fuck,
fuck
fuck

But I felt a warm hand on the neck of my shirt and somehow found myself pinned in a triangle between my group of three. I bounced around between them, forced to stay standing as we made our way to the back of the club and all four squeezed into a restaurant-style booth. I remember Noah ordering us drinks but I don't remember them being brought out or drinking them. Noah and Korie were cuddling and kissing, Jasmine scooting up next to me too. I felt her hand rubbing up my leg and across the contents of my pocket. The last thing I remember seeing was her right eye winking at me over and over again at random intervals.

Someone told me that we can only remember one dream every night. The rest of them go into some kind of liquid dream repository where they swim around in a clear gel until called up to the surface of our subconscious again. I don't know if there's a way to flush the repository, to get a clean dream-slate, but if so I'd be first in line. Because the only dream I've ever remembered is a reoccurring one, though always with different variations. And it would always come right before I woke up so it was fresh in my mind, like it was still happening somewhere else, everything part of a multiverse. I'll spare you the details, but the particular variation that morning involved small explosions and sexually explicit, visually lurid images of skinless faces. Also bats. And any time I sleep in a different place than I slept the night before, I inevitably wake up disoriented – a regular occurrence that week. With those two components combined, it was annoying but not unexpected when the tiny people inside my head started drumming again, trying to mine their way out of my head as Noah shook me awake. I actually couldn't remember the last time that I woke up without the little bastards trying to crack through my skull. I couldn't blame them for coveting autonomy though. I wanted out too.

"Hey I've got to get to work, and you're coming with me."

I groggily lifted my upper body, stiff and creaky. I was on Noah's sagging green cot in his empty bedroom. I swung my legs – rotted logs, *why so heavy?* – onto the floor and he handed me a glass of water and two long, glossy turquoise pills.

"Take these. You'll feel better." Noah wore a white linen robe that hung loosely on his frame, though his orange shirt from the night before was still visible underneath.

"I really ought to go back home."

"No can do buddy."

"Come on." I covered my eyes with my wrist.

231

"You can't quit the program early or it won't work. Remember? You're doing this for your daughter. You want her back, right?" I nodded, stretching my limbs. "Well if you're gonna stay here to figure things out you've got to do what I say. And I say you're coming to work with me."

"Can't I at least sleep a little longer?" I asked rolling over on the cot away from him.

"Nope. I've let you sleep as long as I could."

I was really in no position to dissent; plus he was right, I was bound by agreement. And even though I was beginning to have my doubts about Noah's intentions and his know-how, you may or may not believe this, but I'm true to my word.

> *and i have to try everything,*
> *have to say that i turned everything over*
> *and if no one does what he says he's going to do, then there is no truth*
> *and if there is no truth then there is no beauty*
> *and if there is no beauty then there is no meaning*
> *and if there is no meaning then there is no purpose*
> *and if there is no purpose then we would all just bleed ourselves out –*
> *or at the very least sleep abundantly,*
> *in huge unchecked chunks,*
> *sleep for days and forget what it's like to be awake and use our bodies*
> *and we have to believe that what people say is true*
> *and i need Luna*

I reluctantly got up and pulled out my last clean shirt and pair of underwear from my backpack. My pants – soaking wet – would have to last me a little while longer despite the mucus-looking stain near the knee cap. The novelty of the stench made it tolerable.

In the kitchen, Noah was on the floor stretched out on his side holding a tall cream candle in his ear, the top end lit. He had fashioned some kind of paper plate device to keep the wax from falling onto his face.

"What the hell are you doing?"

"Cleaning my ears out."

"You don't believe in Q-tips?"

"I believe they exist, but they just pack everything further down into your brain. The ear candle is much better for you. It keeps your brain from getting clogged."

The candle burned down and the wax dripped onto his paper plate rippled at the edges.

"Where's your coffee machine?" I asked opening and closing make-shift cabinets in his colorless kitchen.

"I don't drink coffee, Gumby."

"Come on, are you fucking *kidding* me!"

The tiny people in my head lost their footing and scattered, slamming against every surface.

"You'll be fine." He shook the candle out and started roaming around the house stuffing things into a plastic grocery bag: a bundle of bananas, three pairs of wool socks, two apples, a lighter, a box cutter.

"How far is it to where you work?" I rubbed my fingers across the bridge of my nose down to the tip.

"We'll ride down to Hamilton again and then it's about a twenty minute bus ride."

I literally gagged at the thought of the bus. I associated the image in my mind with the fish-mucus-sweat smell from the night before.

"Why can't we just ride your motorcycle all the way there?"

"Well here's the thing. It's not actually mine, per se. And I don't exactly have the proper licensure, per se," he said rummaging through the cabinets which as far as I could see were completely empty.

"So when you say 'per se' you mean 'at all', right?"

"Basically. I drive exclusively on back roads that nobody travels because I can't afford to get pulled over and taken in."

He looked squeamish, suddenly gauche.

"Why's that?"

"Well there may or may not be a warrant out for my arrest."

"Seriously? What'd you do?"

"Nothing," he answered quickly. He pulled a folded gallon-size Ziploc bag out of one of the cabinets. "I don't want to get into it. But I will say this: when we get to work, don't call me Noah, okay? Call me Berny."

I knew that if I questioned him or pushed the issue any further I would lose his trust, and I couldn't afford to burn another social bridge.

"Where do you work anyway?"

"Plastic Persons," he said while heating a cup of water in a gray handle-less mug. "I know a guy there who got me a job in shipping. You'll need that." Noah nodded towards a pastel green tarp with a hole cut in the top.

"What's this for?"

"Poncho."

I looked out the window. It was raining outside and by the look of the terrain it had been for a while, which explained why my clothes were all so wet. I stepped into the bathroom, tried to turn on the exposed light bulb.

"Is your power out?" I yelled down the hall.

"You don't remember?"

"Remember what?"

"Nothing, Gumby. Hey man, no time for a shower. We're already late," Noah said leaning his head into the bathroom. He had shed his white yoga suit, stripped back down to his orange pi t-shirt. He handed me a portable mug of steaming water.

"What's this?"

"Tea made from red elm leaves. Or you might know it as the slippery elm. It'll settle your digestive system."

It was bland with a fruity sort of after taste and immediately started dissolving the brick settled at the bottom of my stomach. We sprayed some fabric refresher on our clothes and I patted my pockets. We stepped out into the rain wearing our tarpaulins draped over our tired bodies. Outside, the ground touched the rising sun like a tangent line. The sun looked exhausted as it creaked over the skyline, brilliant and slow, stretching but controlled.

we all need to stretch ourselves
and we all need the beauty of exhaustion.

"I'm sort of afraid to ask this, but what exactly happened last night?"

"Well how much of it do you remember?"

Noah and I were sitting on the bus again using our folded tarpaulins as seat covers. The windows had been left cracked open overnight and small puddles of cold rain sloshed in the indent of each seat. Noah and I were the only ones on board other than the bus driver, a scruffy twenty-something who said he had just returned from living "off the grid." He snacked on a bag of homemade trail mix tucked between his legs.

"The last thing I remember was ascending from those underground sex chambers or whatever the hell they were. Then I got lost and thought you guys abandoned me and then somehow you guys found me and I remember we all sat down at a booth."

"That's it?"

"That's it."

"Well, shit, Gumby, you missed all the fun then. All the important stuff anyway."

I waved my hand up in front of his face. "Actually, then, okay, I don't even want to know. Just tell me why the power is out everywhere. And please tell me what all this has to do with helping me get Luna back?"

"Fair enough," he said turning up the left corner of his mouth, causing his cheeks to dimple under his beard. "There was a lightning storm last night, really bad. It was hitting all around us and it was one of those things where I could feel my skin tingling every time it hit, made my arm hairs feel weird. Totally trippy shit."

He pointed out the window. Tree limbs were down all along the sides of the street, and police cars had blocked off a road where a power line had fallen onto several parked cars.

"Anyway, the power went out at the bar and the bus system stopped running because most of the streets downtown were blocked off by debris. So we were going to stay at Korie and Jasmine's place since it was right around the corner."

"We went to their house? Shit. What happened?"

"No we were *going* to do that but you started flipping your shit. I'd never seen you so damn vocal. You started going off about Luna and disrespect and then you started saying how you had to get more data and pulled out your notebook – which, I mean, what the fuck is that?"

"I'm collecting data."

"Still? Jesus weren't you doing that in high school?"

"Yeah."

"Well anyway you said we had to walk back to the motorcycle and ride back to my place."

"So we walked all the way back to Hamilton to get your bike?"

"Well we started too, you started too anyway and I wasn't going to let you walk alone. But you were just totally out of control. It was windy as hell and shit was blowing back up in our faces. And there was lightning everywhere and my watch was going haywire."

I looked down at my watch. The hands were frozen in position at 4:32 a.m.[37]

"And then you started mumbling something about Mira and I had no idea what you were saying, but you pulled this thing out of your pocket." He pulled the flattened, moist origami fortune teller out of his plastic grocery bag. "But of course the wind knocked it out of your drunk hands and you started chasing after it. So I started running after you and I swear to God I don't know how you were moving so fast. But you eventually collapsed on the side of the road and I tracked down your thing here. Anyway thank god Korie followed us in her car because she picked us up. And I figured you'd freak if you woke up anywhere other than the cabin so she drove us back to my motorcycle and then I slung you on the back and drove your drunk ass to the cabin."

---

[37] I still have the watch if you don't believe me.

"Jesus, I don't remember any of that," I said taking the soggy fortune teller out of his hands.

I did my best to return it to its original three dimensions but the paper was torn and thick with moisture. I managed to peel back the paper under each numerical flap. Under number one and three, in dripping blue ink Mira had written "I'm for you" and under options two and four she had written "You're for me".

"This is us," Noah said pulling the string along the window to light the stop sign at the front of the bus. "Well, yeah, you were pretty far gone."

I carefully folded the wet paper and put it into my back left pocket as we stepped off on a two-lane road and turned down a few side streets. Noah walked quickly. His strides were monstrous, his feet massive. His feet were fleshy flippers. I couldn't keep up.

is he trying to shake me?
he's trying to shake me
and that fucker's going to leave me here

I jogged to catch up, jogged in zigzags through puddles, still drunk.

fucking blisters
and fucking black water everywhere

The buildings around me were old, the steel and limestone aging poorly, sagging and chipping like chalk. When I caught up to him, Noah was standing in front of a large, plain looking warehouse with pale siding along the front, the roof black. Across the front a sign read 'Plastic Persons' in large tan block letters. The parking lot was basically empty, maybe a dozen cars. I didn't want to go inside. I wanted to sleep on the sidewalk, maybe roll into the marshy ditch.

let them stare!

237

I wanted to sleep and then wake covered in dried mud and run back for you, Luna. The mud would crack and fall off in the wind as I ran and when I got to you our skin would turn red but no one would stop us, no one could stop us. I want you to know that I never stopped wanting you, that I never stopped wanting us. I know none of this looks good, that I was blacked out in the city, dirty and hung over while I was losing you. Nothing I can say will change that. But I was trying. I was searching. And I promise that you'll see why I'm telling you all this eventually.

"Alright let's go in and see what's happening."

I was more seriously regretting my decision of agreeing to blindly follow Noah – in his smug feyness – as a means of personal rejuvenation. The aluminum front door led us into a reception area lit only from the sunlight through the windows. Noah slipped his plastic grocery bag of belongings into a cubby behind a tall desk, then signed both our names on a piece of paper snapped to a clipboard on the wall. He signed his name as Berny Bartelby and mine as Cetus Guest.

Inside the main warehouse, "the floor" as Noah called it, several dozen flashlights were duct taped to the walls, throwing beams of light across the concrete room at odd angles. Lining the right side of the massive room were dozens of rows of fully assembled mannequins. In another row next to that there were what looked like department store shopping racks with wheels. Hanging from the top bar were fake limbs of all kinds: legs, arms, hands, feet, torsos. Along the far back wall were piles of huge boxes stacked onto pallets on the floor and a steel shelf reaching to the top of the ceiling filled with more boxes. Half a dozen or so employees wandered around in the room taping up more flashlights, clicking them on and off to test them. It looked like a run-down disco club or maybe the filming location for a low-budget horror movie.

Walking – drifting, really, I was still clouded from whatever was in my system the night before – down the main aisle of the warehouse, I saw several side rooms tucked behind the rows of mannequins. Inside one room were several long conference tables covered in prosthetic limbs. A few people in white half-masks were moving in and out of the light, holding spray paint canisters. In another room, there were dozens of half assembled mannequins, some leaned up against the carpeted walls and others standing, waiting to be given an arm or a head.

"Hey Berny, you made it!" A heavy-set, balding man jogged with limp wrists from across the warehouse, carrying a nude, fully assembled and anatomically correct female mannequin in his arms. A pair of massive calico, thick-lensed glasses slipped down towards the base of his nose as he jogged towards us.

"Did you hear about the storm? I heard almost everyone lost power. We did here too."

"Yeah, Stan, I noticed."

"Course you did. But hey, Boss stopped by and said we don't have to work today if we don't want to. He said probably no one was gonna show and since the backup generator is out too we don't really have much light. But he brought a ton of flashlights," he said pointing around the room, spinning on his heels. "He said we can make some more people if we want, but Boss said he's not coming back today."

Noah told me later that Stan was obsessed with Plastic Persons, even naming and befriending the mannequins. Management eventually moved him to shipping, Noah's department, because he would always try to follow the assembly of one mannequin in particular each day.

"Me and Delilah are gonna stay and work. We're trying to save up for a bigger apartment."

Stan held the mannequin upright with his arm around her waist. I tried not to stare.

"They're not people, Stan. They're mannequins," Noah said

Stan arched his eyebrows downward and pushed the middle of his glasses back up the ridge of his nose.

"Let's go Delilah."

Stan – corpulent and squirmy – regained a firm grip on Delilah and jogged back to the other side of the warehouse. Over the past several weeks, Stan had apparently been seen

239

taking Delilah home, and rumor had it, he even ate and bathed with her.

Further down the main aisle in the shipping area, we found Noah's friend Rick behind a pile of boxes stacked like a jagged pyramid. He was slouched in a dented metal fold-up chair by a table of prosthetic arms illuminated by a row of flashlights taped to a shelf above him. Tucked unsteadily under his armpit, he had another flashlight, the light wavering over a prosthetic arm which he was drilling through top to bottom. Noah unfolded two more chairs and we joined him.

"What're you drilling that for?"

"Oh hey, buddy. I was hoping you would still come in," he said looking up. "Boss isn't coming back in today, so I'm gonna hook us up."

He drilled a hole down through the arm until it reached the would-be-elbow where there was a natural bend which he had hollowed out into a little bowl. Rick reached up under the table and tapped his hand around, feeling for something.

"Your stash is still here?" Noah asked.

"Yeah it should be. Unless some motherfuckers found it." He got down on his knees to get a better look. "Bingo."

He came back up with a tiny crinkled baggy covered in duct tape and began packing what looked like wet, sticky weed into the mannequin's elbow. Even from a distance, the mannequin faces around the room looked unsettlingly realistic, like they each might at any moment request a complete body, require arms and legs that bend, or demand to be granted civil liberties. I shifted my legs under my fold-up chair as we watched Rick prepare the prosthetic bong.

"Alright. You wanna do the honors?" Rick asked holding up a lighter.

"But isn't it plastic? Won't that melt if you try to light it?" I scooted my chair out of the shadows. "Also do you think I could ask you a few questions?" I patted my notebook in my pocket.

"Who the hell's this guy?" Rick asked looking at Noah. He had apparently not seen me.

"He's good."

Rick looked back towards me, not blinking, his eyes dry. "It's fiberglass. And no."

"Right."

Things That Look Sketchy
-Stinky's Gas Station
-Noah's mailbox
-The paraphernalia scatter around here.
-My foot blisters
-Realistic Mannequins

I tucked my notebook back into my pocket. Noah took the arm-bong first and put his mouth at the top where it would have, under normal usage, connected to the shoulder. He held his lighter over the lumpy, sticky looking substance that Rick had packed into the elbow and inhaled the smoke up through the arm then held the arm-bong – smoke still shaking out the top – up to me.

"Oh no thanks."

"Remember our agreement?"

"Okay, you're right Berny," I said eyeing Rick.

"Berny? Come on are you serious man?" Rick said looking at Noah. "Seriously. Who the fuck is this?"

"You can call me Noah around Rick. He's the one that got me the job."

I reluctantly took out my gray lighter, balanced the liquid inside and flicked it several times until it sparked a weak flame. I lit the bowl – dark and still wet – and took a hit – the smoke weirdly sour, hot against my throat – that because of the sheer size of the arm-bong, was bigger than I had intended. My body rejected the smoke. I coughed and gagged, spat and wheezed, my nose suddenly on fire, filled with unfamiliar spices.

Across the room, Stan sat in a corner talking to Delilah who he had placed in the spotlight of one of the flashlights taped to the wall, a few of which had begun to dim or fade altogether. Another flashlight illuminated a well-dressed boy crouched in the corner of the warehouse.

241

"Who's that kid?" I asked between smoky burning coughs.

"That's Boss's kid. I guess he left him here to make sure we didn't blow the place up or something," Rick said.

"I heard he's scared to death of mannequins."

I thought about going over to ask the boy how often his father sees him but I thought the data, when reversed, might not be as relevant. Two more flashlights dimmed, taking the boy out of the spotlight, and we heard a faint high pitched whimper coming from his dark corner.

Rick pulled a dollar bill – folded twice long-way and tall – out of his front pocket and a wadded bandana out of his back pocket. He wiped the table clean and folded inside the bill was a white powder that he dumped out. With the side of the bill he lined it up, rolled the bill up into a tight cylinder, and leaned in to snort the line.

"Sorry, that's it," he said looking at Noah, thumbing his nose.

"It's cool man." Noah said. "Hey let's run out and get some more flashlights and batteries and stuff," Noah said looking at me. "I bet all the one's here'll be dead soon anyway."

Noah took the arm-bong from Rick who had just taken another drag. He indicated for me to do the same.

→I don't need another hit.
→I need to find my daughter, fight for her.
→I need to repent, find the door to my old life.
→If I take another hit I'll get sick.
→If I get sick maybe he'll realize he's taken it too far.
→He might stop dragging me around.
→I'll be able to go home, develop a real plan, something practical.
→**Hit Approved.**

Determined to push the limits, to force the seams to burst, I took another hit, focusing on not letting the smoke tickle and burn the back of my throat. Almost instantly, I was in a thick fog, your ghost floating in the far corner of my eye. I remember standing up and walking down the main aisle again, watching men walk in slow motion, watching flashlights click off all around us, the shrill whine of a drill and a whimper bouncing off the corners of the dimming mausoleum.

Rick's weed must have been laced with something unfamiliar to my system because when we got back on the bus again, I felt completely disconnected from my body. It was like I was still seeing the world through my eyes without experiencing anything in live action. I was used to the normal weed-induced spinning, the floating, the spirals, the blood rushing everywhere. But this was amplified, more intense. The sounds and the movements around me didn't match up – a timing delay between my visual and auditory input. Things around me were rearranging. Things inside me were rearranging.

"You okay, Gumby?"

Noah slapped me on the back again. I didn't respond but something boiled inside me, splashed and sizzled against the sides of my stomach. Normally my stomach has a little give to it but it stood firm on its boundaries. My stomach was igneous rock. The acidic lining was dried ash, hot magma burning underneath. My salivary glands pumped and pulsed, trying to put out the fire, and I felt myself repeatedly, though not intentionally, rubbing my hands over my thighs, down to my knees, stuck in a loop.

"We need to get off the bus," I said.

"You're right. This is our stop. There's nothing to do at work so I've got something else in mind for us. Stage Three."

I put my hand over my mouth and ran out of the collapsible door as soon as the bus driver released it open with his lever. Something inside me was bubbling – really fucking boiling and cooking my organs. I doubled over and puked – like breathing fire – in the grass. My head still spinning, I wiped my mouth on my sleeve and turned towards Noah who had gotten off the bus behind me. Still not fully engaged with my body, I was on my knees looking up at Noah.

"I'm sick of you dragging me around!"

New vibrations buzzed through my limbs, resonating in my chest, still steaming.

"I need to do something real! I'm losing my daughter! We need to talk to someone! Find out my rights!"

My inhibitions gone, I yelled with hot breath, with melted knives.

"What's the point of all this?! What's the fucking point?! You never even had a plan for me, did you?"

"Is that really what you think?"

"Absolutely. You're a disgusting…"

I spat on the ground, spat flakes of hot mucus burning on my teeth.

"pitiful…"

I coughed and dry heaved.

"…fucking drug addict."

I stood up and slapped him on the back as hard as I could. He had the same distant look on his face that he had yesterday morning when I found him doing a headstand in his grandfather's cabin.

"Did you get it all out?"

"What?"

He shook his shoulders. "You're right. I'm exactly what you said I am. You and I are completely different. You know how?" I looked back at him getting even angrier that I hadn't gotten a rise out of him. "You and I are different," He leaned in closer to me. "Because I would rather be up front with what I'm about instead of having to be shamefully exposed by somebody else. That's how people end up with cancer."

"What are you talking about?"

"I just think we should be defined on our own terms. It's your body. It's your time. Don't you want to be in control?"

He paused for dramatic effect, leaning forward to create a visual barrier with his body.

"I mean, here is essentially how I think about things. Either I know something or I don't. And I don't have to search for the things that I know because, obviously, I already know them. And as for the things that I don't know, there's no point in actively searching for them. How can you look for something that you don't know?"

I stood up, circled wide, sweeping around him as he spoke, but he continued like he didn't notice I was moving, holding his gaze forward.

"I figure that either I'll find them out along the way or else they're just not essential. And maybe my own hubris will be my undoing, but I don't care."

I circled quicker, spiraling closer into him, shaking the blood back into my hands, into my fingers. My throat was on fire, my skin hardened, made of scales. I was a fucking dragon.

"Because it makes me self-satisfied - going on my own terms. And so the question for you becomes: when are you going to figure out what you are? And when are you going to accept it? Because, I can tell you, things aren't going to turn out how you want them to unless…"

I stopped circling and punched him hard in the jaw. As soon as I connected, I went down to my knees and puked in the grass again. He could have easily ducked out of the way or pulled some yogi-type move on me to soften the blow, but I saw in his eyes when I made impact that he was deliberately choosing to absorb the hit with full force.

And when he fell, he was my father – suit tie flapping in the wind. He was my father when he stumbled back, turning away from me. We were both on all fours in the grass. After collecting himself, Noah pulled a bottle of water out of his plastic grocery bag that was twisted around his wrist and came over to me.

"Here drink this, you'll feel better. The first time I smoked a Buddha I did the same thing. It definitely has the potential and the potency to make people angry. And sick for that matter. This is good. This is progress," he said looking at my piles of puke in the grass.

He pulled a tissue out of his pocket and dabbed at his bloody lip. His reaction didn't make any sense to me. When I push on something, physics tells me that I'm supposed to feel it pushing back – but maybe Noah was right: there are no absolutes.

"And look I'm just trying to help because you asked. And, yes, I have a plan in all this. But we're not done yet. I've got one last place to take you if you still want to come. Okay?"

My back pocket buzzed. My phone hadn't been getting any signal so it caught me off guard. The number flashing on my screen was not listed in my contacts but I recognized the 513 area code so I picked it up and stepped away from Noah still watching him over my shoulder through narrow eyes.

"Hey."

"Brody?"

"Yeah."

I waited for him to say something, to state his cause.

"So hey, did you get my message to check on Tails and to water my plants?"

He was still not saying anything but I heard heavy breathing and these weird nasally plosives coming from his end of the connection.

"Yeah," he finally said but it was not in his normal voice. It was all air and phlegm. He cleared his throat. "Tails is fine. The plants are fine. Look I've been trying to reach you for a while now."

it's not your job to keep tabs
and don't try to make this something that it's not
and don't always have your chin pointed down

"Yeah I've been unavailable. Look, this is kind of a bad time. Do you need something?"

He took another deep, heavy breath, drawing up air from the bottom of his lungs, from the corners only called on during strenuous exercise.

"Dad passed."

He said it quick. Said it all in one word.

dadpassed.

I thought I had misheard.

"What?"

"Dad passed."

248

speak up!
i can't hear you!
speak the fuck up!

"What do you mean?"
"Dad died."
He said it quieter, quicker.

dadied.
dadiedandnowdadisdead.

I thought maybe he was confused, that maybe it wasn't
my brother.

yes, his voice is all wrong
and it's not him
and it's just a weird coincidence
and it's a guy named Brody – not my brother
who called my number by mistake to tell me that his dad died
and it's all a misunderstanding
and oh boy, i feel bad for him
and how will I break the news to him?

--Look I'm sorry your dad died but my dad's fine.
--I mean he's a douche (haha!) but he's alive.
--I'm meeting with him this Fall for the first time in years in fact.
--You must have the wrong number.
--Whoops!

"Hurley are you still there?"

fuck.

I guess our minds, when shown things that we don't
believe in, things that we don't want to be true, instinctively
move to disprove, to inquire, to probe, to verify every detail, to
try to follow the logic and prove it wrong, prove that it was
impossible.
"Are you serious?"

249

"Yes."

"Well when did it happen?"

"Yesterday."

"And how did it happen?"

Whatever was mixed in with that weed was accelerating a rise in my body, on my skin – hot and itchy.

"He had a massive heart attack. Apparently there were two severely clogged arteries that finally gave out."

My fingertips pulsated and the cartilage in my nose froze.

"And so that's it…? Is there a funeral? Did I already miss it?"

When I said the word 'funeral' Noah caught on to the content of the conversation and came over towards me. I waved him off and took a few steps in the other direction, avoiding my first pile of vomit in the grass which I noticed had viscous semi-rivers of black and red snaking through it like veins.

black water is everywhere inside me
and the fucking current is…

"The viewing is tomorrow afternoon."

"In Urbana?"

"Yeah. Arthur's Funeral Home at two o'clock." He paused again, I guess waiting for me to say something. "Look Bailey said that when you called the other day you sounded disoriented and then when the apartment was almost completely empty, that sent red flags up too. So I don't know where you're at or what's going on with you. It is what it is. But can you be there?"

"I'll be there."

I hung up the phone and sat down on my knees in the muddy grass by the bus stop next to my second post-punch pile of puke. My body was heavy, all iron and calcium. It was dense, gravity squeezing and pushing it all down. My body was melting. It was condensing. It was sinking into the rain-soaked earth. The ground couldn't push back hard enough on me. I felt like I would either burst into flames or dissolve into a puddle of watery carbon.

how can people die of heart disease anymore?
and shouldn't scientists have conquered death by now?
and don't we have machines that can pump and circulate our blood
and oxygenate our brains?
and can't we charge him back up
and put him on one of those machines?
and couldn't we have kept him lucid
and wheeled him into a rented boardroom
with a projector screen for my presentation?
and it wasn't supposed to happen this way
and i could have fudged the numbers
and the ground is so wet
and it's gray everywhere
and they say you can drown in a cup of water
if you do it right.

Noah came over, a dinghy in a flood and sat down next to me. I don't know if you inherited this from me or not, but I have never been the kind of person that handles bad news well. My mom used to tell this story about how when I was three, maybe four years old, I pooped on the kitchen floor when I found out that I had to go to preschool. So looking back, I'm glad I was blitzed when I got the news about my dad. My high had slowed and muted the way my synapses sent the information to my nerve endings. It changed the way that my mind related to my body.

My phone buzzed in the grass next to me. Apparently the call from Brody was the first time that I had a reliable signal on my phone since I left Hamilton and a wave of text messages and missed calls poured in: two unread texts from Mira, two missed calls and a voicemail from my mom, two missed calls and a voicemail from Brody, and a call and voicemail from an unknown number. I rolled up off my knees, off my grassy hassock and onto my blistered feet.

"Change of plans Noah." I stood tall, my back stiff and straight. "This time you're coming with me," I said with my shoulders shaking in the wind.

Part III

why all things rise

Noah and I sat alone on the bus riding towards Forest Park just north of Cincinnati. Most of the side streets were still blocked by debris – shards of wet bark and loose metal. Whole trees were down, car windows smashed, everything dislodged. It looked like a tiny tornado had hit.

"We need a vehicle," I said. "Something bigger than your motorcycle."

"Okay perfect. I know what to do."

"Not a stolen one."

"Right. Well there's a rental place just down the road here, I think." He pointed down the street. We got off the bus and walked a few blocks to the only place with any lights on.

I had first-hand experience with Noah's ability to persuade people to bend to his will so even though I was trying to seize control of myself, I deferred to him when we got inside. The main atrium was small, surrounded by glass windows on all sides, except for the back wall which had a series of doors – closets and exits with tiny metal latches. Through the glass we could see the person behind the desk was a middle aged woman – the kind of person who was clearly attractive when she was younger and was desperately trying to hold on to her youthful looks and charm. Her bleach blonde, papery hair hung over the front of her shoulders. Up close, she was clearly in her fifties but trying to reject her generation, giving nature the middle finger, trying to masquerade as a careless twenty-something. But she hadn't picked up the nuisances, didn't play the role convincingly yet. A butterfly bandage was strapped across the bridge of her nose, above her collagen smile.

"Botched nose job?"

Noah nodded. The woman wrung her hands in her lap, twisted and rubbed them while staring at the computer screen in front of her. She didn't look up or acknowledge our entrance. Noah led.

"Hello Miss."

Her head snapped up and she spoke with an accent that sounded British but not convincingly so.

"What can we do for you today sir?"

She visibly recoiled when she saw us. Since trying to hitchhike, I hadn't really considered what I might look like. There were new cuts on my face, I guess from when I drunkenly collapsed trying to walk to Noah's motorcycle the previous night. The old cuts had already begun to close. I rubbed my fingers across the self-sutured scraps.

> *my body closes its own wounds*
> *and i don't need a fucking doctor*
> *and i'm a self-healer*
> *and my skin is made of stitches!*

The cuts, both old and new, were small but noticeable and my hair was thick with sweat and body grease. Noah's jaw was beginning to swell from my punch and his lip was struggling to scab – probably a side effect of whatever drugs he had put into his veins. Our clothes were stained white around the neckline and underarms from dried sweat, our pants dotted with brown patches of caked mud, and I had a patch of dried vomit on my shoulder.

"Well we're in need of your services."

"Certainly."

She smiled and nodded, trying not to look either of us in the eye, compulsively shrugging her shoulders. I patted my notebook and hung in the back of the room to give Noah his space to work the situation.

> *i should ask*
> *and log some more numbers*
> *and it's too late*
> *and it's always been too late*
> *and he's gone*
> *and it doesn't matter*
> *and it never really mattered*
> *and it's so wet everywhere*

I felt in my pocket for your button to make sure I still had it and then pulled out my cell phone, started thumbing through my messages that had started coming in after Brody called. First I opened the texts from Mira.

"call me when ur ready"
"haven't heard anything from you in a while…u okay?"

I didn't know how to respond yet so I exited out. I listened to the voicemail from the unknown number.

"Hurley. It's Al! From the gas station. Anyway, sorry to bother you but I saw your telephone number posted on the refrigerator – oh, I took you up on your offer to stay at your apartment if that's not already clear – so I thought I would give you a call to keep you updated. Some people just came by, didn't say anything, and then left when they saw me. Not sure who they were but I just thought you should know. I also noticed that you have a garden on your porch – very nice by the way – but the tomato plants have wilted. I tried to water them and give them an extra bit of sunlight but nothing seemed to work. But the good news is that the yellow squash is starting to sprout, so at least you'll have something to harvest. Anyway, I'm calling from a payphone so you won't be able to return this call but I'm sure I'll see you soon. Thanks again!"

I saved the message and tuned in to see about Noah's progress.

"…the best car that you have for an urgent, highly emotional quest across the Midwest."

He spoke seriously but with a wide grin on his face. Noah spoke openly with anyone, spoke with temerity, afraid of nothing – one of his more admirable qualities. Though I was still mad at him, I was actually starting to feel a little better, less hopeless. And I had to admit that he was a great traveling partner, that maybe he was on to something. The woman behind the counter laughed and batted her eyelashes too hard.

"Let me see what we have in stock."

"I can tell you exactly what we need."

He pointed through the tall glass window to a covered car – untouched by storm damage - under an awning at the back of the lot behind a red velvet hanging guardrail.

"Sir, I'm sorry but that's reserved."

"You're right. For us."

Out of his plastic grocery bag, he pulled a small wooden box and slipped it across the counter.

> *i really should get him a better bag.*
> *something cloth, maybe.*
> *something reusable,*
> *more sustainable.*

She pulled out a small plaster Buddha with a clasp on the side gripping a match in his hands.

"Baby we're gonna need that car."

She leaned across the counter towards Noah holding her head in her hands propped up on her elbows, held it loosely like it might fall off and roll around on the floor.

"Fine, but you've got to tell me your name is Bert Holland." She whispered flicking her eyes towards a camera in the corner of the room, her faux-British accent gone.

"Yes ma'm. That's right. My name is Bert Holland and we need that elite vehicle immediately. I *demand* that you release that vehicle to us this instant," he said loudly, standing up tall. He slammed his fist on the counter for good measure, which caught the woman off guard again.

"Right away sir," she said resuming her awful British accent.

Using only her two index fingers, she typed a few things into the computer before sliding the key across the counter to us and placing the wooden box in her purse under the desk.

"Enjoy your trip gen'elman."

Noah turned around on point and we walked out of the glass building together, out under the clouds made of charcoal, made of old smoke and soot.

"How the hell did you pull that off?"

"Easy. I could see that her eyes were twitching and she was wringing her hands like crazy. She was practically begging for a fix. Buddha-bing-badda-boom."

I waited under the awning while Noah did a slow lap of admiration around the car. He peeled off its stretch-satin cover, revealing something silver, something sparkly and shaped like a bullet. I don't know what kind of car it was – I'm not a car guy – but Noah said something about R8 and horsepower, I think.

"You want to drive?"

"No you go ahead."

"You sure? Back in high school you loved driving."

"It's cool. I'm too buzzed to drive right now."

We got in – the leather seats warm and slippery – and when he cranked the car, the engine started soundlessly.

"Alright so you're in charge now. Where are we going first?"

"I don't know. What do you think?"

"Come on, Gumby. You said you were in charge."

"Right, okay. Well can we make a pit stop in Hamilton? I'm hoping one more person will be joining us on the trip."

"Excellent! Trips are always best in threes."

Even though the contents of my blood were still questionable and my body was breaking down, my skin buzzed at the thought of seeing Mira. It was like Noah had stretched my body and soul down to such a thin string and when that string was plucked by the death of my estranged father, it started to play a note in tune with the rest of my body. Something felt in balance that had not been there before. I'm not saying that our bodies are like pianos, the wires inside always being plucked and struck by someone outside. It's not like our organs are puppets. Our emotions are not marionettes. All I'm saying is that I felt myself settling into my body as we drove northward towards Hamilton, towards Mira, towards you.

I had forgotten how much I hated riding in a car with Noah, reckless and inattentive, so I was relieved when we crossed B and C streets and parallel parked outside the house that Mira rented from her dad. It was a small faded-chartreuse-yellow house with an old wooden porch out front made of mold and moss.

i never called her back
and i never answered her text
and i will be interrupting something
and she will already have plans
and she is young and she is sexy
but i need her to be available, to be able to make the trip with us.

"So what now?" he asked as we sat parked outside her house in the dark.

"I guess we see if she's home. Wait here."

I didn't see any lights on, but I figured their power was out too. I avoided the doorbell and knocked directly on her door, swallowing an unexpected nervous lump in my throat. Kylie, her roommate, answered, her face illuminated through a candle in her hand. Like the last time that I saw her, she had a boyish haircut, dyed black with blonde patches in the front. It made her look younger than she was and when she was bundled up in winter clothes, concealing her breasts, it made her sex indeterminable. But at the door, she was barefoot, wearing pastel blue running shorts and a fitted, black crew neck t-shirt, revealing her half sleeve of tattoos snaking up her right arm. I had never really taken the time to look at all of them, but it appeared to be some sort of celestially-themed artwork. I wondered if Mira had designed it. Kylie clearly didn't recognize me, which I couldn't really blame her for, given my out-of-character appearance.

"Yeah?"

"Is Mira here?"

261

When I asked for Mira the mental light bulb visibly went on, her eyes fully open.

"Hurley?"

"Yeah. Is she here?"

"I think she's getting a shower. But yeah, come on in. We lost power last night and it still hasn't come back on yet, so sorry it's kinda dark."

I waved for Noah to join.

"That's what you drive?" she asked watching Noah step out of the car.

"Well, no not exactly. It's a rental. Long story." I shook my head loose of the memories from the last few days.

"Noah, Kylie. Kylie, Noah."

They nodded at each other, and Kylie's eyes followed Noah until he sat down on the couch, her eyes darting to the ceiling. She sat on the floor across from us pulling her knees up to her chest. Their house felt small, boxes pushed up against every wall shrinking the room, pulling us all towards the center. A caged, green parrot was in the far corner against a rusted-brown brick wall, the mortar dried dripping down. The parrot was completely still, maybe sleeping. In the middle of the room was a menorah with nine tall candles lighting the room. A little bit of fading sunlight came in through the window shades, but it was dark enough that I could see the flicker of small flames in other dark rooms. Their apartment – smelling of burnt sage – was small and sparsely decorated though there were several useless multi-tentacled, colorful lamps and a tiny elaborate windjammer tucked inside a glass jug on a side table. Somewhere deeper in the apartment, I heard the quiet hissing of running water.

"I thought you could only use the middle candle on a menorah," I said breaking the silence. "Isn't it bad luck or taboo or something to light them all without the whole ceremony?"

"Oh, I'm not Jewish. We bought this at the Salvation Army as a decoration piece, and we needed light so we just lit them all."

"Oh. Cool."

A rough looking white cat, fur thick and matted, walked into the room, sniffed and turned back around.

"So what happened to you guys?" Kylie asked, her eyes back on Noah.

"Suffice it to say it's been a weird couple of days," I said.

"I'll say. It looks like you two got your asses kicked and wiped all over each other. Jesus."

The water pressure noise in the back subsided.

"I'll go let Mira know you're here."

She picked up the single candle next to her and walked back down a hallway.

"So what's up with this Mira girl?"

Noah reached over to slap my back but I saw it coming and leaned out of the way.

"Look, it's not like that, okay? We're just really close friends, that's all."

"Who are you trying to convince?" Noah said as Kylie came back down the hallway.

"She'll be out in a minute. She said she's glad you're here though." She curled her lips into her mouth and puffed them with air like a bull frog. Noah looked at me, wide eyed.

"Free reign," I said.

"So what all do you have tattooed?"

Noah got up and moved towards Kylie. She rolled up the rest of her shirt sleeve and showed him her moons and stars orbiting across her skin. Mira came down the hallway wearing the same cutoff jean shorts that she had on when I last saw her and a vanilla white v-neck t-shirt. In her right hand, on a small black disk, she held a tall cream colored candle. I think it was coconut scented. Her hair hung in wet clumps around her face.

"Hey it's great to see you." She came over and hugged me, pulled her body in close. "Sorry about the power being out."

I interrupted Noah's conversation. He was rubbing his fingers over Kylie's tattooed arm looking closely at the artwork.

"Noah, this is Mira."

"Pleasure to meet you. I've heard so much about you."

I can knock Noah for a lot of things but his adherence to social propriety is not one of them.

"Yeah me too. You were one of the Nicklebee Hot Boxers, right?"

"I guess so," he said making an exaggerated frown at me, his sign of confusion.

"You want to go in the other room and talk?"

"You guys going to be okay?" I said looking at Noah.

"We're fine, Gumby."

Mira and I went back to her bedroom, and walking away I heard Noah ask, "So how far up do these go?"

We sat down on the floor in her bedroom, our backs against the same bare wall. Two paper lanterns, one buttery yellow, one clear-water blue, hung above us.

"Sorry it's kind of lame in here. I haven't really had a chance to decorate much yet."

"No I think it's nice."

She set the coconut candle in the middle of the floor and lit another one on her bedside and one on her desk. Near the foot of her bed she had a turtle tank filled with stones, greeneries, and a small built-in pond. Two turtles stood still inside, watching each other. The three candles lit the room unevenly, leaving the corners and edges dark and gray.

"You look like you've had a rough couple of days," she said.

"No. I mean." I started laughing. "Yeah actually it's been really fucked up."

"So what does this mean that you're here?"

"I don't know." I shrugged, and we sat on her floor, cross legged looking over at each other for a few silent seconds. "It means that I've been thinking about you," I said turning my head away.

"Yeah. Me too."

We both looked in opposite directions, breathed in deeply.

"Hey I read the thing that you gave me." I pulled out the origami fortune teller, dry but crumbling at the edges. With my knees up to my chest, your brown button slid out of my front right pocket. I picked it up, placed it on my knee.

"What'd you think?" She unfolded the origami fortune teller all the way, spread it flat.

"I agree. But here's the thing…"

"I figured there was more."

I paused, avoiding eye contact, looking into the dark corners

"I mean…I don't know…"

"Oh come on, you're going to get shy on me now?"

"It's complicated and it's just that…"

She interrupted my trailed off thought. "Anything goes."

"Okay, this is probably gonna sound weird."

"The weirder the better."

"Okay well how much do you know about black holes?"

"Nothing really. Why?"

"Well there's this thing called an event horizon. And basically the idea is that you can only come within a certain distance of a black hole before you get sucked in. And once you get sucked in, you don't even know that it happened because the singularity becomes your new reality. And so if your body isn't ripped apart you're just sort of stuck in this place that you don't even know you're trapped in."

"So what are you saying? That I'm some sort of trap? A black hole?"

"No, I'm saying that people in paper houses don't light fires."

I smiled, my skin heavy.

"I need you to be more specific."

"Okay." I paused to gather my thoughts. "I guess I'm afraid that I'll just mess this up. I'm afraid that getting too close will ruin it." She looked at me, her lips straight. "I guess I'm just saying that sometimes it's better to keep a safe distance because that way it can stay perfect. "

"Come on. You can't honestly be implying that you're afraid to pursue this because I'm perfect. That's ridiculous."

"Is it?" I looked towards the soft corners again.

"So you're saying that if I can prove that I'm not perfect then you'll be able – at least morally – to pursue this?"

"I guess so. Yeah."

She paused and looked around the room.

"Okay for example, let's take my nose. There's no way it's perfect."

"What's wrong with your nose?"

"It's just. I mean the angle of protrusion is really weird for one. And there's this bump in the middle." She rubbed her index finger down the ridge.

"No way! I think it's…I don't know…proportional. And well-sloped."

"I've just always been really self-conscious about it. That's why I got it pierced. To make it look daintier or something. Does that prove it?" she asked scooting up against me.

"I don't know."

"Or how about the fact that I'm scared to death of Luna? I know it sounds weird – I mean I've never even met her. But I know that if you and I were together I *might*, and please don't get freaked out, might be like a mother-type figure in her life. Which scares the shit out of me."

"Why?"

"I guess I'm just afraid that I have too much of my mom in my body to be a mother – or anything close to it. I mean, I know it's not my fault that she did what she did, but I just keep thinking that maybe I was what put her over the edge. That having a daughter wound her brain or her soul or whatever so tightly that it finally just snapped. And I guess I'm just afraid that might happen to me too, that I'm predisposed or something to behave the same way. Is that enough?"

I put my arm around her shoulder, pulled my chest up against her arm.

"Is that a yes?"

"What?"

"Am I fucked up enough?"

"Absolutely."

"Good. So hey what's going to happen with you and Luna now that Eris is gone? How's that going to work?"

"I don't know. Eris wants to take sole custody. And she'll likely get it."

"Why?"

"She knows I've kept drugs in the house with Luna. And I know that if I fight it that she'll bring everything out in the light. It's sort of been this unspoken agreement. I'll lose my job and everything. So really, either I don't fight it and I lose Luna. Or I do fight it and I end up losing Luna anyway along with my job and everything else."

"Can't you talk to her? I'm sure you guys can work something out."

"Maybe. But it'll ultimately be up to the courts. Do you think I should talk to her about it?"

"It probably wouldn't hurt."

"You might be surprised." I picked your button up off my knee and tucked it back into my empty right pocket. Mira and I paused again, watching the candles flicker, sending our laughably stretched shadows rippling across the white walls.

"As long as we're baring souls and everything there's something else I want to ask you?"

"Sure."

"Okay…well, actually let me preface by asking this: When your mother died, what did it feel like?"

"What do you mean?" she said taken aback a little. We didn't talk about her mom often, not since reading *The Bell Jar*.

"I mean, what did it feel like in your body? In your arms and in your hands and in your chest."

"I don't know. Tight, I guess? Maybe, heavy."

I nodded, thinking that I would soon feel everything once my high completely subsided. I wanted to be ready to feel it all, finish it fast.

"What's the last thing that you remember doing with her?"

She looked at me with inquisitive concern, her eyes glistening.

"Well...okay. I remember a few days before she died, she took me to the zoo and while we were looking at the animals she started acting really weird and hiding her face behind her hands. It turns out she was crying so I asked her what was wrong. I remember she said that she was 'mourning the souls of the captured animals.' Her words, not mine. I was too young to know what she was talking about, but I remember seeing something similar in her eyes that I saw in the animal's eyes. Like a vagueness – a disconnect. I think that's why I like animals so much. Because they remind me of my mom. Looking back on it I think she just wasn't able to connect the thoughts in her head with the truth that she felt in her body. I think she felt like she had to shed her body to free her mind."

She looked down at her feet on the carpeted floor. "Why are you asking me all this?"

"My father died yesterday." Unplanned, I said it like it was a question, my voice inflection high at the end. Her eyes welled up and her lips and nose contorted and twisted. She let out a small squeak. "And the last time I talked to him was seven years ago and I punched him in the face. But I planned on meeting up with him at Thanksgiving this year."

She wrapped her arms around my upper body.

"I'm so sorry," she whispered. "What happened?"

"He had a heart attack, had two clogged arteries. Do you think you could go with me to the funeral? It's in Urbana, Illinois. It's tomorrow."

She looked up at me, tilting her head to the side, reminding me a little bit of Tails, which consequently reminded me of you again. A familiar vibration – a retuned string – shook through my body.

"Of course."

"We'll need to leave first thing tomorrow morning. Probably 9:30 or so."

She buried her face into my stomach, still holding on to my upper body. I must have had a terrible stench but she still burrowed her way into me recklessly.

"Of course I'll go with you."

"Why are *you* crying?"

"It's just really sad. Why are you *not* crying?"

"I don't know. I just don't like to. It doesn't feel manly, I guess."

"Jesus, are you still stuck on that?" she said laughing between reflexive heaves.

"No I guess not."

"Good because I like a guy that can be emotionally vulnerable – being comfortable is the manliest thing."

We sat tucked around each other on the floor before we slowly unwound. I picked up the origami fortune teller, thumb-tacked it onto her corkboard next to a scrap of paper with notes scribbled across it.

"…we only have bodies so we can make more bodies and so we can keep our souls from dissipating, from being spoiled or pilfered by…"

She wiped off her tears and went out to join Noah and Kylie. I pulled out my notebook and quickly tore out the pages containing the Unmasculine category and created a new one.

Masculine
-Emotional Vulnerability

Since the apartment was quickly darkening, the night creeping up, Noah and Kylie – now in black skinny jeans – had moved out to the porch, lit at the corners by tiki torches to keep the mosquitoes away. Each had a beer in one hand – wrists limp – and a freshly rolled joint in the other.

"You guys want a beer?" Kylie asked, looking up at us, adjusting her bra strap. Mira and I both grabbed a beer out of the cooler sitting under the plastic table. I unfolded and sat down in a metal chair propped in the corner.

"So what were you guys talking about?" Mira asked.

"I was just telling Kylie about Hurley's father. I hope that's alright."

"Yeah I guess it's not really a secret."

Kylie passed her joint over and I rotated it between my forefinger and thumb, lit it again with my dying gray lighter. Mira sat on my lap and we passed it back and forth. The tip tasted like lemons every time she passed it off.

"Do you think there's an afterlife?" Noah asked puffing on his own crumpled joint, the edges dark. Mira gave him a look – with her eyes wide and her brows arched – like the question was inappropriate given the circumstances. "Right. Well how about this. Do you think God exists? Not the idea of him but the actual physical self of God."

The air above the porch smelled like sugary tar.

"I don't think so," Mira said trying to keep me from having to answer.

"Why's that?"

"I don't know. I mean I know it's an overdone argument but how could he create something and then just not care about it? I just don't think it's possible to not care about something you've created so I don't think he was involved."

"So are you saying that God doesn't exist or that he does exist but that he didn't create us?"

"What do you mean?"

"Well, I guess I look at it this way. There is a difference between 'zero' and 'nothing'" Mira looked at Noah confused. "What's your favorite sport?"

"What?"

"Just answer the question."

"Baseball, I guess."

"Okay, let's say we both play on a baseball team. And that the opposing pitcher throws a no hitter so neither of us has any hits." Noah paused to take a swig of his beer and a puff. "But now let's say that you're a player and that I'm the coach on that team. It's still true that we both have no hits but I didn't even attempt to get any hits. So yours is a real zero where my zero is a lack of an attempt, an irrelevant nothingness."

"So what are you saying?" Mira took a drag on our joint, passed it back to me.

"I'm just pointing out the options. What do you think Hurley?"

270

Mira repeated her look again.

"No it's fine. I don't know, I guess I think he probably existed. Somehow. There's just no way that our minds – these minds that are wired and designed to question our mind's ability to question our mind's abilities – there's no way that just accidently happened after some tiny molecule blew up or something. The odds of that are insane. I think maybe the best description I've ever heard about God was from one of Brody's co-workers. Brody's my brother. He's a professor of Greek mythology down at University of Cincinnati," I said turning towards Kylie who nodded. "Anyway this guy was talking about this idea called deus otiosus which basically translates to "hidden god." Essentially it's just the idea that God created the world and then withdrew to do other things, leaving us to fend for ourselves. And that was just the plan from the beginning."

"So in your scenario God is '0 for 3' not hitless on lack of attempt?"

"Sure," I said, not really following his analogy. "But I think maybe there's more to it than that," I said. "I don't really think God is always just gone necessarily. I think maybe he is like the sun – not because he's at the center – but because we can see him and feel him even though he's not always visible – he's always moving."

"What do you mean?"

"Like, for example, because of the way the Sun rotates it's only in each constellation of stars for about a month and then it rotates on to another constellation. But at the end of every synodic period it inevitably returns. So maybe we're just a constellation that he moves through."

"I like that," Mira said. "We have autonomy but are not alone. I can subscribe to that."

All four of us took swigs on our drinks, watched each other's faces flash and fade behind the flickering light of the tiki torches guarding the porch.

"So have you figured out what you're going to do about Luna?" Noah asked.

"I don't know. Mira and I were just talking about how trying to get custody is just a lost cause because Eris can totally screw me over if she wants."

"Don't you think he should try to talk to her?" Mira said to Noah.

"Yeah, I mean…" His eyes widened in recognition of something. "Actually yeah that's exactly what you should do. We should all go! We can woo her into making the right decision."

"I don't know man."

"Just look at it this way. Because she has leverage, she has the power. Worst case scenario nothing changes. Best case scenario everything changes." He raised and lowered each palm like a scale. "You've got nothing to lose. Even if she decides to withhold your daughter, at least you'll have given it all you can." Noah started talking louder and stood up. "We have to go win your daughter back! We'll use intricate verbal tactics – possibly even briberies." He circled around the tiny porch stopping every few words to prop his foot on the protective palisade. "What's her favorite type of fruit? Actually, nevermind. Does she like horses? No, we shouldn't have to use force because that would negate our credibility. But we'll need to go now."

"Now?" I asked.

"Tonight is our best chance. I think you're ready Gumby. Close enough anyway. We have to catch her before she makes a definitive decision. And since the power is out all over the place we'll be able to catch her in a moment of vulnerability. And if Eris doesn't agree, we can always kidnap Luna! Let's move out!"

"Do you really think I should go?" Mira asked, still not sure if Noah was fully serious. "Don't you think if Eris sees Hurley with a girl she'll be less likely to agree with anything we have to say."

"Good point. Way to think ahead in terms of the schematics. But you two will come as reinforcements. You can keep us hyped up on the drive over to…where did you say she was staying?"

"Julie's house. Over just past the high school."

"Right. Plus we'll want you both there for the celebration afterwards. Just duck down in the car while we put Eris under our linguistic spell."

"I don't know man."

"Trust me. Have I led you astray yet?"

Eris' Jeep was still parked outside along with John's black truck under the dark street lamps. It was late, well past your normal bedtime, the time of night when everything solid is cloaked in black, turned into a shapely shadow and the only visible color is the deep cerulean blue of the bruised sky.

"Alright ladies we'll be right back. Ready Gumby?"

I thought of when I came here a few days before, when I was unable to act, when I was peering into car windows and listening around corners, when I was only capable of picturing and experiencing things in my head.

"You knock," I said to Noah.

"No way."

"Will you at least do the talking?"

"I'll give you a proper introduction and chime in when necessary but this is all you. It has to be."

He slapped me on the back and knocked on the door. No answer. Noah put his ear up against the door, listened for movement inside.

"Do you hear anything?"

"Not yet."

"You try."

I knocked and something stirred inside. We watched through the window as a candle – blurred at the edges of the light – bobbed and floated towards us. The wood door, painted deep red, opened and Eris stood on the other side. She looked at me, then at Noah, then back at me again.

"Hurley?"

"Yeah."

"What are you doing here?" she said in a harsh whisper. Her voice sounded different, coarser, more friction involved. And even in the dark her face was still so shiny, lathered in smooth film, bouncing off the moon and the candle. "I have nothing to say to you, okay?" She started to shut the door.

"We just have a few urgent matters that we need to discuss." Noah said. "It will only take a few minutes to resolve if we begin presently."

"He does all your talking for you now?"

"No. I mean…look…can we just talk for a minute?"

"Not with your lawyer or whoever this guy is."

I looked over at Noah, not wanting him to leave. "Certainly. I'll wait in the bushes by the roadside while I look over some legal paperwork by flashlight."

Eris came out to the concrete porch and we sat in two white wicker chairs. She smelled like mints, like our bed sheets, the smell sending vibrations all through my throat.

"Are you here to talk about custody?"

> *her face is so bright, so shiny even in the dark*
> *and what is reflecting off it?*
> *and how is it so dark out and her face is so wet and bright?*
> *and it's black everywhere*
> *and this is not how it was supposed to be*

"Yeah."

"Well you're not going to get her. It's as simple as that. I know what you've been keeping around the apartment. I know what you've been bringing around Luna. And then when I went over to pick up my stuff on Wednesday, I ended up bringing John with me. And the apartment was totally wrecked. The whole place smelled like smoke and in the trash, I saw straws and aluminum foil with zigzags burnt into it. And I found a bag of some kind of brown stuff. I don't even know what it was, but John said he knew."[38]

"What? There's no way. That's not from me."

"Well then whose is it?"

"It must've been Al's. I gave him a key."

"Who is Al?"

"It doesn't matter."

---

[38] Even though she was convinced of it, I swear I wasn't into anything hard at the time.

"Hurley. It does matter. You have a daughter. I still think the drugs were yours, but even if they weren't, you shouldn't be giving out keys to people who will bring that around. You can't do that."

It was quiet and cool out, the air hardening and shattering on my skin on contact. Eris had a thin cardigan wrapped over her shoulders and soft red pajama shorts on the bottom. She shifted to pull the fabric between her bare legs and threaded wicker.

"So you and John?" I asked nodding towards his truck.

"Yeah."

"How long?"

"Since the start of the year. At Julie's New Year's party."

"Right."

"What about your new girl?"

"What do you mean?"

"Well I also saw someone's lip gloss at the apartment – which by the way is in my name still – when I went to pick up my stuff. I know it wasn't mine and unless you started using lemon flavored lip gloss then I figured someone else had been there with you."

"Yeah. I mean it's not like that," I said quickly. "I don't know. It's just starting right now."

We looked in opposite directions.

"Listen I don't know why you're here but I've made up my mind about custody. You're not getting her. You're not good for her. Not right now. John took pictures of the apartment when we went over. And he's a cop so he'll be a character witness if you decide to take this to court. I really don't want to drag you through the mud with this, okay? You'll lose your job. So just go. Let's make this easy."

"Can I at least see her?"

"She's not here right now. And I'm sorry about your loss by the way." She stood up to go back inside.

> *where's Luna?*
> *my loss?*
> *does she know about my father or does she mean losing Luna?*

277

Enfeebled, I got up to leave.

i should say something
and i should be able to tell Luna that i said something
and when she asks about this moment i want to be able to tell her
i said something.

I stood up, my blood thickening and I stuck my hand into my right pocket for your button. I turned around to look at Eris.

"Look I'm not going to beg. But I don't think Luna should miss out on having a dad just because this didn't work out and you think I'm garbage." My voice quivered – my throat still weak with vibration – but I raised my volume to try to cover the breakage. "You know I love her and even though I'm not the best and most stable, I would do anything for her. And you know that."

Eris' skin creased across her forehead, taken aback by my assertiveness.

"All I'm asking is that you just think about whatever you do before you do it. If we could just work something out…" I trailed off. "She doesn't need her father to be regulated. That's not right. All I'm saying is just think about what you're doing." She turned to go inside, not saying anything. "And you were right about the button – it popped off."

I took your brown button out of my pocket, flicked it in the air and caught it. "I'll hang onto it so she doesn't choke on it."

Eris carried her candle back inside, and I got back in the car where everyone was waiting for me in the dark.

"How'd it go?" Noah asked from the driver's seat.

"I don't know. Not good, I think."

"Well at least you tried. And you never know. She might come around."

"You don't know Eris like I do. She doesn't back down when she thinks she's right."

"So what now?" Kylie asked from the back seat. "Do we celebrate or mourn?"

"Neither. I've got a better idea."

Noah pulled out of the neighborhood, onto Eaton Avenue which he took out to SR-128 towards New Haven.

"We're not going out to the cabin are we? And you shouldn't really be driving should you?"

"No on both accounts."

I prepared for the worst, submitted – and I'm not proud of this – to the idea that I would not be the father that I wanted to be, would not be allowed to be. I thought it was already out of my control, that I had already sealed my fate, that I was destined to be a repeat.

> maybe i should start a collection for her, in her name, really.
> i could get tons of stamps, or maybe some kind of rare doll.
> yes.
> dolls.
> i will get every doll in the whole damn set
> and i will give them to her when she's older
> and tell her how she used to love these dolls,
> how she played with them all the time,
> couldn't get enough of these goddamn dolls
> and she will pick one up and smell the hair of the doll,
> searching for familiarity
> and smelling for her younger self,
> testing if the smell could take her back to the memory,
> could give her back a childhood that she had forgotten,
> that had existed only in her mind
> and only as a possibility

"Do they still make Beanie Babies?" I asked as we parked the car outside a small deserted fair site fenced off at the road side. I saw a shoddy roller coaster and curvy go-kart track inside.

"Probably. Why?"

"Nevermind. What are we doing here?"

Noah shrugged. "You got anything to eat or drink in here?" he asked Kylie.

"Yeah I think so." She reached under the seats and pulled out a partial bottle of cheap red wine, two unopened rows of wheat crackers in plastic sleeves, and a tied off plastic wrapper of Styrofoam cups.

"Perfect." Noah said.

We all got out and walked up to the fence tied shut with thick metal chain links.

"I don't think we're gonna be able to get in," I said shaking the gate weakly. "We'd better just head back. I mean we're probably not supposed to be out here. What if someone drives by?"[39]

"Relax. We'll just jump over."

Noah leaned his shoulder up against the fence and cupped his hands into a stepping stone which Kylie used to launch herself over. Mira followed.

"You're up buddy."

"I don't know."

"Come on Hurley. It's fine. Just jump over," Mira said from the other side.

I put my right shoe on Noah's hand and he catapulted me over. I landed on my stomach, scrapping my soft palms on jagged pebbles.

"You okay?" Mira asked, helping me up.

"Fine, yeah. Thanks."

Noah put the wine, crackers, and cups in his plastic grocery bag and scaled the fence to join us.

"They don't still run this do they?" Mira asked looking up at the roller coaster.

"I don't know. It looks like it works."

Noah knocked his knuckles against the red and white metal twisting upward about fifty feet at its peak, nearly scraping the ground at its trough. There didn't appear to be any flipping at any points, though it spiraled into a helix towards the end. Noah balanced four Styrofoam cups across the metal bars and emptied the wine bottle across them, filling each one to the brim.

---

[39] From what I hear, you're already more outwardly fearless than I was then.

"To Hurley," he said raising his cup. "The best father I know."

We all took a sip of our wine and got into the cars attached to the coaster – Noah and Kylie in a car in the back, while Mira and I shared a car in the front.

"It's chilly out here," she said scooting up against me, sipping on her flimsy cup of wine. I hesitated and then wrapped my arm around her shoulder. Leaning into her, my gray velvet pouch fell out of my pocket, a few pills scattering onto the metal seat.

"What is it with all the pills?" she asked scooping them up.

"I don't know."

"Come on."

"Guilt, I guess."

"Guilt over what?"

"A lot of things. Too much to condense. It's not worth hashing out."

"Of course it is. I want to know."

"You sure?"

"Absolutely."

"Well I had this really good friend, her name was Kolby, when I was growing up. This was when I lived in Illinois still. And we lived on the same street so I'd walk down to see her all the time during the summers. And so one day when I was seven, summer of '91 I think, we were sword fighting with a stick or something when we stumbled across this weird looking shriveled up boot-shaped nest hanging from a tree. And so being the brave one, she took the stick and started poking it."

I cleared my throat, constricting and causing my voice to squeak.

"Anyway. When she poked the nest a few hornets scattered out. They moved like one body, like one mind and – it's so weird how I can see it so clearly now – one of the bees separated from the body and just hovered – its wings all blurry – and it just kind of backed up and landed on her arm, poking the stinger into her skin all in one quick motion. And her skin started to swell up immediately and I remember her looking at me and her eyes were just like these floodgates getting ready to burst. And so she swatted and killed the wasp on her arm, which – and I didn't know this at the time; I read up on it years later – but it made the wasp release this pheromone that is basically a battle call for the rest of the brood inside the nest. So once they got wind of their fallen comrade they all came rushing out of their cells in the nest and I swear to God it looked like something out of a cartoon. And of course the scent led them straight to Kolby who I don't know if I mentioned this was almost completely deaf. And, I mean, I don't know if you know any deaf people but it seems like since they're missing a sense, all the other ones are more intense. So she always had a heightened sense of touch and was really ticklish. Anyway, so as they started swarming her, she fell over and was shrieking in that terrible pitch that only deaf people have the gall to hit and was signing 'Help Me!' over and over again."

I stopped to catch my breath, subconsciously talking faster. I looked behind us to see what Noah was doing. He and Kylie had moved from their roller coaster seat and were spinning with their arms outstretched on the go-kart track.

"But I just kind of stood there, you know, paralyzed by what I was seeing. I didn't know what to do. But eventually I stumbled away – and I keep thinking now, I mean, why did I just stand there, why was my first reaction to not act and then to run? – because then I ran up to her front door to get her parents. I rang the doorbell and when her mom came she asked me what was wrong. But I couldn't say anything. The words were caught in the back of my throat. I remember the blood in my arms and legs felt thick and spiked, everything inside me clanking together. I could clearly feel my heart trying to push my thick blood and it was making my limbs feel like they were being tickled from the inside. And I just felt really dizzy and nauseous. But I couldn't say anything. It was like my brain synapses were just refusing to fire. I guess eventually Kolby's mom heard her in the backyard because she pulled me inside and ran out the back door. Anyway, it turns out that Kolby was deathly allergic to the Northern Paper Wasp and she was stung well over a hundred times and died on the way to the hospital."

"Jesus."

"So anyway I guess that's the root, everything happening now stems and grows out of that somehow. Basically anytime I hear anything that buzzes, like the white noise of a crowd or something, or anytime I ring a doorbell or see something boot shaped, I get triggered, feel everything slow down inside me, feel the viscosity of my blood change. And with everything with my father and things with Eris and Luna now, it just adds up and it's just better to dull it out."

She looked at the bottom of our metal seat, looked down at our crumbs, then up into my eyes – old and dark.

"Why haven't you told me any of this before?"

"I don't know, I mean, it's fine. It was a long time ago. And I'm just not the kind of person who likes to drone on about my baggage. Everyone has baggage right? And everyone thinks that theirs is the heaviest. And I just don't want to add to the cycle of self-imposed pity. There's enough of that going around already."

We looked up into the intricate curvatures of the metal roller coaster and sat quietly in our seat sipping on our wine, which stained the inside of the Styrofoam red. I pulled out my notebook.

Sketchy
-Stinky's Gas Station
-Noah's mailbox
-The paraphernalia scatter around here.
-My foot blisters
-Realistic Mannequins
-Roller Coasters and Styrofoam

Masculine
-Emotional Vulnerability
-Accepting the Past

Mira and I split a row of crackers, huddled up in the cool summer night. I felt her muscles quivering and wrapped her up tighter against my ribs, pulled her into my body. Kylie came up to us winded and sniffling from running around the track. Her arm veins were bulging, her eyes blackening, the top button of her pants undone.

"We're getting cold and the wine is gone. You guys want to head back to our place?"

So we reverse-hopped the fence and drove back to their dark apartment where we all sat around late into the evening drinking skunked beers and smoking stale cigarettes, loosening ourselves. But it wasn't a morose or angry, my-father's-funeral-is-tomorrow kind of drinking. We all drank in relative moderation punctuated with cigarettes to get the beer taste off our tongues. I drank just enough to maintain my constant mental sedation of the past few days.

The conversation was alternatively light and heavy, especially between Noah and Kylie who were engaged in some kind of sexual, intellectual bantering. But the community and the companionship were comforting. At around two in the morning, Mira stood up and stretched.

"I think I'm gonna head to bed."

She put out her cigarette in a half-size glass Mickey Mouse cup that doubled as an ashtray on their porch.

"Yeah we should probably all turn in. We've got a big day ahead of us," Noah said.

"You guys can stay here. I'm sure you don't want to go back to your place tonight, right?"

"No, not really. You sure you don't mind if we stay?"

"Not at all."

Mira tested the light switch when she walked in and the whole living room lit up in watered-down yellows and blues from their twisty-armed lamps.

"I guess the power's back on now."

We all shrugged with tired indifference. Mira offered me her bed, though not in a sexual way.

→She has invited me to her bed.
    →She's at least comfortable with the idea of sex.
        →Though I don't think that's what she's after.
        →I don't think I want to either.
            →It's too soon.
        →But it would be nice to at least sleep next to someone.
            →Not just someone; her in particular.
        ←But I don't deserve that.
    ←She's just being polite.
        →No.
        →This is real. This is right.
    ←But I should take it slow, not come on too strong.
←And I'm drunk and smell like a dead rodent.
    →True.
    →I should be sober and smell good when we get in bed together.
    →**Offer Denied.**

"No thanks. I'll just sleep on the couch."

We hugged again, this time longer, before she went to her bedroom and turned out the lights. I was too tall to fit lengthwise on the fake-leather couch so I slept on the floor in the living room draped across two seat cushions partially covered with a yellow hand-me-down quilt. On the opposite side of the room, Noah slept face up, spread eagle on the rug. Since hiking the Appalachian Trail, he had been a heavy, powerful sleeper that could fall asleep in an instant and could sleep through anything. But he only slept in small doses – three, maybe four hours at a time. Even though I was exhausted and had slept less than him these last few days together, I never once heard him complain about being tired. I guess his mind and body would shut down in his sleep in ways I was incapable of replicating.

what is it like to live in that kind of body?

I don't know what time it was when I woke up shivering, the room smelling like baby powder. I thought about what my life would look like without you as a constant presence, thought about how the shape of my purpose would wilt and curve without you. I listened to the low hum of the air conditioner, the low hum of my heart. My back, sagging in between the two cushions, began to ache again – the bottom tip of my spine sending out circular pang-waves evenly throughout my body. I wasn't cold but I couldn't stop my muscles from convulsing and my teeth from clanging together.

I got up and tucked the cushions back into the couch before I went into Mira's room. The door was already cracked – a quiet invitation – but the hinges squeaked as I tapped it open all the way with my knuckles. Mira, apparently a light sleeper as well, stirred in her twin-sized bed.

"Are you coming in?"

I crawled into bed wearing only my boxer shorts, tried to keep my arms at my sides. But the bed was too small, so the spaces between our elbows and knees disappeared – her feet, imperfectly cold. We didn't kiss or talk but just lay there locked like fingers on opposite hands of the same body until she fell asleep. I knew she was out when I felt her body twitch, felt her body resist the fade into her subconscious, felt her heart slow and tap rhythmically on the cage of bones that protected my own.

We woke up the next morning in the exact same position – fetal, each cocooning the other. No one, tiny or ghostly, shuffled in my head, and I knew exactly where I was. And though we had slept in the same bed together once before, this was the first time I remembered it. I don't want to aggrandize it too much because I'm sure you're not really interested in hearing about Mira after all that your mother has said, but it was just nice waking up with someone who I knew wanted to sleep next to me. I looked at her bedside clock: 9:43 a.m. EST.

> *a good time.*
> *not too early and not too late*
> *and maybe i'll cook us breakfast –*
> *eggs, both scrambled and sunny;*
> *toast, both French and American;*
> *tea of all flavors and nationalities*
> *and maybe i'll even bake banana bread.*
> *do i know how to make banana bread?*[40]

286

I untangled my limbs and stretched out, my feet hanging off the end of the mattress.

→I hate being tall.
    →I hate being tall because he is tall.
        →Now I have to say that he WAS tall instead of IS tall.
            →Though I guess his body is the same height even if it's dead.
                →And in the ground.
                →SHITFUCK!

"We're late."

I scrambled out of the tiny bed.

"Shit, his funeral starts in four hours," I said pacing around the walls of her room looking for my clothes. Mira sat up rubbing her eyes. The light of the morning bounced off her empty white walls causing us to both squint.

"What're you doing?"

"We need to leave now. My father's funeral. If we leave right now we can still make it on time."

"God. I forgot to set my alarm. How long will it take to get there?" she asked, still groggy.

"Four hours. Three and a half hours if we haul ass. Good thing we have that rental."

I went out into the living room, still in my boxers, to see if Noah was awake. He was not there but I found my dirty clothes that I left out in the living room folded neatly on the arm of the couch. Out the window I saw our rented vehicle was gone too. Mira, sleepy-eyed and smooth-skinned, joined me by the window, yawning, her hair thick and dry.

"Where's the car?"

"I don't know. And I don't know where Noah is either. That dipshit better not have bailed and stranded me here."

"Why would he do that?"

"Let's just say he doesn't have the best track record."

---

[40] I do not.

"Well let's get ready to go. We can take Kylie's car. She's still asleep, but she lets me borrow it all the time."

Mira went back to her room to get ready and just as she did, a green Explorer turned into the apartment complex, parked where the rental had been. Noah got out of the car looking smug.

"Where the fuck have you been?!"

"Cool it, Gumby. I was trading in the car for something more appropriate for the spirit of the journey." In the direct sunlight, Noah looked more unstable, his skin gaunt and loose over his bones. "Plus we needed more room for our third traveler. Sorry I took a little longer than expected. I had to help someone with a flat tire on the side of the road. They were having some problems getting it jacked up but I set them straight."

"Whatever man, are you ready to go? We can still make it on time if we leave right now."

"Ready when you are captain."

We went back inside to get Mira who was walking down the hallway dressed in a loose knee-length black rippled skirt. I had never seen her in a skirt before. I had never seen her in black before either. She was looking down at the ground fixing her hair.

"Hey Hurley have you seen my…hey you're back Noah," she said looking up. She also had on a vintage-Mira white v-neck t-shirt with words written in fresh permanent marker.

"So it goes…"

"Yeah and all your stuff is already loaded up in the get-away car. So's yours Cetus. Shall we?"

We all looked around at each other, though their eyes both ended on me, waiting for me to either call it off or on.

"Alright then. Let's go. I'll drive," I said taking the keys out of Noah's hand.

When I first got my license, I loved driving. For a lot of people it's the symbolic freedom that comes with getting a license, but I really just loved the actual act of driving. I loved taking round turns, loved that trippy centrifugal feeling where my body and organs shifted angularly without my consent, loved the way the car shook and tried to resist while I steadied the wheel. And I always loved the way the turn signal clicked in whatever time signature I wanted it to click in, loved the squeak of the windshield wipers against the dry glass, loved how driving connects everyone, how we're all dependent on each other to follow the same rules, to play the same game. I loved the idea that a red light meant stop to everyone. It was a huge uplifting trust game, everyone agreeing to stop so the people with the green arrow could turn, everyone deferring to the rules, all of us in it together, in on the same joke. I would never let anyone else drive, always took the wheel without asking.

But something happened with the internal mechanisms of my first car, something to do with the steering components. And so right before I graduated high school, my car stopped being able to make right turns, only went left. It was fine for a while. It just took me longer to get places because I had to go in a round-about sort of way. But after reading *Silent Spring* my senior year, I developed stronger environmental convictions so I sold my car for parts and just started using my bicycle. And after that I just never had a reason to drive, outside of occasional short trips with Eris in the passenger seat. So driving on the interstate towards Illinois was a nostalgic rush.

Crossing the border into Indiana, the entrance placard read "Crossroads of America" but, to be honest, it felt more like an erasable afterthought full of corn and skinny trees – trees like telephone poles, like slingshots. I wanted to skip the whole state, to teleport across it. It was the only state standing between me and my dead father.

The scenery went by the window unchanged – a massively bland, flat landscape spotted with painter's trees blurring on unreachable hills. I don't know if this is unique to Indiana but I'll always associate the practice with the state since I first noticed the peculiarity on this drive. They like to spell out the name of each town on the roadside with various forms of creative landscaping – shrubberies, stonework, perennials – that created a well-labeled sky grid.

Mira sat in the front next to me and Noah, who had developed a habit of pointing out grammatical mistakes on street signs and billboards, sat in the back seat, leaning up towards us like a little kid with his elbows on the front arm rests. Mira and Noah had picked up on a buzzed conversation from the night before. He had been antagonizing Mira about her love for animals. I was trying to zone out, to avoid all conversation, but I inevitably picked up a few lines of their discussion between thought bubbles.

"So you think that animals have thoughts?" Noah asked.

"No I didn't say that. I don't think they do, at least not in the same way that we do," said Mira. "But that doesn't mean that they don't have feelings."

black hole.
brown button.
black hole.
brown button.

"See I think they can experience pain but that they can't suffer."

"That makes no sense!"

"Alright, hear me out. I don't think animals fear death. Yes, they still have a survival instinct, but they don't fear death in the same way that we do so they can't suffer in the same way that we do."

dead father.
brown button.
dead father.
brown button.

290

"But if you think they can feel pain then why can't they suffer from the fear of feeling more pain."

"Interesting. I don't know. Maybe you're right. Are you siding with her?" Noah turned towards me.

"Sure," I said trying to focus on the road. I tried to feel – in my body, in my chest, in my platelets, in my strings and loops – the friction of the tires on the pavement underneath our feet, tried to feel more connected to what was happening.

dead father
and our bodies are a continuum
and our souls are a conduit to other souls

"What do *you* think Noah?" Mira said sarcastically, unbuckling and turning around completely in her seat.

I focused on the lines on the road and the quivering needle on the speedometer.

things are more easily measured at high speeds
and variations are more noticeable
and do i feel the same about my father at this velocity?
and where is the threshold?

It was hot outside, everything moving in waves, in quick tiny ripples. The pavement at the edge of the moving horizon looked like glass, like melted windows.

"…Descartes' opinion on the subject…"

→Physics tells us that nothing – save light – can travel at the speed of light because it would require an infinite amount of energy to be exerted on the object.

→My inner string, plucked by the death of my father and the thought of losing my daughter, is vibrating with an infinite amount of energy.

→I should be able to travel at – or break – the speed of light.

what does light look like as you pass it in the fast lane
and would it give me the finger as i speed by?

291

"…rationis capax, I believe he called it…"

no matter when i get there, it will not stop him from being dead,
but the sooner i arrive, the higher probability i have of seeing him
before his soul leaves his body
and is there a soul?
and no one can ever know
and is there free will?
and did he decide this or was this decided for us?
and we can only do what our bodies our capable of doing
so our freedom is limited from the beginning
and it's so god-damn sad to never know
and is the fucking set of all sets self-contained?

"…only parts of the sensory experience are available to different…"

Mira put her hand on the back of my neck, which felt cool against my red, sunburnt skin. But for some reason it annoyed me, shoved me deeper into my head. I followed the curves of the road with the tires on the inside line, maxing out my speed and angle. I looked at the car clock: 11:34 a.m. EST. As the four ticked to a five I felt myself getting angrier, felt my ears heating up and my mind catching back onto their conversation.

"Blue Sky."

"Cow."

I think they had finished their discussion about animals and were playing the game where each person alternately has to name a visible object that starts with the next letter in the alphabet all the way to 'Z.' By my calculation, they were on the letter 'D.'

dead father

"Duck," Mira said.

"Hey, can you guys just fucking cool it!"

I instantly regretted snapping at them, thankful that they were both there to distract me and keep me company. They both quieted down and Noah leaned back in his seat.

"I'm sorry. It's just. I don't know. I'm sorry."

My outburst pulled me out of my head and back into the moment.

"Don't worry about it," Mira said. "I know this day sucks. When I went to my mom's funeral, I remember feeling really angry. The smallest little thing would set me off. I remember my dad wanted me to wear this flowery dress and I wanted to wear jeans and it made me so mad that he wanted me to wear something else. But I knew I wasn't really angry about the dress. I should have been mad at my mom, if anyone, but really I was mad at myself for some reason. Like there was some unnamed thing that I could have done differently that would have changed the outcome."

"Your mom died?" Noah asked.

"Yeah she killed herself when I was eleven."

"That's some heavy shit." His eyes looked glazed and he was slouching over in his seat, his arms at his sides.

"But you have to remember," Mira said picking up on her previous thought, "that it has nothing to do with you. Whatever is going to happen is going to happen no matter what. I don't know if you believe in that kind of existentialist shit, free will vs. fatalism and all that, but I have to believe to be able to keep going sometimes."

Her eyes welled up again so she took the conversation a different direction to avoid full-fledged tears.

"Tell me something about your dad that you liked. Sometimes it's better to think about the good times rather than what you would've liked to have done differently."

"My father didn't really like me. There weren't a whole lot of good times."

"Come on, I bet there was something. Maybe when you were really young?"

"Well I guess when I was little he taught me how to swim. I remember he would take me and Brody to the pool on the weekends in the summer. I was maybe four years old or something so Brody already knew how to swim. He would go play with his friends in the deep end, jumping off the diving board and all that. But my father stayed with me in the shallow

293

end right by the stairs. The first thing he taught me was how to do the 'dead man's float' – that's what he called it."

We both laughed uncomfortably, turned towards our windows.

"Is that a real thing?"

"Yeah, sure. It's when you hold your breath and float on your stomach for as long as possible. I have no idea what you would ever use that for, now that I'm thinking about it, but that's the first thing I remember learning. I guess, maybe, he was trying to get me used to being under water and to holding my breath, I don't know. But I would do it for like fifteen or twenty seconds and the whole time he would have his hand underwater on my chest. I remember feeling his massive hand over my heart while I was under. And when I would come up gasping for air, he would congratulate me like I had really accomplished something. God, I haven't thought about that in a long time. But yeah, I guess that's one of my first memories of him, one of the good ones."

"I don't know but he doesn't seem that bad."

"I mean you're probably right. I think more than anything he just didn't know how to accept things that were different than him. I was always into art instead of athletics and I was naturally reserved rather than aggressively outspoken. And I think he just didn't know how to relate to me. He just had a very clear idea of what he wanted his boys to be and I messed up that image for him."

"Not that it's any of my business, but what exactly is the deal with your dad? I mean I know he just basically ditched you guys when you were…what? Eleven."

"Yeah."

"But he made amends with everyone except you, right?"

"Yeah." She raised her brows. "I don't know, I mean I just felt like we didn't even matter, like we were completely expendable to him when he moved out to California with some younger girl. It just seemed so selfish."

"But I'm sure everyone felt that way and they've all patched things up. There's got to be something else."

There was a grunting noise coming from the backseat. We both looked back over our shoulders and saw Noah with his eyes closed, arms splayed across the seat, his mouth wide open, tongue visible.

"He's kind of a weird dude – sort of gets under your skin," Mira said.

"Yeah but he's alright, I guess."

"And he smells terrible. Actually you guys both do to be honest. It's seriously like the asshole's asshole in here."

"Yeah sorry, I haven't been able to shower properly in a couple days. I wish I had time to shower this morning." I rolled both the front windows down.

"Thanks," she said leaning her face out the window. "Why don't we stop and pick up a change of clothes at least for you?"

"There's no time. We'll barely make it as it is."

I looked at the clock: 12:34 p.m. EST.

"So back to your dad. What's the real deal there?"

"I know you're right – that there's more to it. And I've actually been thinking about it a lot lately. Because I agreed to meet him later this year. And I had all these statistics that I've been collecting for – God like a decade I guess. Jesus has it really been that long? Anyway I had these probability charts and graphs with all this data collected from people about how often they see their kids and stuff like that so I could somehow prove that my father's decision was not only immoral but a numerical aberration. But the data just wasn't there so I kept putting the meeting off. But eventually it just got to the point where it felt like I just had to release him because the resentment was like a toxin in my blood or something."

"Is that why you resented him so much?"

"No I think the reason I resented him so much was because I felt like I had to live a double life growing up. And I just felt like I couldn't be myself. But I'm realizing now that really that's my fault just as much as it was his. If I had just been up front about things he might have been fine with it. I don't know. I guess I'll never know now."

Mira dozed off in the side seat, her feet tucked under her skirt, her eyes darting around under her eyelids. And so I was left quietly to my own thoughts, which I did my best to push away from my father, away from losing you. So I thought about driving. I typically don't like to switch lanes as I drive. But if ever there was a time to drive erratically, this was it. I weaved in and out of cars, always posturing for better position, for a clearer path. Each time I changed lanes, somewhere ahead of me, a car would switch in my previous lane. It was one of those quirky phenomenons that I had always noticed since I first got my license, even if I was in the passenger seat. And I dismissed it on the grounds that I probably only noticed it when it happened and just overlooked the normalcy of it not happening. But while I was driving towards my dad's funeral, it kept happening, lane-switch after lane-switch. I couldn't help but wonder if there was some kind of microcosmic universal balance going on.

what if i only laugh because someone else is crying?
and had someone been born the same moment that my father died?
and is the human population trying to be static?
but hasn't the population risen over time?
but what if the balance manifests itself in different forms?
not like some kind of reincarnation type thing
but what if it is just some universal emotional ecological energy?
and so what if my dad is never gone?
and what if no one is ever gone?
and so what if i…

I forced myself to stop thinking, to stop over-analyzing[41] because it was getting me nowhere. I switched lanes again and drove in silence until we crossed the Illinois border thinking

---

[41] If you have a tendency, maybe a dormant one, to do this too, now you know where it came from.

instead back over the events of the last few days, of the people I'd met and the things I'd felt[42]. Despite my attempts to block it, I spiraled into a series of semi-related questions.

is life just a book in desperate need of explication dropped into my lap?
and should i be mapping out the themes?
and are there patterns in nature that i am supposed to be seeing?
or is the non-pattern the actual pattern?
but there are patterns everywhere;
pick up a leaf or truncate a tree –
swirls and veins, maps and ripples
are all different versions of each other
and if pi is calculated out far enough will it ever repeat?
and does it matter?
and are we supposed to keep calculating it out
until we catch the melody

I reigned myself in again. The air coming in through the cracked window on the front passenger side lessoned as I finally let up on the accelerator and veered right towards our interstate exit. It must have been the change in air pressure or lack of white noise that woke Mira.

"How long was I asleep?" She unfolded her feet out from under her skirt.

"I don't know." I looked at the car clock above the stereo: 2:27 p.m. EST. I had completely lost track of time.

"Fuck! The funeral started half an hour ago! God-fucking-damnit!"

my driving failed
and i failed
and i failed
and i failed
and
fuck
fuck
fuck it.

---

[42] And intentionally not felt.

I slammed my hands on the steering wheel causing us to swerve onto the shoulder of the exit ramp. My respiratory system started malfunctioning and the organs in my chest tangled and turned, coiling inside. The symptoms were coming in full force: blurry vision, hot skin, slippery skin, heavy head, light head, no head.

fuck it and bring in the hard ones
and let's do this right

The commotion broke even the heavy sleep of Noah. Through the rear-view mirror I saw him pull one of my missing blue cylindrical pills out of his pocket, place it on his tongue. His face was white, thinner under his beard, his lips colorless.

"What's going on? Calm down Gumby," he said from the back. "Just pull the ship over and we'll figure something out."

I made a right turn and pulled into a gas station, shutting off the engine.

"I can't believe I missed it."

"Come on we might still have time to catch the end of it. What time did it start?" Mira asked.

"There's no point. It started at two o'clock sharp."

Noah pulled a flask out of his plastic grocery bag on the floorboard, took a heavy drag and then passed it up to me. Mira glared at him. I took a long drag as well. It tasted like burnt wood chips and brown sugar: whiskey – hot in the back of my throat and warm at the bottom of my empty stomach.

"What? I came prepared for both success and failure," Noah said sticking his neck out. "Well *he* seems to appreciate it."

Noah nodded at me slapping my lips together. I pulled my lighter out of my pocket and pressed my thumb hard against the rippled trigger, pressed down until I had lines in my skin.

"Wait, you said it starts at two, right? That's local time I assume isn't it?"

"What?"

299

"Well I'm guessing that Brody told you it was at two o'clock local time. Which means…"

"Which means we're actually early! We still have half an hour to get there!" Noah yelled too loudly. He was easily excitable, always wearing his emotions on his sleeve. I was still confused with the whiskey beginning to dizzy me. Mira read it on my face, contorted and wrinkled.

"Illinois is on central time. When we crossed the border, an hour fell off the clocks," Mira explained.

"Central time! We can still make it?!"

"Yes!"

"Yeah? Fuck yeah!"

I took another swig of the whiskey, this time celebratory, and cranked the engine again. I felt like clapping and chanting again, singing an intricate paean.

"I think we need some more victory whiskey," Noah said shaking his empty flask.

"Isn't the idea of showing up buzzed at your father's funeral a little depressing?" Mira asked.

"I think it's fitting," Noah said.

"I think it's necessary," I said.

Noah got out of the car and walked into the gas station. While my organs returned to equilibrium, I got out as well and circled around the car a few times, energy steaming off my buzzing skin. I stopped by Mira's window.

"Do you have a black marker? Or whatever you use to write on your shirts?"

"Yeah sure. What do you want it for?" She leaned down in the floorboard to dig through her duct tape purse and resurfaced with a black marker in her palm.

"I'm gonna make my own."

I took my gray shirt off and laid it across the front of the Explorer and wrote across the chest.

"A Manuel for Sons"

Noah walked out holding a bottle of bourbon whiskey in the air like a trophy in one hand and a row of plastic cups in the other. He filled up his flask using a tiny metallic funnel that he also carried in his plastic grocery bag. Mira poured a few shots worth into a cup. I grabbed the bottle around the neck. We all held up our drinks sitting around in the green rented Explorer, the engine running.

"What are we drinking to?" Mira asked.

"To dads everywhere," I said.

When we pulled up to the funeral home, the parking lot was already filled and it was five till two.[43] Thanks to the whiskey, I was quickly losing control of my finer motor skills, losing sight of the details so I was glad to have the car safely parked.

"You want to all go in together or do you want to go in alone?" Mira asked.

"Come on, you guys came all this way. I'm not gonna ditch you here."

We all got out of the car and looked up at the tall stately white building which stood on a small hill. Visually it had the look of a chapel, with an elaborate stone lintel over a colonnade of white pillars that jutted out from the main door, holding up a wrap-around porch on a second level. At the end of a hand-laid stone path, a wide line of sharp gray stairs led up and then took a hard right turn up towards the entrance.

"You go on ahead," Noah said touching my back. "We'll follow behind you in a few minutes."

"Okay, see you guys in a few."

My muscles itched under my skin. They needed to be worked, needed to deny the laws of inertia. I jogged up the stairs two, then three -- *can I do four? I cannot* -- at a time. My body which had been feeling creakier than it should have, felt young and efficient again. I was well-oiled, lubricated, double jointed everywhere. When I walked – chin up, eyes active – into the funeral home, I was still breathing heavily and the salty-white sweat stains on my shirt were moist anew. The door opened to an atrium that was white-dominated. There was a small bouquet of baby's breath and anemone sitting on a white side table with a picture of my father, who looked younger than

---

[43] Central Standard Time!

I expected. I imagined it being at least five years dated, though I really wasn't sure what my father had looked like in recent years. Next to the table was a half-open door which lead into another room crowded with people. Brody stood by the door in conversation with an unfamiliar man. We made eye contact from across the room and when he saw me he shook the man's hand, patted him on the shoulder twice before he came over to me. I immediately regretted not being better-dressed, became self-conscious. He had on a black three piece suit with a thick knotted tie tight under his white collar. People were gawking at me, turning up their noses at my filthy clothes, my muddy skin. I felt for my gray lighter, my pockets feeling too empty, weightless.

FRONT LEFT: FRONT RIGHT:
lighter (nearly empty)   pen
pouch of pills (nearly empty)   brown button

BACK LEFT: BACK RIGHT:
(empty)   notebook

"Hey, I'm glad you could make it," he said shaking my hand, pulling me close to him. His greeting was docile, actually appropriate. He patted me on the back, man-hug style. Up close, I saw that he was clean shaven, glass-eyed, and smelled of musk and pine.

"Have I missed anything yet?"

"No. Things are just getting started. The casket is through that door." He pointed to where he had been standing. "It looks like there's a line starting to form. You missed the viewing but you can go in and see him before we start."

I wanted to ask if it was open casket, if I would have to see his face up close. I had no interest in seeing his beard whiskers, didn't want to see his creases and skin folds and compare them to my own in the mirror. I feared our wrinkles were conjugates.

"Great."

"So how are you? Where have you been?" He looked me over, eyes crossing.

"Oh yeah, I'm fine."

"This is not a good look for you Hurley. Would you want Luna to see you like this?"

I ignored his questions, shuffled my feet and rubbed my wrists.

"Is that pasta sauce on your shirt?"

I looked down at the vomit stain on my shoulder.

"Yeah, I guess I'm a messy eater. So anyway, what is this exactly? I mean how do these things work? Is there a ceremony? Are we burying him right after? What's the plan?"

I wanted to put him in the ground as soon as possible, to make official what I'd already convinced myself was true.

"Let's go sit down for a minute."

"Come on, man. I'm fine. We don't need to have a sit-down."

I curled my fingers to imitate air-quotes as I said the hyphenated phrase. But he took no notice and was already walking out the back door, so I followed. The door opened into a circular courtyard with a small birch tree in the middle. Several leaves had fallen on the ground.

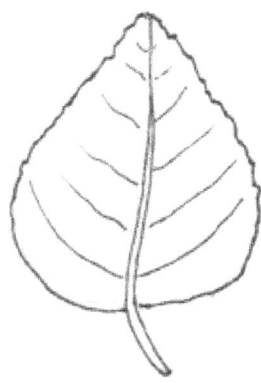

I sat next to Brody on a block of limestone jutting away from the outer wall.

"So where's Mom?"

"She didn't want to come. She said that she had already said all the goodbyes that she needed to get out. She's having his ashes delivered in an urn to their place where she'll keep them."

"So he's being cremated, not buried?"

> --I'm an ash sitting in an aging urn
> --Or dusted onto a brown lawn
> --Or dumped onto a makeshift tombstone.

"Right. This is just a ceremony and there are a few *designated* people giving speeches and then they'll take him away...and, well we'll get his ashes later."

He wanted to make it clear that I was not to speak publicly, that I was not to say anything negative. He chewed his gums with his lips.

"Do you know what happened to Dad?" he asked.

"Well you said that he had a heart attack."

"Right. But...," he paused to gather his thoughts, trying to decide the best way to articulate what he was about to say. "But do you know what happened to him in California after he left? Do you know why he left and why he came back and why Mom and him got back together?"

I shook my head. I wanted him to stop talking. I wanted to remember my father as I had framed him. He was a selfish man that died trying to atone for his sins. I wanted to be done with him. I didn't want him to be explained, to have behaved rationally, to become a martyr, to gain dignity. I'm guessing these feelings all sound familiar to you. I stood up to leave the circular courtyard, but Brody put his hand on my shoulder.

"Just hear me out." He didn't give me a chance to refute. "Well, like you know, he moved out there with Cassie, his girlfriend."

"And she was like twenty-three when he was forty?"

"Something like that, but that's not the point. That is what it is. And, trust me, I was upset about it too, but he really hated leaving us."

"Well if he hated it so much then he shouldn't have done it."

I turned to get up again.

"Look just let me finish. So he was out there for about seven years when he found out that she was making a cuckold of him. He left immediately because he couldn't deal with another betrayal like that. So that's when he came back to the Midwest."

"What do you mean *another* betrayal?"

"Right," Brody paused. "So the reason that he left in the first place was because Mom was unfaithful to him. When he found out, it really broke him. He decided that it would be best to leave so that they could both move on. He didn't think he could see her with someone else. Not every day. Right after that he met Cassie and they went to the West Coast. He had been trying to cover for Mom and that's why he never came around much. Because he wanted to protect her."

"Why are you telling me this now?"

"Because this is what Dad was trying to tell you when you punched him in the face a few years ago and what he's been trying to tell you ever since – despite Mom trying to stop him. He made us all promise not to tell you because he felt like he had to do it himself. He was just waiting for you to give him the chance. But I know he would have wanted you to know the truth and to know that he never stopped loving us. He wanted us back in his life more than anything. And especially after we both had kids. He hated that he was never able to see Luna."

"He wanted *you* back in his life." I wasn't sure what else to say but I felt myself getting angry so I just started an argument. "You were always his favorite. I mean, he went to you first right?"

"True. But I wasn't his favorite. He just knew that if he had me on his side he might actually have a chance of getting you back. It was the loss of you, the lack of a relationship with you that he regretted more than anything."

"Why has no one told me any of this before?"

"Well, like I said, Dad had tried to tell you several times, but..."

nothing is right and nothing is true
and nothing is stable and nothing is real
and no one is true to themselves
and no one is true to anyone

"Look I don't know why you're telling me this like it's some kind of casual addendum to his life. But it doesn't even matter now because…"

"I know you're angry, and trust me, I was too at first, but it is what it is."[44]

"…he's gone and I never knew him and regardless of why it happened or whatever, it won't change now because he's gone."

Fuming and confused, I stood up feeling dizzy, booze-loosened, whiskey-eyed. I stumbled on the metal grate under the tree. The roof was sinking down on me, the courtyard was shrinking, compressing, the air thick, every breath filled with tiny invisible flakes, heavy shards scraping the corners of my mouth, cutting my throat.

"Hurley…"

"I'm fine damnit!"

I grabbed the side of the wall and circled my way out of the courtyard, back through the main atrium, past where Mira and Noah were standing and out to the white pillars on the porch.

why had she never told me the truth about why he left?
and why had she let me falsely harbor my negativity?
and why had she let me believe a lie?
and does this absolve him for leaving?
and i was an asshole to him
and i didn't make it easy
and i haven't made it easy
and i've never made anything easy
and that's why the water is so black
and new growth follows every fire

---

[44] I hate that phrase. He said it all the time, and I couldn't stand it.

306

I wanted to leave, wanted to yell at my mom for not being at the funeral, wanted to bathe and scrub the skin off my muscles. I pulled out my notebook.

Masculine
-Emotional Vulnerability
-Accepting the Past
-Being honest

An urge to look at my father – to see him and be finished – buzzed around my skin.

→If I see him that way – dead – I will always picture him from that point on as a dead body.
    →A dead body would at least be more honest than the picture I had been carrying around of him in my head.
        →Which has just been shattered.
            →So I need a new, more accurate picture.
                →Which means I need to see him.
                    →Even if dead.

Mira stood at the doorway – the bottom of her loose skirt blowing in the breeze – sensing that she shouldn't say anything just yet. We went back inside, looked into the room past the white table where a line was forming, snaking its way up to the casket opened on the top half, flowers covering the bottom half. People were fanning themselves, shaking their collars. It was hot and we were all dripping. Another picture of my father bordered by a wreath made of purple statice flowers was on the left side of the casket. In the middle of the room there were white plastic fold-up chairs set up in rows, curved into a half oval with an aisle split down the middle. Behind the coffin was a short black podium.

Looking around the room, I first noticed how many men there were. Everywhere I looked, I saw fathers that were still alive. In every pair of hunched shoulders, I saw sons that had given their fathers a chance, that had given their lives a chance. I saw men with secrets, men with insecurities, men trying not to cry because men don't cry. I recognized few of them – a knifing reminder of my non-relationship with my father. They were probably friends that he had accumulated through our years of estrangement. It had been easier believing that none of them existed, that my father didn't have any kind of life, that he lived on an island as a recluse, chose to live in seclusion pondering penance.

and it's the most reclusive continent that powers us all

But I forced myself to look into as many faces, into as many eyes as possible. Most of the men looked sun-beaten and weather-worn though well-dressed, like old stones taken out and carefully polished. One man in particular caught my eye. He wore a black tweed jacket with a top hat and a gold-chain monocle on his right eye. The few hairs that poked out from the back and sides of his hat were a light gray, almost white color.

"This is beautiful," Mira said quietly from behind me.

Noah, who had followed us into the room, nodded in admiration, harnessing his buzz as the three of us stepped to the back of the line which would lead us up to my father's casket. I watched the people walk by my father's body trying to get an idea of what to do when I got there, of what behavior and mannerisms were normal and acceptable, searching for a prescribed way to act. Some said a few words, some just paused to look, others placed their hands on the casket. I think they were weighing the image of my dead father up against their memory of him – an image based on experience, on real-life sensory input. The only thing that I had to weigh him against was the image I had chosen to draw in my mind, an image based on a decayed lie. I wanted all the people in the room to have a personal projector screen attached to their head so each person could display an image of my father, the image of who he had been to each person. I wanted us all to walk around the room looking at each other's images of him– comparing and contrasting – so we could discuss and rest on some kind of agreed upon consensus of who he had been – an amalgamation of the images that he left behind in the minds of others.

The line shrank and I moved towards him, swaying sideways from right foot to left. I kept anticipating unbearable vibrations, some kind of anger to boil up to the surface and itch on my skin and for me to try to check out, to reach for a pill. But I forced myself down into the scene, forced myself to locate and identify my emotions, to feel and know each vibration so I could fully participate in the moment. Only when it breaks down can you be fully aware of your body, and only when you're fully aware of your body can you be fully aware of your emotions. I wanted to name each emotion and then concentrate them all, consolidate them into something more easily manageable. Writing about that moment now, writing about preparing to see my father's body, I still remember the emotion, the vibration, how my body felt while I was standing there. And when my body remembers how it felt, I feel that vibration again and my mind remembers the details of the scene. So I guess our minds – or at least my mind – stores memories in the body, in those hidden vibrations, those tiny quivering loops.

When I got up to my father's body, I had all the filters turned off, ignored anything synthetic, anything distilled in my system. My first reaction was how light his body looked, like it might float out of the coffin at any moment. Kolby, the only other dead body I had seen up close, had looked heavy, like she might fall through the bottom of her tiny casket, like gravity was finally going to win and that she would break through the ground, slide down into the molten lava and burn together with the other bodies expanding the Earth's rock-iron core. But my father's body was unburdened, his limbs like helium balloons.

is he tied down to the casket?
and how do i know if the soul has flown?
and are souls insoluble?
and are we all just a hologram?

His skin was pale, his eyes shut. I looked at his eyelids, looked at the tiny creases, the closed curtains. I waved my hand a few inches over his body to see if I could feel the magnetic energy floating outside his skin, some sort of static attraction that might snap my hand onto his body, something to indicate he was still there. But nothing was there, nothing tingled. Though as I held my hand over his body, I felt new vibrations, felt things rippling through my body, contracting my muscles, turning my blood to silk. With my body loosened, I felt an unexpected kinship, saw wavy images of your mother, of her with John and felt a vague, ethereal sense of empathy for my father, trapped in some kind of modern day fablio, secretly cuckolded – wrong but well-intentioned in his covering of tracks.

He was clean-shaven, looked foreign without the beard. And someone had dressed him in a well-pressed navy blue suit with a matching blue tie pushed cleanly up against his throat. His collar was buttoned tight, containing the clean skin around his neck which was pinched in the fabric to avoid drooping. I rubbed my fingers against my throat to see if my skin was loose, to see if we had that in common. He still had a full head of hair. His head, like mine, had always resisted balding. Growing up, I hated that our bodies had things in common, hated that our bodies had the same blood inside them. I rubbed and tapped my knuckles on the coffin, made of solid, deep brown and heavily lacquered wood. Brody had said he was being cremated anyway so I figured there wouldn't be a fancy casket, just something temporary.

Someone told me once – and I don't remember who – that ghosts are created, trapped somewhere, when life is cut short, when we leave things unresolved.

did he accomplish everything that he wanted to accomplish?
and did he leave satisfied?

I realized the one glaring incompleteness immediately after the thought.

he did not
and i prevented him from doing so

310

I rubbed my left palm against the wood and walked away, unsure of what else to do or say. Noah and Mira joined me in the corner of the room where we watched stragglers walk by the coffin, watched them find their peace. Eventually a familiar-looking woman went up the podium to test the microphone and everyone in the room migrated towards the seating area while the speakers in the room buzzed and clicked. She had on a black pantsuit, with her dirty blonde hair pulled back tightly. She said a few words, though I don't remember what. Then Brody, who was sitting next to me, went up and said some things that I'm sure were heartfelt. His head was lowering, his mouth was moving, he was licking his lip, but I couldn't pay attention to what he was saying. I kept watching the black suit lady as she sat on the edge of the front row, listening intently, artfully twisting her face into a look of forced solemnity.

why do i know her?
and why does she look so god-damned familiar?

A few other strangers came towards the podium and read prepared statements from folded pieces of lined notebook paper, statements written quickly, written from their sleeves. I didn't recognize any of them. I watched as the woman in the baggy pant suit returned to the podium and made some closing remarks.

she left me at the side of the road
and she saw me in the sun
and the sun was fucking made of gold, liquid gold
and my toes were dipped in the gold, flush on the white line
and she saw me
and yes she saw me
and she changed lanes
and she fucking knew
and she flexed her leg
and turned the liquid into sharp gold flakes

"And now the Tyde family would like to invite us all back to their house for the reception."

311

I leaned over to Brody.

"Where are we going?"

"We're going back to Mom's for the reception."

The crowd dispersed but I stayed in my seat. Mira, Noah, and Brody stood at the exit door waiting for me.

"You guys go on out. I'll be down in just a minute."

After the building emptied of everyone but the employees, I walked back out to the circular courtyard and unpocketed my notebook.

~~Masculine~~ Human
-Emotional Vulnerability
-Accepting the Past
-Being honest

> *if someone were to tell me that gravity is not what holds me down*
> *would i still stay stuck to the ground?*

I thumbed through the pages, some of which had useless categories on one side and meaningless probability charts and tabulations on the reverse. I opened the grate under the birch tree and dug a shallow hole in the dirt next to the exposed roots. The dirt was hard and dry but I dug as deep as I could and set the notebook down into the hole. Then I pulled my gray lighter out of my pocket and covered them both up together. The loosely coiled wire spirals along the binding still showed through the dirt.

> *what is the probability that these stupid probability charts,*
> *these meaningless statistics and interview notes,*
> *these categories failing to provide any self-clarity –*
> *what is the probability that these will grow into the tree?*
> *and that the attempts to find numerical fault with my father will*
> *photosynthesize into the fronds like a sugary nutrient?*

When my mom moved back to Urbana after I left for college, she bought a house bigger than she had any business buying. Six bedrooms upstairs. And she decorated the whole thing herself, stripped all the wallpaper down and painted every room a different eccentric color, all oranges and bright yellows, sky blues and amber reds. For several years, she lived there alone, and in an attempt to shrink the house, she slept on the futon in the living room, only really lived on the first floor. Even after my father came back from California and moved in with her, she still slept on the futon downstairs while my father slept on the floor next to her by the oversized bay window. At some point they started sleeping together upstairs, though I'm not sure when or who initiated it. I always pictured that my father came to his cold spot on the floor one night to sleep and found my mom asleep there, a white sheet twisted around her legs, the top bunched under her head as a makeshift pillow. Maybe my father carried her upstairs, still sleeping, tucked her into bed, and slept next to her over the sheets. And it grew from there. That's how I like to imagine it anyway.

The driveway was already full when we arrived at the reception. I pulled the Explorer up onto the curb behind Brody's car which had just parked in front of us. We – Brody, Bailey, Noah, Mira, and I – all walked up to the front door together.

"Where's Colton?" I asked.

"Grams has been watching him." Bailey said. I hated when she referred to my mom as 'Grams' especially when Colton was not around. "Since she didn't want to go to the ceremony, she agreed to keep an eye on the kids."

"The kids? Plural?"

"Oh Brody didn't tell you?"

"Tell me what?"

Through the secondary glass door on the house, I saw you with your face pressed against it, your nose scrunched up.

313

My first inclination was that I was hallucinating – that the pre-funeral whiskey was going to my head, that some of the pills were still floating – dissolved – somewhere in my body. I jogged up to the door and you pushed through the broken latch, grabbed onto my leg.

"Daddy!"

You loved saying that, said it all the time with different creative inflections. You were so creative.[45] I picked you up under your arms and looked at you to make sure you were real. Your face, perfectly round and evenly-halved, was pink, your cheeks dark, and your thin blonde hair curled across your scalp aimlessly, proudly wild.

Again, I had an overwhelming urge to put you in the car and drive away with you. We could live as fugitives, move to the savanna and live off the land. We could change our names and dye our hair. I could create an artistic rendition of what you would look like in five, ten, twenty years and we could make sure you never matched the picture. We could drain all the rivers and live in the dusty trenches. We could melt our bodies together so that no one could ever take you away from me. Maybe it's selfish, maybe this whole thing is selfish but I think you should know that's how I felt.

"Who brought you here?"

You shyly pointed at Brody who was entering the house with everyone else. I blinked my eyes hard, opened them wide trying to siphon off the tears, hot and dry against my cheek. My eyes were open underwater directly in the path of a jet stream.

maybe the tears can wash out the toxins
and my eyes can look clean-white and healthy
and i can look everyone in the eyes
and see everyone for real
and Luna will see them and know

"Well we went over to feed your cat and water your plants and all your furniture was gone and there was a homeless man sleeping on the floor," said Brody coming over.

---

[45] I'm sure you still are.

"Al."

"Okay, well we didn't know *Al* so we tried calling you and couldn't get through. So we called Eris and she told us everything," he said looking towards Mira. "Anyway it took some convincing but she let us bring Luna along. We picked her up yesterday. And it was definitely an interesting conversation." He held his head up high and fixed his tie. "It took some wheedling and wangling but I worked it out. She'll be driving here tonight to pick her up."

I hugged Brody, and though I was much taller than him, I pressed hard against his chest – a repressed outburst of fraternal solidity.

"It is what it is," he said.

My mom came down the hallway behind us carrying two-year old Colton on her hip.

"Oh look at you two!"

She put Colton down and squeezed herself in between Brody and me, wrapping an arm around each of our waists and pulling us towards her, though I leaned my upper half away. The top of her head barely reached my underarm.

My mom was a small leathery-skinned woman, and though pushing sixty at the time she still looked athletic – thin and toned. She wore black leggings under a form fitting sock-like dress that barely touched the tops of her knees. Ever since my father had moved to Urbana and they had gotten back together she had been dressing much younger than her age.

"You two look so handsome."

Through the warped lens of her mother-goggles, I apparently looked healthy and stable, clean and reasonable. She pulled me away first, putting her hands firmly on each side of my face. I looked at her forehead, couldn't look directly in her eyes. I wanted her eyes to be moist and bloodshot. I wanted the skin underneath to look red and irritated.[46] But I wasn't sure if either was true so I avoided looking closely altogether. I could smell her hairspray – gluey and made of chemicals.

"I've just missed you."

"I just saw you a few months ago."

---

[46] Probably the same way that you want my eyes to look when you see me.

"It's just nice that you're here," she said quietly to me before making an announcement. "Well, let's everyone come on in. There's no need to stand around the front door all day."

We all headed down the hall led by you and Colton, both of you ran wildly, you skidding in pink socks.

"And who is this young lady?" Mom whispered to me, nodding towards Mira.

"Oh right. This is Mira."

"It's a pleasure to meet you, dear." She shook her hand, squinted to read her shirt.

"And you remember Noah right?"

"Of course. How could I forget? It's been a long time. How are you?" she said giving him a hug.

"Namaste." He folded his hands in front of him and bowed. "I'm fantastic, Daisy. It's great to see you, though I wish the circumstances of our reunion were different."

My mom has always been a difficult person to dislike or to be angry with because, at least publicly, she cloys with everyone. So I just tried to avoid her. We all moved to the kitchen where a crowd of people stood shoulder to shoulder around the tableau of dishes centered around an oversized bowl of Everlasting Syllabub. Their chatter swelled into a collective buzz and I began to sweat. I didn't want to stand around and hear people talk about stories whose prefaces and denouements I should have known, so I hung to the fringe of the room. In the corner, hovering over a trembling tray of pigs-in-a-blanket was the man with the top hat. I went over and stood next to him.

"Excuse me, sir. How did you know Cliff?"

The man looked up from his plate of food, seemingly surprised that someone was talking to him. Up close, he looked even older, his face wrinkled, the skin folding in unusual ways, his cheek bones too pronounced. He was much skinnier, though not by intention, than any human had a right to be. His severely convex Adam's apple protruded out several inches from his neck. I watched the large shapeless mass bobble as he talked in a deep voice, the register almost too low to be audible.

how can this man be alive and my father be dead?

316

"Cliff was a dear friend of mine."

"How long had you known him?"

"Oh, let's see – I guess almost fourteen years now. How did you know him?"

"He was my father."

"Oh you must be young Cetus then, correct?" The paper plate shook in his unstable hand.

"Yeah but I prefer to be called Hurley."

"Right, right. Your father spoke quiet fondly of you."

my father spoke fondly of me?

"How did you say that you knew my father again?"

"We worked together out in California. Said you were a bright young man, lots of potential."

The idea of my father talking positively about me to his friends, especially after what I did to him was unsettling.

he's confused
and he's mistaken
and it's just a bit of senile dotage

I back-pedaled, his head and neck oscillating, nodding and shaking in constant indecision while he watched me walk away. I went back into the living room, peopled and noisy, buzzing with nonsense.

how did my father know so many people?

You were standing in the middle of the room entertaining everyone with a song. And you were spinning with your arms outstretched singing "Skidamarink" – a song I taught you, though you always misplaced the syllables, turning 'skidamarinky-dinky-dink' to 'didaskaminki-dinky-donk' which everyone in the room found funny in an endearing sort of way. When you finished bellowing the last chorus of "I love you" I scooped you up and sat on the floor with you in my lap. I hate that there were still drugs dissolving inside me, that I was still

317

whiskey-drunk while I sat there with you because in my memory I can't feel the full effect of that time with you, of one of the last free moments we had together.

"You smell bad," you said scrunching your nose. "Can I go play?"

I nodded and you ran out of the room, sliding around again on the hardwood. Back then you ran with your arms out in front of you, ready to hug anything or catch yourself if you tumbled. I wanted to harness your childlike enthusiasm, encapsulate it and dole in out anytime you were feeling down.

"Have you had her baptized yet?" my mom asked nodding towards the hall you had just skidded through.

"No."

She pulled me aside with her eyes, led me into the empty dining room. The swinging door that separated the rooms, waved on its hinges squeaking as it swung, slowly coming back to equilibrium. A tall deep brown china cabinet on the far wall was filled with delicate plates that I had never seen in use. She sat down at the thick brown table – also rarely used – and pointed to the chair next to her.

and she has no right to ask me anything
and has no right to talk to anyone

I was not in the mood or stable enough to field inquiries about my future plans or the quality of my character, and frankly my mom repulsed me after what I'd heard from Brody. But I wanted to hear it from her, wanted her to finally be fully honest. She had her hands folded on top of one another laid across the table. In the corner of the room I saw a stack of Cosmopolitan magazines, where I assumed she got all of her fashion tips to try to stay young, fresh, interesting.

"Hurley I'm worried about you. I heard from Brody that Eris moved out. Is this true?"

"Yeah. I think so, anyway. I haven't been by the apartment the last couple of days, but she said she was moving all her stuff out. So, yeah, I think it's over."

"I won't ask you what all you've gotten yourself into," she said looking me up and down, "Because that's none of my business anymore. I know you and Eris have had your disagreements over the years and that she's not always the easiest person to get along with but you have a daughter to consider."

"I'm familiar." I saw her bare feet, her toe nails painted in purple swirls. "What's your point?"

"My point is that you need to get organized. You need to have some accountability. You need to be a fit father. You're not a fit father right now." She spoke confidently, pointed at my clothes, covered in mud and puke, waved her hand in the air around me. "And I know you don't want to make the same mistakes that your father made." I wiggled in my chair, ruffled my hair – thick and matted. "You can't just run away from your family and expect everything to work itself out behind you. That's not how life works. And that's not how this family works."

She spoke with eyes like glass balls, eyes ready to shatter.

"Really? I feel like this is emotional manipulation or something."

"What are you talking about?"

"I just think I'm finally realizing that 'how this family works' is in disguise. We all just sort of tip toe around each other being polite. But being dishonest. Being secretive."

"You don't really mean that."

"I absolutely mean that. Look, all I'm saying is that Eris is leaving and that's what's real. And she's probably going to get sole custody of Luna because of some bad habits I've developed. And it's really all just a misunderstanding. But all I can do now is either sign things over or fight it and leave it up to a judge. Those are the options. And there's nothing I can do to change that. But I think that's okay," I said shrugging, fully loose. "I think it's okay because being a parent is really just about being honest – about teaching your kids to be true to themselves. And maybe I'm not going to be able to be as present as I'd like to be with Luna, but I'm always going to be

319

honest with her. That's all I can control. So I'm just going to be what I am and that's the best I can do.[47]"

"Well that's your decision to not fight for Luna. But is that what a father would do, what a *man* would do?"

She lowered her chin, firmed her jaw.

"I'm not having this conversation with you right now." I got up from the table.

"You're just like…" she said but I had already walked out, left the door swinging and squeaking.

My body buzzed. My emotional landscape vibrated underneath my skin, the tip of my left ring finger suddenly numb again. I needed to be clean, to flush out all the bile and toxins, to widen my aperture and absolve everything in view. I walked around the house looking for you. It was so loud everywhere, somehow more crowded, all the corners covered with bodies. People were laughing in the kitchen, laughing loudly, splintering cackles.

are people allowed to laugh at these events?
and what's so funny?
and what's so goddamn funny about all this?

Dizzy, I wanted to storm into the kitchen, flip tables, and smash windows.

--Is it still fucking funny now!?--

I came around the corner, saw your mother standing by the door with John – in full uniform. She had a manila folder in her hands, papers sticking out, a pen tucked behind her ear.

i'm not ready to sign anything away
and this isn't the right time
and i'm not ready to fight

---

[47] I've always been doing my best. I've always tried to be better than I've been.

You saw her too, came running, clasped onto her leg. She hugged you, leaned down and into your ear, cupped her hand.

"Sweetie, go play with Colton. I need to talk to your dad," she whispered.

You ran down the hall, arms still out in front of you.

"Can we go outside and talk?"

"Sure."

Suddenly charming, John walked over to my mom now in the living room, sat down next to her, immediately drew out a smile and a pat on the forearm. Eris and I went out to the porch, sat on the gray concrete stairs – cold and sharp.

"Is that your car?" she asked pointing towards the Explorer.

"It's a rental."

"Have you been driving?"

"Yeah."

"I saw an open bottle of whiskey in the console." I turned away, rubbed my fingers through my patchy beard, pressed my temples. "I keep wanting to give you the benefit of the doubt. I keep wanting to think that I'm wrong about you. But you're making it too easy, Hurley."

"Are those for me to sign?"

"You can either sign these or there is a court date. The choice is yours. And before you say anything, speeding this whole thing up is what's best for Luna. The last thing we need to do is drag it out and make this ugly. She needs stability."

this is only temporary
and i only need a few days
and i'll be fine in a few
but one day leans into another
and our toes begin to wither
but i can look firm
and make steady claims
and clear-headed rebuttals
and grow to fill out a suit
and i will be irresistible
and believable

and i can't lose her,
not now, not ever,
not even partially.

"I can't sign anything."

"If you change your mind..." she left the sentence hanging, handed me the folder.

I want you to know that I had a choice in that moment. I could choose to sign you over, to see you once a month at best. Or I could choose to fight a battle I knew I would likely lose, a battle that I knew had the potential to destroy me, professionally and personally. I chose to fight, Luna. I lost everything, but I fought for it. Despite what you've heard, I am a warrior.

"We have to go. We need to be back in Hamilton by dark."

"Can I at least say goodbye to her?"

She nodded, got up, went back inside to sit by John. I saw you sitting in the bay window, your cheek pressed up against the dusty glass, and I started to calm down. My blood settled, smoothed out, and I tried to listen in, to listen to my blood. I sat down next to you and put my face up against the window, the glass warm from the sun.

"That feels good doesn't it?"

You nodded and scooted over to me. I don't know if you remember this conversation or not.

"Look, sweetie, I'm probably not going to be able to see you quite as often."

You blinked.

"Do you understand?"

You nodded.

"I'm hungry," you said.

Eris would have had snacks. I had no snacks. I had nothing to give you, nothing to offer.

"I'll get you something. But I want you to know that even though I won't be around as much, I'll always come back okay?"

"Promise?"

"I promise."

We walked into the crowded kitchen and you picked out two single serving plastic cups of applesauce.

"You want two?"

"One's for Colton." You shrugged your shoulders like I should have known. Then you put your hand on my knee. "You look sad."

"Yeah. I'm a little sad."

You tugged hard on the freezer door, the suction too strong for you. I pulled it open and you grabbed out a bag of frozen corn on the bottom shelf.

"Put this on your chest. It'll make your heart feel better."

You walked back towards the living room where Colton was sitting on Bailey's lap and you ate your applesauce without a spoon, just sort of squeezed the plastic cup, pushing the sauce up and out all over your face. Eris came over and cleaned you up, took charge.

I couldn't watch you get in the car with Eris, couldn't watch John holding your hand, helping you into your car seat. I knew I would see you again, would see you in the courtroom dressed in bright red flower-prints, tiny flowers pinned in your hair. I knew it was not over. I knew it would never be over. It's still not over. Not to me.

I signaled to Mira and Noah – both wobbling by the food table – and we left my mother's house, frozen corn in hand. I don't think you even noticed I was gone.[48] Still vibrating, I didn't have a destination in mind, just knew I needed to get away, knew that I needed to feel a rush of open air in my chest – just above the heart and behind the pectorals – that comes when things fit together, when the grooves meet and roll smoothly.

Instinctively I drove by my old neighborhood, by the place where I watched Kolby get stung and die. I hadn't been back there since I moved away. Pulling into the neighborhood, I idled, hovered along the curb, everyone quiet. I wanted to get out of the car so I could walk around my old back yard, walk around Kolby's old back yard. I wanted to see if another hive had been built on that limb, to see if the limb was still sagging

---

[48] Do you remember any of this?

from the weight of the hive. I wanted people to know what happened, wanted to organize a community sit-in, wanted to hold up provocative signs or start speaking at seminars about the dangers of wasps.

do her parents still live there?
and is it still her yard?
and if we stop seeing things everyday
do they stop being ours?

I wanted to wipe my memory and walk around on my knees – *tabula rasa* – so I could see the world like I did when I was a child. I wanted to see the world like you saw it Luna, full of potential, boiling with love and hope.

I looked over at Mira sitting in the passenger seat, and she suddenly reminded me of Kolby, of how I imagined she would have grown up to be, of the creative energy she would have possessed, of the life she could have lived.

do the living absorb the spirits of the dead?
and do the dead live inside us?

Instead of getting out, I looped around and drove a few miles down the road where I spotted a small pull-off that lead into a park labeled Crystal Lake.

→I've never been here before.
    →Al would approve.
        →Al has known all along.
        →He is a fucking genius.

I had been scared of new experiences, but at the same time I was dissatisfied with familiar experiences. And you can intuit where that left me: constantly scared or dissatisfied. So I had to push through, not for me, Luna, but for you. I'm still pushing, still trying.

I pulled the green Explorer up a hill and into an empty gravel parking lot. Still quiet, we pulled down the tailgate and sat on the end, passing around the bottle of whiskey that Noah bought before the funeral, throwing tiny jagged pebbles of gravel at blades of grass, at trunks of thick trees.

"You said after I punched you in the face – so sorry about that by the way – that you had some kind of plan in all this. So was that just bull shit?" I asked Noah.

"No, of course not."

He was calm but clearly drunk, his eyes shining, a red plastic film rolled over them.

"So what was your plan?"

"Well the plan – like I said, though you didn't believe me – was to simulate a rite of passage for you. We needed to empty you out completely so that we could fill you back up with something good. Mission accomplished I'd say."

"But didn't you say that you had one more place to take me?"

He looked around and churned his jaws, chewing on nothing.

"Right. Actually I bet we can do it here. This'll be good. Better actually." He jumped off the tailgate and took one last swig out of the bottle. "Everyone be really quiet."

Mira and I looked at each other unsure of whether Noah knew what he was doing. I think we both just figured that he was too belligerently fucked up to have a clue but we followed anyway.

"Why not?" I said looking at her. She shrugged.

"Okay, follow me," Noah said whispering and hunching down.

We walked onto a man-made path of soft wood chips – our padded footsteps reminding me of Noah's foley studio – that led into a densely vegetated area next to the gravel parking lot. Every ten feet or so Noah stopped and held his hand up and tilted his ear towards the trees. Eventually he signaled for us to follow him off the path. We high stepped over broken limbs and molded logs, plastic trash and busted lawn furniture. It was still several hours before sundown, but as we went deeper into the woods it got darker and blacker and harder to see.

it's all so black
and it will always be so black
and no one will ever know what's under the water
and no one can ever see the bottom of the ocean
and the bottom of the ocean is just a theory
and i'll live inside an idea
and Luna can never be lost inside an idea

"Do you hear that?" he whispered.

"I don't hear anything Noah. Look, come on, do you know where we're going?"

"Wait, yeah I actually do hear something," Mira said.

"What do you hear?" Noah asked.

"It sounds like running water."

"Exactly."

In a drunkenly campy gesture, Noah skipped and waved his arm like a windmill through the darkness, mouthed for us to keep moving.

"Come on, man, seriously. Where are we going?"

He jogged up ahead of us, pulled back a green branch revealing a small, bright waterfall running over a flat rock into a circular cove surrounded by thin rocks – coquina. Our eyes collectively squinted as the vegetative canopy opened up over the foamy water, allowing the sun to come in and reflect off the surface.

"Perfect," Noah said. "Now I had originally planned on doing a Hindu cleansing ritual but now I actually have something else in mind."

"What's that?"

"You'll see."

"I don't know what – if anything – you have planned," Mira said coming through the clearing, blinking her eyes, "but whatever it is, it needs to involve you two washing off because you both still smell like ass."

Exhausted and on stimulus overload we all three laughed. The vibrations pushed up from deep down, shaking my whole body, everything natural. I couldn't stop and the corners of my eyes started to leak. It felt good to be so out of control under my own volition. I took off my filthy shirt and

326

patted my pockets – your button the only thing left to carry – before taking off my pants and jumping into the cove after Noah.

"Come on, Mira, get in!" I yelled. "The water feels good!"

> the water is right
> and it is clean
> and it is blue
> and soft and clear
> and made of melted glass – soft, smooth
> and there is no bottom
> and no one will ever know
> and no one is ever meant to know

She laughed at Noah and me splashing in the water like feral children, free and unashamed. I put my head under the waterfall, ran my fingers across my scalp and combed through my silly-looking beard. Noah signaled for me to join him, suddenly serious.

"I want to do a Buddhist ritual for your father," he said with sincere severity.

He cupped his hands under the running water and as it spilled over the sides of the hand-cup he repeated a mantra.

"As the rains fill the rivers and overflows into the ocean, so likewise may what is given here reach the departed."

He let the water spill over his hands for a few more seconds and then submerged his head in the water. When he came back up he had his hands twisted into the shape of bird wings which he flapped in the air before wrestling me under. The clean water was in my eyes and up my nose and on my skin and I felt it all over me and moving inside me.

"Come on. Get in," he yelled towards Mira.

I swam on my back over towards her and watched as she slipped out of her skirt and jumped in with us, the words written on her shirt dissolving into the water. I know it probably sounds ridiculous or way too idealistic – which is fine because that's just a part of who I am – but I swear I felt my dad in the cove with me. There was an unannounced presence that I felt with my curled toes in the mud at the bottom. I breathed him in through the trees, let him open the walls of my capillaries, felt him crafting a home inside those tiny elastic tubes that stretch and keep everything alive.

And I guess even if it's not true, even if it was just in my head it doesn't really matter. Sometimes the intensity of what we feel in the moment is truer than what actually happened. And I think our hearts remember things stronger than our minds anyway.

Our faces reflected off the rippling surface of the water. The full moon was cracked-white – a ghost – and the sun – round and hot orange – shared the clear day sky with it while the three of us[49] splashed and swam and talked until our abdomens ached and the skin at the tips of our limbs turned pale and wrinkled-white.

I'm trying hard – Luna – not to make this feel over the top, not to drag it through clichéd language, not to debase the grounding gravity of that moment. I just consciously let everything in. And I'm not saying that happiness – or self-assurance, whatever you want to call it – is exclusively a choice, but I hadn't really felt like I deserved to be happy.[50] I had felt compelled to disallow things like that, to keep my chest an empty cavity – reasonable voices bouncing off the stone walls unheard – because of my decisions. And it took so long to fill it back up, to reorient my thinking, to recalibrate my body, but this was the start. This moment was the center. I don't care what anyone says. This moment was the only center. I chose to listen to the water gurgle and chose to see the tiny bubbles and white froth pool at the edges of the cove. I chose to fight for you.

While I washed my dirty clothes – the text dissolving off my shirt – I felt the green wisps, the carbon particulates in the air, the ashes and flowers, the gray steam and smooth iron. I felt it all bumping up against my thin skin. I felt the clouds – the firmament – dissolving onto my head. I felt all the friction I had

---

[49] Also accompanied by – at least I believe – the monadic spirit of my father.
[50] And you might still feel this way about me too.

been avoiding, all the beautiful friction that tells us we're alive and that it's okay. We all just float without the friction.

no one can ever really be gone
and it's never over
and we're always growing
and we'll never learn enough
and we were never meant to
and i know you feel all these same vibrations
and i know you feel the energy buzzing on your soft skin
and even if we don't connect now
our souls will find each other in other incarnations
and we will always recognize each other
and we will always feel the pull
and i love you

your father

about the author
michael lives in portland, oregon
and he lives with his wife
and she is an admirable girl of immeasurable compassion
and he mumbles
and he is not a father
and this is his first novel

For more information visit
www.deusotiosusetc.blogspot.com

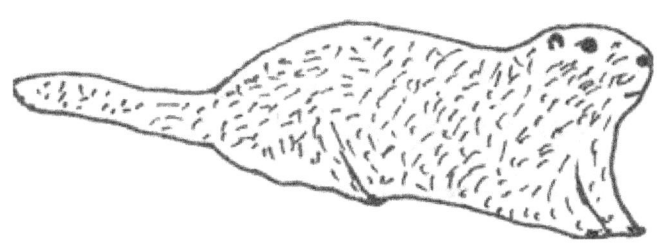